Reap a Wicked Harvest

Reap a Wicked Harvest

Janis Harrison

THORNDIKE
CHIVERS

This Large Print edition is published by Thorndike Press®, Waterville, Maine USA and by BBC Audiobooks, Ltd, Bath, England.

Published in 2004 in the U.S. by arrangement with St. Martin's Press, LLC.

Published in 2004 in the U.K. by arrangement with Robert Hale Limited.

U.S. Hardcover 0-7862-6285-0 (Mystery)
U.K. Hardcover 0-7540-9852-4 (Chivers Large Print)
U.K. Softcover 0-7540-9853-2 (Camden Large Print)

A Gardening Mystery.

The text of this Large Print edition is unabridged.
Other aspects of the book may vary from the original edition.

Set in 16 pt. Plantin by Ramona Watson.

Printed in the United States on permanent paper.

British Library Cataloguing-in-Publication Data available

Library of Congress Cataloging-in-Publication Data

Harrison, Janis (Janis Anne)
Reap a wicked harvest : a gardening mystery / Janis Harrison.
p. cm.
ISBN 0-7862-6285-0 (lg. print : hc : alk. paper)
1. Solomon, Bretta (Fictitious character) — Fiction. 2. Women detectives — Missouri — Fiction. 3. Nurseries (Horticulture) — Fiction. 4. Women gardeners — Fiction. 5. Gardening — Fiction. 6. Missouri — Fiction. 7. Large type books. I. Title.
PS3558.A67132R43 2004b
813′.6—dc22 2003071180

Some people come into your life for a reason. They are there to assist, to give you guidance, and support. They might aid you physically, emotionally, or spiritually. They are there for a reason.

Some people come into your life for a season. They bring experience of peace or make you laugh. They teach you something you have never known. They give you joy, but only for a season.

This book is dedicated to my mother-in-law of thirty-two years. Pauline Chaney Harrison passed away on July 8, 2003. Her reason on earth was her family. Her season was much too short.

A special thanks to

Chief Deputy Steve Catron of the
Henry County Sheriff's Department.

Steve Parks of the Clinton
Fire Department.

My agent, Lori Pope.

And my editor, Kelley Ragland, who
helps make each book special.

Chapter One

"Death plays havoc with my social life," I said. "It's after five o'clock. We've missed all the scheduled events." I peered through the windshield, searching for passing landmarks that would show we were getting closer to Parker Wholesale Greenhouse. "We might as well have stayed home."

"Where's your compassion, Bretta?" said my father from the passenger seat of my SUV. "I'm sure Mr. Tyler would prefer a few hours' festivities over his present location."

Since Mr. Tyler was stretched out in his casket prepared for burial, I knew my father was right. But neither fact kept me from being grumpy. My flower shop closes at noon on Saturday, but just because the doors are locked doesn't mean the work ceases. Lois, my second in command, had a sinus infection. I'd had no choice but to design and deliver the sympathy bouquets for Mr. Tyler's funeral service. I'd put in seven straight days at my flower shop business and looked forward to having this day off. I'd hurried every chance I could, but we were still late for Dan and Natalie's Customer Appreciation Day Celebration.

We were headed south of River City, smack dab in the middle of the Missouri Ozarks. The road twined and clung to the hillsides like a serpentine trumpet vine. Fleeting breaks in the wall of foliage revealed the Osage River flowing at a leisurely pace in the valley. It was a peaceful, relaxing ride through the sun-drenched August countryside, and one I'd anticipated for weeks.

"There's the sign," Dad said. "See it? Up ahead on your left."

"Got it," I said, flipping the turn-signal lever. We rolled off the highway onto the private road and through an elaborate gateway made of wrought-iron curlicues. On each side of the entry a natural outcropping of limestone rock was landscaped with bright spots of sun-loving annuals tucked into soil-filled crevices. Purple verbena trailed over rugged stones. Hot pink periwinkle, portulaca, and the rich autumn tones of the rudbeckia gave a domesticated feel to the untamed tract of land.

Dad tilted his head so he could look up the bluff. "I see a flash of sunlight on glass. Is the house up there?"

I nodded. “The lodge where Natalie and Dan live and the commercial greenhouses, too. It’s another mile to the top of the bluff where the ground levels out.”

“Will there be parking?” Dad touched his walking stick that was propped against the SUV’s console. “My arthritis is bothering me. I’m not up to hiking long distances.”

“Natalie promised she’d reserve a place for us close to the lodge,” I said and tried not to roll my eyes. Arthritis might be the excuse, but knowing him, he was more concerned for the condition of his clothes.

My father, Albert McGinness, was a natty dresser. Before we left home, I’d explained a white suit might not be the best choice for an outing to a greenhouse. Jeans or shorts and a T-shirt would be the order of the day. But he’d gone ahead and decked himself out like Colonel Sanders.

I glanced at him. He was a handsome man in his seventies. His hair was thick and gray, his eyes blue. In his younger days he’d been lean and wiry, but age and good living had added a paunch to his middle. He’d only recently come back into my life — when I was eight years old, he walked out on my mother and me. My feelings toward him were complicated. I cared about him, but I wasn't always sure I liked him. I was making an effort, but sometimes he irritated the living daylights out of me.

We topped the bluff and saw cars, vans, and trucks parked everywhere. "Do all these vehicles belong to florists?" asked Dad.

"No, though I'm sure many of them do." The lane was shady. I turned down the AC and lowered my window. "The greenhouse delivers potted plants in a radius of two hundred miles to garden centers and retail outlets as well as flower shops."

Dad nodded. "What's in store for us this afternoon?"

I reached into the side pocket of my purse and pulled out a folded paper. "Here's the invitation, but as I said, we've missed all the tours."

Dad took the paper and smoothed the wrinkles. With gusto he read: " 'Come join the fun! Meet our growers. Tour the Parker facilities. Whole hog roast with fireworks to end the day's gala.' " Turning the paper over, he squinted at the smaller print used for listing the schedule. "You're right about the tours, but we can still wander through the gardens."

"And," I said, "we can eat."

Dad chuckled. "What about your diet?"

I'd lost one hundred pounds after my husband, Carl, had died two years ago. Since then I'd lost and gained the same ten pounds over and over. My struggle with food was a war with daily skirmishes against my foes — ice cream, potato chips, and chocolate.

I grimaced. "It's August. It's hot. I'll be walking and sweating. I can get by with a few extra calories."

Dad stuffed the paper back into my purse. He made a sweeping gesture toward our surroundings. "When you said we were going to a greenhouse, I pictured some glass huts filled with plants. I had no idea it would be so big or so beautiful."

I slowed the SUV to a crawl, partly because of the parked cars that lined the roadway, but mostly because we were ogling. A long building that served as loading area, potting rooms, and offices fronted the fifteen greenhouses. To our left were the gardens and around the curve of the driveway would be the lodge.

Dad touched my arm. "I hope your friends won't mind that I've tagged along."

"They'll be happy to meet you. You'll like Natalie. She's fun-loving and outgoing. Dan is the typical absentminded professor. He's developing his own hybrid orchid and would rather be with his plants than socialize. Natalie says he's so involved in his work, she can hardly get him to the house to eat or sleep."

"Hey, Bretta!"

Hearing my name, I stepped on the brake. A young man dressed in the Parker Greenhouse uniform, emerald green shorts and a jade-colored T-shirt, drove up to my window in a golf cart. "Hi, Eugene," I said. "Looks like a good crowd. Natalie promised she'd save me a parking spot."

Eugene was lean and tanned. His teeth, exposed by a wide grin, were white and strong. "I wasn't sure if you were going to make it," he said. "Follow me, and I'll move the sign I used to save the space."

"Who's he?" asked Dad.

Since my window was down, I spoke softly. "His name is Eugene Baker. He phones Parker customers and takes their orders. I talk to him every week."

I followed Eugene up the drive and waited for him to move the sign. I parked the SUV and hopped out. Eugene said, "I'm glad you're here. The day wouldn't have been the same without you."

My father snorted rudely.

Eugene leaned down so he could see in my window. "You must be Bretta's father.

It's a pleasure to meet you, sir. *You* have a fine time here today, and if there's anything you need just look me up." Eugene winked at me and drove off.

I went around to help my father out. When I opened the door, Dad said, "Eddie Haskell."

"No," I said patiently. "That was Eugene Baker."

My father frowned as he got out. "I mean he's a suck-up like that kid on the *Leave It to Beaver* show. Remember? Eddie Haskell was Wally's buddy."

"Yeah, well, put Eugene, Eddie, and the Beav out of your mind. Enjoy yourself, just don't get too hot."

Dad smoothed the lapels of his summer suit jacket, then reached for his walking stick. Straightening his shoulders, he gazed around him. "I'm glad I brought my sketch pad. This place is a wonderland of subjects. My fingers are itching to get started, but I think I'll meander first."

"Do you want to meet someplace later?"

"I'm not here to cramp your style, daughter," he said as he walked off.

I gazed after him and shook my head. Since my father had reentered my life he'd taken to calling me daughter every so often. It sounded formal, but I'd decided he used it to remind me that he was the parent. It also helped to verbally establish our kinship — a fact that *never* slipped my mind.

Happy that my father was content to be on his own, I scanned the area for my hostess. I spotted Natalie under a shade tree, telling a story to a group of children. Short and chunky, she wore her hair in a Dutch boy's bob. And she loved color. Today she was dressed in Day-Glo orange shorts, shirt, socks, and sneakers.

Natalie told her tale with comical facial expressions. She puffed out her cheeks and crossed her eyes. Leaning forward she flapped her arms, then looked around, pretending to be amazed that she hadn't taken flight. The children responded with wild giggles. Flushed with pleasure Natalie glanced up, saw me, and flashed a happy grin before she beckoned the children closer.

"She's in her element," said Emily Thomas, coming to stand near me.

I turned and smiled at Natalie's aunt. A stout woman, Emily usually had a capable air about her, but at the moment, she appeared frazzled. Her dark hair had been pulled back in a bun, but several pins had come loose and the knot had worked itself free. Her white shirt was stained across the pocket, and her blue shorts were wrinkled.

I shifted my position so I could see Natalie. The picture of her surrounded by children was sweet and cozy, but it made my heart ache. Natalie couldn't have children, a fact that devastated her. I sighed. "She would have made an excellent mother. I wish they'd adopted a child."

"They've talked about it, but the red tape involved is invasive to their personal lives. Private adoption would involve less people and paperwork, but the cost is prohibitive." Emily made a dismissive gesture. "After the last five hours, I've decided kids are overrated anyway." She reached up and anchored a couple of pins in her knot of hair. "I'm exhausted. I was elected medic for the day."

"No serious injuries, I hope."

"Just the results of a bunch of rambunctious city kids turned loose in the country. I've given first aid to three skinned knees, a bumblebee sting, and a little girl who had hysterics when she saw a snake. Turns out a Popsicle is the best medicine." Emily glanced down at her stained blouse. "Grape is the flavor of the day."

"I don't see Dan or your husband. Where are they?"

Emily stopped fussing with her hair. "Haven't you heard?"

I shook my head. "I just got here."

"Dan's mother in Portland fell and broke her hip. Then in the ambulance on the way to the hospital she had a stroke. Donovan took Dan to Lambert airport in St. Louis so he could catch a flight to Oregon. They arrived early, but the plane was late. My husband's car was towed — too much time in the wrong zone." Emily grimaced. "I just got a call from him. He's finally on his way back from St. Louis, and he's hopping mad. He was supposed to do rope tricks for the kids. We improvised with Harley giving rides in a wagon hitched to the back of the greenhouse's all-terrain vehicle."

"How's Dan's mother?"

"The news isn't good. Natalie wanted to go with Dan, but it would have been more trouble to cancel today's celebration than to go ahead."

I glanced back at Natalie. "She seems to be holding up okay."

"Yeah. She's doing great." A squeal erupted over by the swings. Emily sighed. "Duty calls," she said and hurried off.

I made my way slowly across the drive, stopping to visit with people I knew. Once

I entered the garden, I strolled along the path, enjoying the sweeping borders of plants, seeking out the hidden seats tucked under rose-covered arbors. Pieces of statuary added focal points to flower beds that were a combination of perennials and annuals.

The garden was divided into elements within a more general design. I turned a sharp corner and left the formal scheme, entering a Japanese-style landscape. Dan Parker had educated me on the fine points of Japanese design — a combination of green upon green with blooms incidental to the overall theme. The use of stone was essential for the success of the garden. No better example could be found than the area that lay before me.

The Garden of Contemplation was an abstract composition of gravel that gave the impression of an open sea. A special rake had made an undulating pattern on its surface. White Rugosa roses rambled over a craggy stone wall. My inventiveness saw them as sea froth. Ornamental grasses of every height, blade width, and variegation edged the perimeter. The plumes waved gently in the breeze, giving movement to the stoic setting.

"Bretta," said a voice from behind me.

"You missed my tour of the garden."

I turned and recognized Dan's lab assistant, Marnie Frazier. She'd taken a summer job at the greenhouse before entering college this fall to pursue a degree in finance. She was petite with red hair and large blue-green eyes. The Parker Greenhouse uniform fit her snugly and complemented her vivid coloring.

"Hi, Marnie," I said. "I'm sure you did a wonderful job." I smiled at the young man at her side. He appeared to be about eighteen. He was dressed in the regulation green shorts and shirt. He was handsome, clean-cut, and seemed familiar. When our eyes met, he dipped his head in a respectful manner.

"Hello," I said to him. "Have we met?"

"Yes, but it has been a while," he said quietly.

His gentle way of speaking triggered my memory, but I couldn't get a handle on it. I felt I knew this young man, but the clothes — shorts, shirt, and sneakers — weren't right. In my mind I saw dark trousers, a light-colored shirt, and suspenders.

Marnie said, "Bretta, this is Jake."

"Jake?" I repeated. The name didn't help me make a connection.

He shrugged. "That's what I'm called

around here, but you know me as Jacob."

I stared into his face, searching the sharp angles, trying to read the expression in his solemn brown eyes. My knees almost buckled as recognition dawned. "Jacob Miller?" I said. "You're Evan's son?" When he nodded, I said, "I don't understand. You're Amish. What are you doing here?"

Jacob said, "It's complicated, but I'll try to explain."

Marnie interrupted. "Before you get into that, I wanted to ask you something, Bretta. Jake says you helped solve his uncle's murder. I find that absolutely fascinating. How did you know what questions to ask?"

I couldn't take my eyes off Jacob. Why was he working at Parker Greenhouse? Had something happened at home? Was his family all right?

Impatiently, Marnie said, "Bretta, come on, how do you solve a mystery? Did you read a book on how to conduct an investigation?"

The intensity in Marnie's voice finally broke through my shock at finding Jacob in these surroundings. I focused on her and tried to explain. "Before my husband passed away, he was a deputy with the

Spencer County Sheriff's Department. We often speculated on some of his cases, and he coached me on the fine points of detection. Since his death, my amateur sleuthing has put several criminals in jail, but I'm hardly an expert."

Marnie studied me closely. "How do you know where to start on a case?"

I shrugged. "Why? Are you thinking of investigating something?"

Marnie's smile had a brittle edge. "Nothing in particular," she said and backed away. "I have to go to the lodge. Dan left some papers in his study for me to look over. I'll see you all later."

She disappeared down the path. I wondered what was behind Marnie's interest, but was more concerned with Jacob. I turned to him. "So, you're working here? Is something wrong at home? Is your family well?"

"I do work here and have for the last week. My family is fine. Mother will be canning vegetables, and my father will be baling hay, when he's not praying for my return." Jacob studied the closely cropped grass. "But I cannot go home right away. I have much to think about before I make the decision to spend the rest of my life as an Amish man."

I was bewildered. "Decision? Aren't you already Amish?"

He looked at me. "It is my right to decide if I want to be baptized into the Amish faith. I was born of Amish parents, but until I take my vow to follow that life, I am merely Jacob Miller, son of Evan and Cleome Miller."

"Hey, Jake!"

Jacob and I turned and saw Jess McFinney striding toward us. Jess was in charge of greenhouse plant production. Though in his fifties, he moved as if he were wired to his own personal generator. The few times I'd been around him, he'd exhausted me with his limitless energy.

"I need help loading some plants," he said. "Can you lend a hand?"

Eagerly, Jacob said, "Are you using that four-wheeler machine? I'd like to learn how to drive it."

"This is a greenhouse, not a driving school."

At Jacob's crestfallen look, Jess grumbled, "One day after work, I'll show you, but right now we've got plants to tend." Belatedly, Jess turned to me. "Hi, Bretta. Good to see you." Without another word, he spun on his heel and galloped away.

Jacob brushed by me. "I've got to go. See you later."

"But I want to know why —" I stopped in midsentence. Jacob was gone. I shook my head. He might be new to the Parker payroll, but he'd already learned that when Jess spoke everyone snapped to attention.

I wandered toward the back of the garden where boulders formed the outer boundary. On the far side of them was the road Dad and I'd taken up to the greenhouse. In front of the rocks was a bridge that arched over a stream. A man-made pool contained a circulating pump that pushed water uphill, where it cascaded over the limestone boulders. After a tumultuous rush, the water flowed back under the bridge and into the lagoon, where it languished in the sun until its next surge over the falls. Crags and crevices were home to rock-hugging sedum. My gaze traveled over the green leaves of the deciduous trees, touched gently on the blue-green needles of some junipers, but lingered on the lime-colored hosta lilies with their rounded, puckered leaves.

I moved to the center of the bridge and leaned against the railing. Cleome, Jacob's mother, was a staunch Amish woman. She would be frantic with worry over her son. Evan would be upset, too, but he'd keep his concerns to himself. I thought about those gentle people and wondered what they would do if Jacob decided not to take his Amish vow.

I crossed the bridge and walked beside the pool. A school of Japanese koi, a colorful species of carp, swirled the water in hope of a treat. Since I had nothing to feed them, I moved on, following the stepping-stone path. At my leisure, I enjoyed the plants and when a particular specimen caught my eye, I pulled the copper identification tag from the ground so I could accurately copy the botanical as well as the common name of the plant into a small notebook I'd brought with me.

As I pushed the sharp prongs of the marker back into the dirt, I heard voices off to my left. Still on my haunches, I swiveled around and saw Irma Todd wrapped in Harley Sizemore's embrace.

I scuttled over to a patch of shade and watched with unabashed interest. Irma was stoop-shouldered, round-faced, and had a tangle of shoulder-length brown hair. Her bangs had been teased into a crested wave. She was in her late forties and had been the Parkers' bookkeeper for several years. I'd considered her a dull, tedious woman, but there was nothing boring in the way she caressed Harley's brawny back.

Harley was maintenance man for these gardens. He was in his early forties with a classic Fu Manchu mustache. He'd elected to wear blue jeans instead of shorts, but his jade green T-shirt fit his muscular torso like it had been painted on his skin.

Unobtrusively, I left the garden, wondering if Natalie knew that Irma and Harley had a romance going. Feeling guilty that I'd left my father alone, I went back to the lodge. I found him on the front porch, entertaining a group of people. With a pad of paper on his knee and a pencil in his hand, he was sketching and talking. I couldn't hear what he was saying, so I walked closer. My lips thinned into a grim line at his words.

"From an acorn a mighty oak tree can grow," he said. "That's the way I feel about investigations. A tiny clue can bring a criminal to justice. The smallest slip-up and BAM!" He slapped the paper with the palm of his hand, making his audience jump.

My father smiled. "When a culprit is apprehended he has that reaction — total surprise that his scheme has been exposed. My daughter, Bretta Solomon, has experience rousting worms out of the woodwork, but she's often busy with her flower-shop business. I, on the other hand, am footloose and fancy-free. I have cards with me. Take one and if I can be of service, please give me a call."

My accomplishments as an amateur detective had been played up in our local newspaper, which I'd learned my father had subscribed to during the years he was away. Dad had come back to River City with the idea of us partnering a detective agency. I'd quickly put the kibosh to that idea — or so I'd thought.

Amazed, I watched interested people pick up the cards and tuck them into pockets or wallets. While the others moved on, one woman lingered. I gave her a hard study. It took ten seconds before I recognized Allison Thorpe. She owned a flower shop and was my biggest competitor. But this was a new and improved Allison. Her tanned legs were displayed in a pair of white shorts. Her blue T-shirt was neatly tucked under the waistband. Her eyebrows, which were usually as bushy as a squirrel's tail, had been plucked and shaped into gentle arches.

My father offered Allison his arm and the two of them strolled off, gazing into each other's eyes. Not once had he looked in my direction. "There must be something in the air," I muttered. I stepped to the end of the buffet line and filled my plate. Searching for a place to sit, I saw the size of the crowd had dwindled from when Dad and I'd first arrived. I made myself comfortable at a table with some out-of-town visitors.

Natalie was everywhere, making everyone feel welcome. On one of her trips past me, she stopped and gave me a brief hug. "Emily said she told you about Dan's mother."

"Are you flying to Oregon?"

"I don't know. I haven't had a chance to call the airlines about a flight." She gave me a tired smile. "I've got to go, but I'll talk to you tomorrow and tell you my plans." She hurried off.

The shadows lengthened. Plates were discarded and a sudden quiet fell over the gathering. It had been a nice afternoon, a pleasant change of pace from my structured life. I get so wrapped up in my flower-shop business that I sometimes forget how to relax. I leaned back in my chair, staring up at the sky, waiting for the first burst of pyrotechnics.

It wasn't long until the air was bombarded with sparkling stars, flashes of bright light and loud explosions. Comets streaked across the night sky and detonated into shapes that resembled large allium blossoms. The crowd was appreciative with frequent and enthusiastic applause. When the display came to a loud, riotous conclusion, yard lights were switched on and people headed for their vehicles.

I was ready to leave, too, but I hadn't seen my father. To make myself useful, I folded some chairs and carried them to a storage shed. I was on my way back for another load when Allison Thorpe burst out of the garden entrance. My father tottered after her. Allison rushed for the lodge, but my father came to a standstill, frantically searching the yard. I waved. When he caught sight of me, he limped forward.

I braced myself. His face was pale, his gait unsteady. I figured we were in for a trip to the Emergency Room because he'd eaten something that hadn't agreed with him.

Before I could speak, he grabbed my arm and gasped. "There's a body in the garden, blood everywhere. There's a killer on the loose."

Chapter Two

My father's words brought immediate action. All around us cell phones were drawn like six-shooters. Electronic crickets chirruped as 911 was punched in.

"Wait! Wait!" I said. These people didn't know my father. They didn't know that his imagination could be as rampant as hen bit on fertile soil. He might have seen something, but then again, it might be nothing at all.

"Don't call —" I started to say, but the deed was done. Turning to the man next to me, I said, "Wouldn't it have been better to check his story before placing that call?"

"Not if a killer *is* out there." He gestured to a woman who was huddled with four kids. "Let's go."

"You made one of the calls," I said. "You have to stay until the authorities arrive."

The man brushed past me. He picked up the smallest child, grabbed the woman's arm, and they jogged down the drive with the rest of the kids in tow. Others were making a hasty exit as word spread. I heard snatches of conversation as people hurried past.

"— bloodbath in the garden."

"— several are dead."

"— there's an eyewitness, but he got away to warn us."

I studied my father — the eyewitness. He seemed to have aged ten years. His shoulders were hunched, his face pale and drawn. "Dad," I said gently. "Are you sure about the body? Could it have been a shadow? A trick of the light?"

"All the lights were shut off, but it isn't a matter of having *seen* the body, Bretta. I touched the leg. I don't know if it's a man or a woman. I don't know who it is, but there's definitely a body in the garden."

I couldn't hide my skepticism. I'd just spent a relaxing few hours. I was ready for a good night's sleep, not the horrors that faced us if what my father said was true.

He stared at me, then sadly shook his head. Pointing to his trousers, he said, "If you need further evidence, daughter, there it is." The white material was streaked with what could have been blood, but in this light it was hard to tell. "I stumbled over something in the dark. When I reached down to see what it was, I touched a leg. It was still warm. The air was heavy with an acrid odor." He gulped. "I'm a farm boy. I know the scent of freshly spilled blood."

I couldn't dispute that claim. If my father said he'd smelled blood, then I had to believe him. I touched his sleeve. "Are you all right?"

He whispered brokenly, "I'll recover, but I might not ever be the same. It's one thing to smell an animal's blood, but quite another to smell a human's."

Natalie rushed up. Her eyes were enormous in her round, pale face. "Bretta, Allison says your father found a body in the garden. What are we going to do?"

I stared at the matte of foliage that had been welcoming in the sunlight but looked threatening by night. Shivering, I said, "Wait for the authorities."

Natalie's fingers gripped my arm. "Who is it? Shouldn't we do something?"

"Dad didn't see who it was. I think the safest place for us is right here." I swept the area with a worried gaze. "People are leaving. The authorities will want to question everyone. You should try to keep them on the property. Those gates at the bottom of the hill need to be closed."

My father hobbled to a golf cart parked in the driveway and slid behind the wheel. I thought he'd taken the closest seat available because his legs ached. I should have known better.

"Don't give those gates another thought," said Dad. "The bastard isn't getting away."

"No! Dad! No!" But he didn't stop. My father headed down the drive. His gray hair shone in the headlights as he recklessly drove between cars, cutting them off. Gravel rolled under tires as brake lights flared red.

"Your father is a brave man," said Natalie.

"Brave?" I heaved a sigh. "He's nuts. What was he doing in the garden, anyway? Why wasn't he watching the fireworks with the rest of us?"

Natalie smiled shakily. "From what Allison said, she and your father were having a clandestine meeting."

"Clandestine? Why? They're both *way* beyond the age of consent."

I hadn't noticed Allison standing nearby. At my words she stormed over and set me straight. "I'll have you know, Bretta, we had your best interests at heart. I told your father you don't like me, and we'd best keep our friendship a secret."

I spluttered. "*I* don't like you? What about how you feel about me?"

Allison's tone was haughty. "That's immaterial at the moment."

Natalie held up her hands. "This is *all* immaterial. I want to know who is in my garden. Who's dead?"

Allison shook her head. "I don't know. I didn't see the body. Bertie and I didn't have a flashlight."

I gasped. "Bertie?" Not by any stretch of the imagination was my father a *Bertie*.

Allison tossed her head. "Bertie stumbled in the dark. I grabbed him around the waist to help steady him. He put his arm around me and we —" She stopped and shot me a quick glance.

I kept my face impassive, but inside I cringed. Of all the women my father could have chosen, why had he picked Allison? I motioned for her to continue. "Go on," I said. "We get the picture."

Knowing that it would annoy me, Allison said, "Once Bertie and I came up for air, he told me he'd tripped over something. He reached down and touched a leg. That's when he hustled me out of there."

"Dad says there's blood."

Allison lifted a shoulder. "I didn't see it, but the grass was slick under my feet."

Natalie and I looked at her shoes. My stomach lurched. The white leather was heavily discolored. This time there was no doubt. It was fresh blood.

Allison bent over to get a better view of her feet. Her voice held an incredulous note. "How much blood does a human body hold? It looks like I waded in it." She stood up and the realization of what she'd said sank in. She screeched. "I want these shoes off. I want —" She gagged. And gagged again. "I'm gonna be sick," she mumbled, her hand clasped over her mouth.

I never thought I'd have anything in common with Allison Thorpe, but at that moment I was in total agreement. Bile burned my throat and made my eyes water. Natalie grabbed Allison's arm and guided her to the privacy of a gangly forsythia bush. As I listened to Allison eject the contents of her stomach, I wondered if I'd have to join her behind the shrub. Waves of nausea rolled over me. I shut out the sounds of Allison's retching and focused on the people.

They stood in tight groups, watching and waiting. I wished for more light so I could study the faces, but the glow from the yard and porch lights didn't extend to where most had congregated. Donovan had arrived. His arm was wrapped around

Emily. I thought I saw Harley, but in the dark I couldn't be sure. I searched for Jacob, but didn't see him. Jess, however, caught my eye and started toward me. I shook my head at him. I didn't feel like talking.

Time crawled as tension mounted. The greenhouses were twenty minutes from River City. Help would be at least that far away unless a patrol car happened to be cruising in this part of the county. That didn't seem to be the case, as more minutes passed. My heart's rhythm settled into a wait-and-see pattern. Then I caught the unmistakable sound of sirens in the distance.

The cacophony increased as the cars got closer. My pulse thudded with dread at what was coming — the disclosure of the body's identity, the questions, the piecing together of information. I hadn't used the word *murder* even in my thoughts, but that was the logical conclusion.

Tires squealed at the bottom of the bluff, but the sirens didn't cease. We traced their route up the hill by the flashing lights that shone against the treetops. As the entourage rolled toward us, I swallowed uneasily. The third car in the parade of emergency vehicles belonged to

Sidney Hancock, sheriff of Spencer County.

From the moment Sid stepped from his patrol car he made it known that he was in charge. He issued orders to his deputies. They fanned out along the driveway, facing the fortress of foliage.

A paramedic shouted, "Where we going, Sheriff?"

"I'm about to find out," said Sid. He went around his car and opened the passenger door. Only then did I see my father sitting on the front seat. He tried to get out, but his movements were stiff and painful. Sid reached in to assist, but my father quickly shrugged away his offer of help.

Once my father was standing, Sid said something I couldn't hear. My father replied, "I think I remember."

From his answer and given the circumstances, I figured Sid had asked my father to take him to the body. I was pretty sure what my reception would be, but I didn't want my father to face that task without moral support. I walked toward them, my shoes crunching on the gravel.

Sid spun around. He proves the adage that redheads have fiery tempers. His was in control at the moment, but he was as volatile as a keg of TNT. My husband had been one of Sid's deputies and a good friend. I couldn't make that claim. Sid didn't approve of my amateur sleuthing, even though I'd had favorable results.

He faced me with his hands on his gun belt and his shoulders bowed in an aggressive manner. In a fairly pleasant tone, he said, "I assumed you'd be here when I saw your father. Whose idea was it to station him at the gate?"

"His."

Sid nodded. "Let's hope he can be just as resourceful when it comes to leading us to the body. He's told me the story, but he's a little hazy on the location. From his general directions, I've sent two officers into the garden, but we may need him to narrow the search. Since you're here, you can come with us."

"What do you mean *hazy?*"

"He says he found the body near a piece of statuary."

My heart sank. "I can think of at least six different statues in this garden."

Dad said, "It was a big piece of marble."

"That's helpful," muttered Sid. "Let's get started." He motioned for my father and me to follow him.

When Natalie, Allison, and several others

fell into step behind us, Sid roared, "Holy crap! This ain't no sideshow. You all stay put. Deputy, I don't want anyone in these gardens except authorized personnel. Got it?"

"Yes, sir," said the deputy. "Let's go, folks. Everyone up on the porch where I can keep an eye on you."

As we entered the garden, I glanced back. About thirty people were being herded toward the lodge. I wanted to see who was present and who was missing, but Sid nudged me. "Keep walking," he said. "Stay next to me. Don't go off on any of your wild tangents."

I had no intention of doing anything except making sure my father was all right. He was shakier than usual, unsteady on his feet. I realized he didn't have his walking stick.

Sid had his head turned, talking into his walkie-talkie. In an undertone, I asked Dad, "Where's your walking stick?"

He cast a swift look ahead of us. I had no doubt that he'd dropped it when he'd stumbled over the body. I decided it would be in my father's best interests if I explained before Sid put his own spin on the situation.

"Uh . . . Sid," I began. "My father —"

"Shh!" he hissed at me. Into the radio, he said, "Yeah. Go ahead." He listened intently, but all I heard was gibberish and static.

Sid finished his conversation and turned to me. "We've had an unexpected stroke of luck. We've located the body, so I don't need your father's help in that respect. But I need an ID. I can have Natalie Parker brought to me, but since you're this close, will you do it?"

The nerves under my skin crawled with apprehension. I didn't want to perform this gruesome task, but I didn't want Natalie to face it either. I took a shaky breath. "I'll try, but there were people here today I didn't know."

Sid's voice was grave. "According to one of my deputies it's bad, Bretta. We're dealing with a savage murder. Prepare yourself."

Sid's concern increased my anxiety. How was I supposed to prepare? As a florist I deal with death on a regular basis, speaking with bereaved families, delivering flowers to the local funeral homes. But those events were after the fact. After the body had been cleaned and dressed in his Sunday best. After makeup had been applied to conceal the harsh reality of what had led to his demise. On the other hand, my amateur detecting had unearthed a few victims, but none had saturated the ground with freshly spilled blood. It was the blood that was getting to me.

We turned the corner of the path. In a quiet voice, Sid explained, "I've called the fire department to bring their halogen lights so we can make a thorough search of the crime scene. They should be here pronto, but I'm not waiting. My deputies have flashlights, and we also have these little path lamps to help light the area." He nodded to the spot ahead of us. "I think you'll be able to see enough to try to make an identification."

Six deputies and two paramedics watched our approach. Flashlights cast an eerie glow on their faces, revealing the heightened tension. I kept my gaze off the ground and on the marble cornucopia that loomed ahead of me. I'd always admired this piece of statuary. Dan's grandfather had commissioned a sculptor to create a piece of art that would commemorate the productiveness of this land. The horn was approximately fifteen feet in length and about eight feet wide. It was cantilevered on a base with washtub-sized fruit and vegetables spilling forth.

These thoughts raced through my head, but I never lost track of what I was about to do. I glanced down briefly and saw a bare leg splattered with blood. The sight made my knees weak, and I wobbled.

"Bretta," said Dad, grabbing my arm, "I don't think this is a good idea. Let someone else do it."

I patted his hand. "I'll be fine, Dad, but you stay here." When he started to protest, I said, "Please. It will be easier for me if I don't have to worry about you."

He nodded and gave my arm a gentle squeeze. I moved forward, trying not to drag my feet. In my mind I repeated the words, *Let it be a stranger. Let it be a stranger.* Perhaps I thought if I didn't know who'd been killed, the horror would be lessened.

As we neared the body, Sid moved closer to me. "This is as far as we go. I don't want the scene contaminated by our footprints on the grass. Don't try to take in details," he cautioned. "Give the face a swift look, then another to make sure. Don't stare. Don't commit anything to memory."

I tried to do as Sid suggested. One swift look and I could leave. But my eyes refused to zoom in. Slowly my gaze traveled over the blood-splattered grass, up the shapely legs, to a pair of shorts and a jade-green T-shirt drenched in scarlet.

"You're taking too long," said Sid. "For your own peace of mind, Bretta, give her face a look. Do you know her?"

Tangled ringlets of red hair. Blue-green eyes wide and staring. I nodded because I couldn't speak.

"Who is it?" demanded Sid.

I blinked back tears. "Marnie Frazier. She . . . uh . . . was Dan Parker's lab assistant."

Sid asked, "Without a doubt?"

Numbly I repeated, "Without a doubt."

"Okay, let's get you out of here."

Sid tugged on my arm, but I couldn't move. A copper plant marker lay near Marnie's head. A jagged hole marred her smooth neck. "There's so much blood," I murmured.

Grimly, Sid said, "The tines of the marker probably pierced her carotid artery. Blood would've spurted like a —" Abruptly he stopped. In a brisk tone, he said, "That's enough, Bretta. Come on."

My feet felt as if they were glued to the path. I stumbled when I turned. Sid took a tighter grip on my arm. "I told you not to stare," he said, and practically dragged me to where my father waited. "I have work to do here. I'll have an officer escort you both to the house. There's to be no talking to each other or to anyone else. I don't want the victim's name revealed." He stared at me. "Is that understood?"

"Yes," I said. "I won't say anything."

Sid summoned a deputy and ordered, "Keep Mrs. Solomon and her father away from each other and from the others. I'll be there shortly."

We headed single file back down the path with the officer bringing up the rear. The path lights cast our bodies' shadows into deformed, unrecognizable shapes. The eerie sight merged with the horror I'd seen. Had Marnie been killed while we'd watched the fireworks? Had the bright flashes distorted the killer's face so she hadn't realized she was in danger?

I felt sure Marnie had known her attacker. There was no doubt in my mind that she'd come here to meet someone. She'd wanted me to explain how to conduct an investigation, and I'd let her down. I hadn't warned her that the most innocent of inquiries could have devastating results, especially if evil is at its crux.

In that paralyzing moment before the killer took her life, had Marnie realized her mistake? By then it would have been too late. Just as it was too late to explain that in such a confrontation, the only one to remain unscathed was the shadow of death.

Chapter Three

Back at the lodge, Dad was asked to make himself comfortable on a bench. I was taken to the sheriff's car. Peering through the bug-splattered windshield, I counted thirty-three people standing on the porch. The deputy, who had escorted Dad and me from the garden, waited on the gravel drive. The other deputy, who had been assigned to watch over the people on the porch, gave instructions. I couldn't hear what he said, but the group divided. Parker employees went to the west end of the porch. The guests remained at the east end.

This was the first time today I'd seen the employees — Harley, Jess, Eugene, Irma, and Jacob — together in one place. They were actually a fraction of the greenhouse work force. The regular workers had the day off while management had hosted the day's celebration. Natalie stood with her uncle Donovan, who worked at the greenhouse. Emily hesitated on the steps, unsure where she should stand. She wasn't an employee, but she was Donovan's wife. She probably didn't feel like a guest either. Donovan waved her to his side. She nodded and slipped into the curve of his arm.

I had my gaze on Natalie, saw her take a head count, and knew the exact moment when she missed Marnie. She twisted and turned, searching for the young redhead. Donovan turned to say something to her, but the deputy quickly called for silence.

Natalie touched her lips with her fingertips, and she stared across the driveway at me. I met her gaze. All I had to do was nod, and she'd know it was Marnie's body in the garden. I fought the urge and didn't move a muscle. Natalie shook her head sadly.

After forty-five long minutes, Sid strode from the garden followed by two deputies. He motioned for me to get out of the car. I went to stand near him as he addressed the group on the porch.

In a clear, authoritative voice, Sid said, "There has been a murder. In order for me to do my job, I need your cooperation. I understand there were a number of people here today. Just because they aren't here now doesn't mean they won't be questioned. I will ask Mrs. Parker to give me the invitation list. Everyone on that list will be contacted.

"As we proceed with the questioning, it *will not* be up to you to decide what is relevant and what is not. My deputies and I will sort out the information, but you have to do your part. We need facts. We need your assistance."

"Who's dead?" called someone from the guest side of the porch.

"I'll get to that later," said Sid. "Right now, I want your names and addresses. My deputies will collect that information and then we'll take your statements."

Annoyed murmurs rose from the group. Sid held up his hands. "I know it's late. We'll make this as quick as possible, but I'm not going to jeopardize my investigation to accommodate any of you. Is that understood?"

His answer was a restless shuffle of feet. Sid seemed satisfied. He turned to me and spoke quietly. "Look at everyone up there on that porch. Have any of them changed their clothes?"

I bit my bottom lip. He was asking because so much blood was involved. "I don't know, Sid. I didn't pay any attention —"

"Just give them a look, okay?"

I did as he asked, which meant I had to stare at each person, feel his or her eyes bore back at me. I squirmed. "Sid, all the employees have on their Parker uniforms. Natalie was dressed in orange, and she still is. Donovan was gone to take Dan to the airport, so I don't know what he was wearing. His wife, Emily, has on the same clothes. As for the rest of the guests, I haven't got a clue as to what they had on."

Sid heaved a sigh. "Didn't figure that hope would pan out, but thought it was worth a try. You and your father can go home. I'll come by tomorrow and talk to both of you. Until then keep your mouths shut. Don't discuss this case with anyone and that includes each other. Got it?"

"When are you going to tell them Marnie is dead?"

"When the time is right."

"I think the employees already know." Sid's eyebrows drew down, and I hurried on. "When your deputy divided the group, Natalie immediately missed Marnie."

"They can surmise whatever they please, but they can't know for certain until I tell them. That's the way I want it. That's the way it will be done."

Unexpected tears filled my eyes. "I feel terrible leaving Natalie alone to cope with this. Her husband, Dan, had to go to Oregon because his mother is gravely ill."

Sid frowned. "Don't fall apart now. You

did good in the garden. You made the ID and spared Mrs. Parker that loathsome chore. Tomorrow after I talk to you, you can come back and be with her, but for now, go on home."

My father hobbled toward us. I asked Sid, "What about Dad's walking stick? Can we have —"

Sid's tone was firm. "It's part of the crime scene. He'll have to buy himself a new one."

Every eye was on me as I helped Dad into the SUV. I climbed behind the steering wheel and started the engine. Before I put the machine into gear, I gazed at the porch. One by one I scanned the faces, wondering if a killer stared back at me.

The pleading look Natalie gave me tore at my heart. Eugene nodded. Jess frowned. Donovan shook his head sadly. Irma's arms were folded protectively across her chest, but she'd edged closer to Harley. Jacob's slim shoulders were stooped. I moved my gaze to the guest end of the porch and encountered Allison's stony glare. Roused into action, I put the gearshift into drive.

As we left the lodge behind, my father said, "Who, what, when, where, why, and how. We know the where, the when, and the how. But *what* went on in that garden? *Who* was with Marnie? *Why* was she killed?"

"Dad, you heard Sid. We can't discuss the case." Under my breath, I added, "But those are damned fine questions. I hope Sid is primed to find the answers."

That night I slept little. I got up at seven, which was unheard of for me on a Sunday morning. I like to start my day of rest at a slow pace, leisurely waking, puttering around in my robe, and drinking coffee on the terrace. Since I didn't know what time Sid would arrive, I was dressed in shorts and T-shirt before eight o'clock.

I came down the back staircase, which put me near the terrace doors. I stopped and stared at the half-finished project that ultimately would be one of the finest gardens in this area — or so boasted Eddie, my landscaper. I couldn't see it yet. The place looked as if it had been terrorized. All that remained of the original garden were the concrete lily pool, some century-old trees, and a few group plantings that Eddie hadn't been able to identify. Before he uprooted them, he was doing some research.

The rejuvenation of my garden had been

put on hold because it was August. The weather was too hot, the ground too dry for planting. All the main features were in place. The raised beds waited for rich soil to be brought in. The old brick walkways had been re-laid with new grouting so the crisscross pattern was distinctive. A tire swing stirred lazily in the hot air. An arbor had been constructed of lattice. The stark white boards fairly begged for some green vines to curl over them, softening their sharp angles.

I might have gone out to look around, but the house was deliciously cool. I wasn't in the mood to sweat or fight the bugs. The offensive little critters always mistook me for their next meal.

I wandered down the hall, pausing in the foyer. My home's architectural style was Greek Revival. The exterior was pure southern hospitality. Lovely fluted columns supported a veranda that I'd outfitted with comfortable chairs and a chaise longue that I rarely had the opportunity to use.

Inside the house, a horseshoe-shaped staircase curved elegantly to the second story. The foyer was the height of both floors and was illuminated by a crystal chandelier. The main floor contained a state-of-the-art kitchen, a dining room, a library, and a ballroom. The west wing served as employees' living quarters. The east wing was a three-car garage.

I'd spent plenty of time and money renovating the downstairs. My father was supervising the remodeling of the upstairs. The work was coming along nicely. By Christmas I hoped to have the extra rooms rented to my first boarders. I had plans to turn this big, historic home into a boardinghouse to help defray the expense of renovation. I'd thought about running a bed-and-breakfast, but I didn't have the time to devote to keeping track of reservations, and I didn't want to hire anyone to do this task. Besides, I liked constancy. I wanted to get to know the people that stayed in my home.

My stomach growled, reminding me that it was time to eat. I moved into the kitchen where I had the place to myself. Normally, my housekeeper, DeeDee, was up and cooking. At twenty-three, she was passionate about the process of creating fine cuisine. She especially liked to revamp ordinary recipes into fabulous edibles, while keeping the calorie and fat grams to a minimum. Since I was forever watching my weight but loved good food, I encouraged her to cook up a storm.

I had the refrigerator door open, studying the contents, when I heard DeeDee enter the kitchen. I glanced around. She'd recently had her dark hair trimmed and permed into a neat cap of curls. Her shoulders were square, her waist dainty. In a pair of shorts and crop top, she looked fresh and cool. I might have complimented her, but I had other things on my mind. I pointed to a shelf that contained several covered bowls.

"What's in those?" I asked. "I'm hungry."

DeeDee rolled her large, expressive brown eyes. "What's new about that?"

I grinned. When I'd first met DeeDee she stuttered so badly she rarely spoke. It hadn't helped her situation to be tethered to her mother's protective apron strings. Leaving home and coming to work for me had broadened the scope of DeeDee's life. Learning to cook, keeping my household running smoothly had given her poise and confidence. I loved her like a daughter. Hearing her speak without stuttering was gratifying. I couldn't have been more proud of her had she been my own flesh and blood. I wanted to give her a hug, but that would have embarrassed her.

Teasingly, I said, "You're becoming a gabby, brazen little hussy, aren't you?"

DeeDee spoke slowly. "It is the fault of the people I associate with."

I lowered my eyebrows and frowned. "I knew my father would be a bad influence on you."

DeeDee chuckled. "Albert isn't the problem." She moved past me and reached into the refrigerator. Removing a casserole dish from the bottom shelf, she said, "You're up early. It'll t-take fifteen minutes to w-warm up this c-crustless quiche." With her knee, she gave the door a nudge.

Fifteen minutes? My stomach craved food now. Just as the door was about to close, I saw a hunk of Colby cheese wrapped in cellophane. I made a successful snatch and took my appetizer to the table. After I'd sat down, I removed the wrapping and munched in silence, staring off into space.

"You're not t-talking," said DeeDee. She picked up the piece of plastic I'd left on the table and tossed it into the trash. "That's not a g-good sign. Neither is your being up early. What's going on?"

"Sid is coming by later."

"The s-sheriff?"

I nodded. "He's taking my statement. A young woman was murdered yesterday in the Parkers' garden. My father found the body, and I made the identification."

DeeDee's eyes grew round. "O-oh, n-no. T-that's t-terrible."

DeeDee's stuttering always increased when she was worried or nervous. I wanted to reassure her that everything would be fine, but how could I? Marnie was dead. A killer was free, unless Sid had made an arrest, which seemed unlikely this early in the investigation.

DeeDee checked the oven temperature. She fussed with the dial, picked up a potholder, and smoothed the calico-print fabric. When she spoke, it was on a different subject. "Bailey c-called last night. H-he said to t-tell you he w-would see you t-today."

I heard DeeDee, but steered my thoughts away from Bailey Monroe and concentrated on what my father had said last night as we drove away from the lodge.

Who? What? When? Where? Why? How?

I skipped the *who* and wondered about the *what*. What had Marnie known or suspected that made her a threat? She had wanted the answers to what kind of questions? Nothing came to me. Perhaps I should approach the possible motive from another angle. What was the driving force behind her murder? Was the emotion rage, fear, or revenge?

I sighed softly. I had more questions than answers. I lacked information. When it came to the victim, I knew very little. Marnie had planned to attend college this fall and major in finance. She'd worked for Dan since the first of June. I'd heard him say that Marnie was an excellent lab assistant. Her interest in numbers and accuracy had coincided with his need for exactness when it came to keeping records on his hybridizing program.

DeeDee set a cup of coffee in front of me. "I just t-told you B-Bailey called last n-night, but you're thinking about that m-murder."

I didn't deny it.

DeeDee frowned. "If my b-boyfriend was c-coming to see me, I'd be thinking about h-him. Not m-murder."

I wrinkled my nose. Boyfriend? That sounded juvenile. I was a mature woman with her forty-sixth birthday due in three days. My hair was more gray than brown. I leaned forward so I could see my reflection in the glass-fronted china cabinet.

I touched the lines that framed my blue eyes. I liked to think those creases came from smiling too much, not from getting older. Lately I'd taken to smoothing on globs of night cream, which advertised the reversal of sagging, aging flesh into the elasticity of youth. I lived in hope that some morning I'd wake up to a complexion that had the texture of a magnolia blossom. So far the only change I'd noticed was the oily stain on my pillowcase.

I took a sip of coffee and watched DeeDee check on the quiche. Curious, I asked, "What would you have me do to prepare for Bailey's arrival?"

DeeDee closed the oven door and stepped back to lean against the counter. Speaking slowly, she said, "This is the first t-time he has c-come over since the accident. After he called, I fixed s-some s-special treats."

I gestured to the refrigerator. "Now I understand the covered dishes. You think we should have a party to celebrate?" When she nodded, I said, "That's a good plan. I wish I'd thought of it, but the last few weeks have been trying. His daughter made it clear I wasn't needed while he was recuperating."

"Jillian l-left three days ago."

"Which is my point. Bailey could have called me earlier in the week. I've waited because I don't want to push myself on him."

DeeDee made a face and went to the refrigerator.

A couple of months ago the truck Bailey and I'd been riding in had been viciously rammed by another vehicle. I'd had my seat belt on. Bailey hadn't. He'd been thrown from the truck, sustaining a broken leg and trauma to his brain. For several days he'd been in a coma, and I'd visited him daily.

My cheeks grew hot as I remembered how I'd taken advantage of his condition. I'd used the time to hold his hand and talk to him in total honesty about my feelings for him, and how lonesome I'd been since Carl's death. When Bailey came out of the coma, I was nervous about seeing him. But he never mentioned those times when I'd sat at his side, pouring out my innermost thoughts.

Since Bailey owns the cottage that's located at the edge of my property, it had been convenient to see him as often as I liked, but Jillian had put a stop to my dropping by. The dutiful daughter had guarded Bailey with zealous jealousy, letting me know that my help wasn't needed, and that I shouldn't make it a habit of stopping by unannounced. I was hurt that Bailey hadn't taken a stand. Why hadn't he told Jillian that I was always welcome in his home?

I heaved a sigh. I was pretty sure I loved him. He knew and I knew there was something special between us. But his being in the hospital, his lengthy convalescence, and Jillian living in his house had put our relationship on hold.

For the last few weeks I've ached to see him. To gaze again into his coppery brown eyes. To feel the heady rush of being near him. It didn't make it any easier that he lived less than a quarter of a mile away. Last week I'd finally given in to my urge to see him.

One evening I'd walked across my driveway and taken the path that led to his cottage. I wasn't going to upset Jillian by knocking at the door. On tiptoes, I'd approached the window and peeked in. I thought Bailey was asleep in his recliner. I'd stared at him like a love-struck teenager. His hair curled boyishly around his ears and needed to be trimmed. Jillian was seated at his desk, her fingers rapidly tapping the keyboard of his computer. She stopped typing and said something. Bailey opened his eyes and laughed. He turned his gaze to the window, and for a moment our eyes had locked. Bailey could have motioned for me to come in, but he had deliberately shifted his position, giving me a view of his broad back.

A piece of quiche perched on a saucer appeared in front of me. I glanced up to say thank you, but found DeeDee glaring at me. "What?" I said.

"Are you still thinking m-murder?"

I snorted. "Nope. You've driven that subject clean out of my head."

"Good."

I frowned. "What's good about it? Sid will be here sometime today. I'd like to have my statement straight so I don't sound ditzy."

"You are never d-ditzy. What you really want is to h-have a theory in m-mind so you can get h-him to d-discuss the case with you."

I leaned back in my chair to stare at her. "That sounds like manipulation. Gosh, I don't think I had that planned." I shrugged and picked up my fork. "But it sounds like an excellent idea." I grinned at DeeDee. "Thanks."

She sniffed disdainfully. "Your s-subconscious is always at w-work. It's f-feeding you information all the t-time."

"And speaking of feeding —" I cut off a chunk of quiche, gave it a couple of puffs to cool it before popping the bite into my mouth. Closing my eyes, I chewed blissfully. "Mmm," I said after swallowing. "Green peppers, smoky bacon, sweet onions, and tangy Swiss cheese. Delicious. Another culinary masterpiece. How many calories?"

"Too many, but for b-breakfast, I thought it w-wouldn't hurt. You have the r-rest of the day to w-work them off."

I sighed and cut off another bite. "Wrangling with Sid should raise my metabolism."

DeeDee snickered. "Burning with d-desire for Bailey could d-do it, too."

I shook my head at her. "Very funny."

My fork was loaded with another bite of quiche. I had it poised, ready to pop into my mouth when the doorbell rang. My hand jerked at the sound. The lump of quiche tumbled down the front of my shirt.

"Hell and damnation," I muttered, wiping at the greasy blotch. I gathered up the crumbs and dropped them on the saucer.

DeeDee started across the kitchen but stopped. In an ominous tone, she said, "Who w-will be at the d-door?" She widened her eyes in mock terror. "The sheriff?" She rearranged her expression, fluttering her eyelashes. She cradled her hands over her heart and put a seductive note in her voice. "Or the prospective lover?" Giggling, she went into the foyer.

I came slowly to my feet. Sid or Bailey. It didn't matter who it was at the door. Both men represented an upheaval to my life, just from opposite ends of my emotional spectrum.

Chapter Four

I peeked around the corner and watched DeeDee open the door. I didn't realize I'd been holding my breath until I saw Sid. Releasing the pent-up air, I walked into the foyer. I wasn't sure how to greet him. I would be lying through my teeth if I said I was glad to see him. When he was involved in a case he could be as abrasive as an emery board. When he *wasn't* involved in a case he could be just as grating.

Food usually took the edge off his crabbiness, so I said, "Come on in. Are you hungry? Do you want something to eat?"

"Yeah. Yeah. That would be good," Sid said as he crossed the threshold. "It's been a long night."

"Do you want to sit out on the veranda or in the —"

"We're staying inside. I've had my fill of nature. Damned leaves and twigs." Sid scratched his arm. "I've been itching like a son of a — I think I'm having an allergic reaction to some of that vegetation."

I looked at DeeDee. "Will you fix Sid a

tray and bring it into the library?"

She nodded, shot Sid a quick glance, and then skedaddled into the kitchen. I led the way into the library and motioned Sid to one of the wingback chairs. I took a seat on its companion.

He ignored my invitation and slouched on the sofa, staring around him. It was a comfortable room. Moss green, cream, and gold upholstered furniture brightened the dark walnut paneling. An Oriental rug picked up the same colors with a dash of peacock blue for panache. I hadn't opened the drapes so the room was shadowy and cool.

"Nice," murmured Sid. He closed his eyes.

I waited a few minutes. When he didn't move, I whispered, "Sid, are you asleep?"

He didn't stir. "Was I snoring?" he asked grumpily.

"No, but —"

"Then I'm not asleep." More minutes passed before he groaned and pulled himself upright. "I guess you've had a good night's sleep and are eager to talk."

I shrugged. "We can wait until you've had something to eat."

"Tempting offer, but I haven't the time. You can give a formal statement later.

Right now I want to hear your rendition of events."

I held out my hands. "What can I say? Yesterday went well, as far as I could tell. I didn't get there until after five o'clock. Everyone was congenial and seemed to be having a good time. I didn't overhear any arguments or rude comments. I didn't notice any friction. It was just a relaxing day."

"That ended in murder. What else?"

"The only thing that comes to mind is that Marnie expressed an interest in how I went about solving a mystery. When I asked her what she wanted to know, she tried to act as if it was no big deal, and she beat a hasty retreat."

Sid wasn't impressed. He took his cap off and laid it on the cushion next to him. Running a hand over his springy red hair, he said, "My deputies and I have tracked down witnesses either by phone or personally all night. We have statements out the wazoo. Two hundred people were expected for the Parker celebration, but that many didn't show up. We still had to contact them all, ask if they attended, and then get verification from those who were there to make sure we weren't getting the runaround."

Sid leaned back and rolled his eyes.

"And speaking of *the runaround*. You won't believe the responses we got when we asked about the victim." His tone turned sarcastic. "Accolades. 'She was thoughtful, kind, and generous.' I was even told she was punctual." Sid's voice was grim. "This was one appointment when it would have behooved her to be less than dependable."

My interest quickened. "Appointment? You've found out that Marnie was meeting someone in the garden?"

"Yeah, that bit of evidence was a real kick in the ass. We could have zeroed in on the employees instead of pussyfooting around with the guests, if we'd found that note right at the start."

Sid was spouting information like an uncapped volcano. I didn't want to halt the flow, but I wasn't clear on this point. Tentatively, I asked, "What note?"

Without hesitation, Sid said, "About four o'clock this morning, Deputy Meyer found a wadded-up piece of paper under a plant on the path near the crime scene. By that time, we were all sleep deprived, but Deputy Meyer was alert. She brought that scrap of paper to me."

Before I could think of a way to finagle the contents of that note out of Sid, he said, "I've got the damned thing memorized. *'Life is precious. There are choices. Meet me at the cornucopia sculpture tomorrow during the fireworks.'* "

" 'Life is precious. There are choices.' That sounds like an argument to stop a possible suicide."

Sid gave me a disgusted look. "The victim didn't die from a self-inflicted wound, Bretta. By the note saying 'tomorrow' I figure it was typed on Friday."

He stretched out his legs and sighed. "In the olden days we'd have looked for a typewriter that had a key askew. We'd match up the machine to the owner, and we'd have our man. Only now we have computers. No crooked key to lead us to the culprit."

To my amazement, he shot me a grin. "But technology isn't foolproof. Near the loading dock we found an old dot-matrix printer and computer. Because of the dirt, dust, and humidity of the greenhouses, the set-up is basic — no frills or thrills. That printer has a habit of spitting a dab of extra ink every time it makes the letter 'e.' It isn't a crooked letter, but it's just as distinctive."

I'd been saturated with information. Why was Sid feeding me these facts? Apparently, he wasn't finished.

"Because of the wording on that note,"

said Sid, "and the location of that printer, we've narrowed our list of suspects down to the Parker Greenhouse management team that worked yesterday."

Suddenly Sid sat up straight and stared at me. To my utter confusion, he actually expressed a theory. "Maybe what Marnie said to you *is* important. What if *she* wrote that note to the killer? What if *she* made the date to meet in the garden?" He looked at me expectantly.

Shocked that he would be interested in what I had to say, I mumbled, "Gosh, Sid, anything is possible."

He made a circular motion with his hand, encouraging me to continue. Feeling my way, I said, "In my opinion, I think you're on the right track. I don't know if Marnie wrote that note, but I thought from the start that she knew her killer and had met him because she wanted some answers to some questions."

He leaned eagerly toward me. "Do you have any idea what subject she was tackling?"

I shook my head. "I haven't got a clue. But why are you filling me in on this case? Why are you interested in my thoughts?"

From the doorway, my father said, "That's obvious, Bretta." He came into the room carrying a tray, which he carefully placed on the coffee table. "It's an election year. The sheriff won the August primary last week, but he still faces the November ballot, and his opponent is closing the gap. In town the word is out that if our present sheriff doesn't solve this case in a jiffy, he'll be looking for a new vocation." Dad quirked an eyebrow at Sid. "How's your appetite . . . now?"

Sid scowled. "Go peddle your sleazy gossip somewhere else. I'm taking Bretta's statement."

Dad cocked his head. "Funny, but the only voice I heard in here was yours, Sheriff. Sounds to me like you're trying to cover all the bases. My daughter has a knack for observation and you know that. Admit it. You want her input. You want to pick her brain, but first, you had to give her something, so she'd feel obligated to reciprocate."

I looked from my father's narrowed eyes to Sid's red face. My shoulders sagged. *Here we go again,* I thought. When Dad arrived back in River City, he and Sid had gotten off on the wrong foot. Sid didn't like the idea of Dad opening a detective agency, and Dad didn't like Sid's brusque manner. Last night they'd tolerated each other, but I guess that was due to the situation, not a newfound benevolence.

In a soothing tone, I said, "Dad, please. Marnie is dead. Her killer has to be found. Regardless of Sid's motives, I'll help any way I can."

Dad snorted. "The sheriff knows that. What I find annoying is that he didn't come right out and ask for your help. He's been skirting the issue."

I braced myself for Sid's angry roar. It didn't come. He reached for the tray and poured himself a cup of coffee. The only hint I had that he was holding himself tightly in check was the slight tremor of his hand. The man was seething, but he presented a well-controlled exterior.

Sid sipped his coffee. Cradling the cup in his palm, he finally nodded. "You're right, Albert. Right as rain. Carl always said I'd come to recognize Bretta's talents. I'll admit she's done some fine work in the past, but she leaps into situations and then wonders if there's a safety net to catch her. I promised Carl I'd watch out for her. I've been her *net* a couple of times, but that doesn't mean I'll be there in the future. If I'm not reelected, the next sheriff might not be so accommodating."

Dad threw up his hands. "Who are you

trying to kid? You're not here because of any promise you made to her deceased husband. That's a bunch of malarkey. You're here for selfish reasons. You think Bretta can help you."

Carefully, Sid set the coffee cup down. He looked at the tray wistfully. The plate contained a thick slice of country-cured ham, two fried eggs, and a blueberry muffin split and oozing melted butter.

Nodding to the tray, Sid said, "Bretta, the price of that breakfast is too damned steep. I won't pay for it by taking crap from your father. This time I thought we could work together where it might mutually benefit us." He stood, picked up his cap, and fit it on his head. "That was a mistake on my part." Without another word, he strode out of the room.

I stumbled to my feet and hurried after Sid, but he was out the front door and into his car. I stood on the veranda and watched him speed down the drive.

"Well, I guess I told him a thing or two," said my father from behind me.

I whirled around. "Why did you do that, Dad? Don't you realize how hard it was for Sid to say those things? He's a good man. A good sheriff. I want him reelected and if I can help, I'll do it."

"Then my vote will cancel yours because I think Spencer County needs a new sheriff."

I didn't answer but went back into the house. Dad trailed along behind me. I was wondering how I could set things right when the phone rang. I hollered to DeeDee that I would get it. It was Sid.

"Bretta," he said in a clipped tone. "Mrs. Parker knew I was coming to see you. She asked that I tell you she'd like for you to come to the lodge as soon as possible."

"Sid, I'm sorry —"

"I've given you the message. Good-bye."

My father was at my elbow. "What did *he* want now?"

"He didn't want anything. He was passing a message on to me from Natalie."

"What was it?"

"Dad, I'm not in a very good mood right now." I stepped into the kitchen doorway. "DeeDee, I'm leaving. I'll be back after a while."

She turned away from the bowl she was stirring. "What a-about Bailey? What if h-he comes over?"

"Start the party without me," I said recklessly.

I went upstairs, grabbed my purse, and then headed for the garage. I backed my

SUV out and drove down the lane. Glancing in the direction of Bailey's house, I wondered if I was using Natalie's invitation as an excuse to get away before he showed up. I gritted my teeth. Maybe it was best this way. I wasn't in the frame of mind to be patient and understanding.

The twenty-minute drive gave me plenty of time to think. My thoughts skimmed and skittered over the information Sid had disclosed, but I couldn't focus on any particular point.

It would narrow the scope of the investigation if Sid could dismiss the guests as suspects, but that had its downside. Dan and Natalie looked on and treated their employees as though they were part of one big, happy family.

Would Bailey have a reasonable explanation as to why he'd slighted me?

Why did my father have to interfere in my life?

Sid hadn't mentioned Jacob. How was the young Amish man coping with Marnie's death?

Was the November election going to be close? What would Sid do if he didn't win? At one time he'd done investigative work for an insurance company, but he loved being sheriff.

How was Dan's mother?

Why was Bailey coming to the house to see me?

Bailey. Sid. Dad. Natalie. Jacob. Marnie. Murder.

I wanted to stomp my feet in anger and frustration, but I was driving a high-powered vehicle. Not the time to do any stomping. On a straightaway piece of highway, I pushed harder on the accelerator and watched the speedometer needle climb. When it hit seventy-five, I lowered the windows and jacked up the volume on the radio. With the hot wind in my face and Bob Seger blaring from the speakers, I pretended I was a rebel, a renegade, who didn't have to worry about anything or anyone.

That flash of defiance lasted for about a mile before I eased off the gas pedal so I could take a switchback curve safely. By the time I saw the Parker sign, I was a law-abiding citizen again, tooling along at a modest fifty-five miles an hour, worrying about my family and friends.

I turned into the private lane and drove up the bluff. Jacob sat on the loading-dock steps with an open book. I slowed down but when he saw me, he shook his head and waved me past.

He'd probably had enough conversation, which was fine — for now. But at some point, he and I would have a talk. I took the drive to the lodge, passing three parked patrol cars. I didn't see any deputies, but I was sure they were close by. I stopped my SUV where I had yesterday and got out.

I didn't go immediately to the door, but stared at my surroundings. The Parker estate covered approximately a thousand acres of limestone quarries, scrub brush, trees, hills, and valleys with the Osage River cutting a broad path across one corner. Dan's grandfather had bought the acreage so he would have a private place to hunt small game. Canada geese and mallard ducks were attracted to the water pits that were home to large-mouth bass, catfish, and crappie. Squirrel, rabbit, deer, and quail were prevalent in the woodlands.

Dan's father, the second generation, had found hunting distasteful. He loved the birds and the squirrels and the rabbits. From what I understand, Dan's father, Calvin Parker, was a master gardener. According to Dan, Calvin had proceeded with caution when he planned his garden. He'd sat for hours watching the sunlight. He noted that when it rained, the run-off made rivulets along a natural drainage channel. He'd designed the garden by preserving the essence of the land, by keeping the spirit alive.

Dan, the third generation, wanted to make money off the land. He'd used his knowledge of plants to establish the present business. Like his father, Dan was cautious. He'd begun with a single glass structure and had built more greenhouses as the profits allowed. Dan used that original glass house for his orchid hybridizing program.

I turned toward the lodge. Dan's grandfather had built a four-room cabin so he could have a place to sleep while on his hunting expedition. During his tenure, Calvin Parker had moved his family to the weekend retreat. He'd added the upper story and covered the exterior with limestone quarried from the property. Dan had put his mark on the house by adding a study with floor-to-ceiling glass windows that looked out on a fenced swimming pool.

I walked up the sidewalk and reached for the doorbell, but Natalie opened the door before I could press the button. I grinned. "That's service. Surely you weren't watching for me."

Natalie took my arm and ushered me

into the hallway. "I was at the living room window and saw you turn off the highway. God, but I'm glad to see you." She burst into tears. "Dan just called. His mother died about an hour ago. He was already in shock over Marnie's murder. Now he's totally brokenhearted."

I put my arm around Natalie and let her sob.

After a few minutes, she stepped back and wiped her face. "I can't fall apart, but I'm worried about Dan. He has to make the funeral arrangements by himself. He sounded guilty for even asking, but he's worried about his orchids. He'd planned on Marnie taking care of them."

"He'll be fine, Natalie. He's used to making decisions. As for his orchids, surely there's someone here to look after them."

"I promised him I'd do it."

"And did that ease his mind?"

She gave me a watery smile. "Sort of. Dan knows I'm not enthused by his project. I don't even like going into his lab."

I stared at her. "Good heavens, why not?"

Natalie shrugged. "It's silly in view of all that's happened. I don't want to talk about it. I'll be right back. I'm going to get a Kleenex."

While she was gone, I looked around. Carl and I had spent many an evening here with Dan and Natalie. I was happy to see that nothing had changed. The floor plan was unique. An eight-foot corridor ran the entire length of the front of the house. Directly in front of me was the staircase that led to the upper floor. To my left and off the hallway were the kitchen, dining room, and a side door that led to the garage. To my right was the sunken living room and further on Dan's study. From the foyer I walked down the corridor to the living room. I could have stayed on the platform that surrounded the conversation pit, but I went down the three steps.

As with her clothing, Natalie fancied bold, vibrant colors in decorating. The room was painted cobalt blue with accents of persimmon, peach, and mandarin orange. Spacious windows flooded the room with sunlight. The ceiling was vaulted with wooden beams, hewed from trees taken from the property. A massive limestone fireplace was the centerpiece of the room.

I cruised across the floor, stopping to touch the chair Carl had usually occupied. I sidestepped a coffee table, another chair, and sofa before I went up three steps to the outer landing. My goal was the windows that overlooked the bluff. Normally, heights scare me senseless, but I never had that phobia here. I felt like a bird perched in a finely feathered nest. The ground was far below, but I couldn't see it for the treetops.

Hearing footsteps, I said, "You know I hate heights, but this doesn't bother me. I guess I feel safe when I'm here." I turned to face Natalie. "It must be all this rock. It's like a fortress."

"Well, it's not," she said, dabbing at her eyes. They were red-rimmed and bloodshot. "I don't feel safe even with those deputies patrolling the estate. Early this morning, an intruder came into the house."

I gasped. "You're kidding."

She clutched my arm with an icy hand. "I'm scared, Bretta. If someone could get in with police everywhere, what will happen when they leave?" She bit her lip and shook her head. "I'm sure there will be a guard, but what good will that do?" Natalie took a deep breath. "I know this is asking a lot of our friendship, but would you please come stay with me?"

Chapter Five

Natalie wouldn't discuss the intruder until I'd agreed to stay with her. She told me she felt safe enough during the day. It was the evenings and nights when she wanted company. I had the rest of the day off, but tomorrow I'd have to go back to the flower shop. We decided to make a run to my house for some clothing.

We stepped outside and an officer appeared. I recognized him and said, "Hi, Jon. We're going to my house so I can pack a bag. I'm staying with Natalie for a few nights."

Deputy Jon Whaler nodded. "I'll pass that information on to dispatch." He turned to Natalie. "Is the house locked?"

"Everything except this door. I was going to leave it open, in case you guys get hungry. There are sandwiches in the refrigerator and a plastic container of chocolate-chip cookies on the kitchen table."

Jon tried not to smile. "Ma'am, we aren't guests."

"But you have to eat."

Jon's voice was firm. "Please lock the door."

Natalie sighed and did as the deputy had directed. I grinned at Jon, then Natalie and I got into my SUV. As we drove down the drive, Natalie said, "They're working so hard, I just wanted them to know I appreciate everything they're doing."

"They know. Now will you tell me about this intruder?"

Natalie stared out the side window. "Everyone had given their statements and gone home. From my room I could see the fierce glow from halogen lights in the garden. More officers were at the greenhouses."

Natalie rotated her head and massaged her neck muscles. "I was exhausted. It had been a horrendous day from start to finish. I locked up and went to bed, but I couldn't sleep. It was about four in the morning. I came downstairs and sat in the study, but I didn't bother turning on a light. I guess I dozed off. I woke up when I heard a footstep in the hall."

I glanced at her. "What did you do?"

"I was still groggy from sleep, and my reaction was pure reflex. I called out, 'Is that you, Dan?' " Natalie made a face. "Wasn't that silly? Of course it wasn't Dan. But by the time I had *that* rational thought, whoever it was had gotten away."

"How did he get in? Better yet, how did he get *off* the estate?"

"There are several ways off the bluff by old roads used when the quarry was operable. As for entry into the house, it wasn't forced. He used a key to come in the side door and through the garage."

I raised an eyebrow. "The obvious question is, who had a key?"

"Not any one person. We keep a set of lodge keys at the greenhouse. If Dan and I are gone, we need someone to check on the house. The keys are labeled, and Uncle Donovan keeps them in his desk. The keys were right where they should be when the sheriff checked. He was pretty disgusted at our negligence. He pointed out that anyone could take them at any time, make a copy, and have easy access to our home."

"But what did the prowler want in the house?"

Natalie shook her head. "I don't know. We don't have fancy jewelry, valuable antiques, or works of art. I can't think of a reason unless he was trying to get to me."

I jerked upright. "Is that the real reason you want me to stay? Do you think you're in danger?"

She lifted a shoulder in a casual gesture, but her hand shook when she ran her fingers through her hair. "I don't know what to think, Bretta. Maybe whoever it was only wanted to talk to me. I've always felt that my employees liked and trusted me. The guilty party might come to me, hoping I'd help him out."

"We're talking murder, Natalie. What could you do?"

"Listen. Be compassionate. I don't know." Turning, she stared at me. "I used to envy your ability to solve crimes. I thought what you did was an adventure — a departure from the doldrums of everyday living. Here I am with a front-row seat, and I hate it. There's nothing entertaining or adventurous about murder. The sheriff has narrowed the list of suspects to greenhouse management. I don't know how or why he's made this leap of judgment, but I don't like being suspicious of these people."

I spoke quietly, trying to offer comfort. "Look at it this way. The person who committed the murder isn't the same individual you know and care about. He or she has a dark side that you've never been exposed to, and pray you never are."

"I know, but just because you learn

something terrible about someone doesn't necessarily mean you stop caring about him. I've almost decided I don't want to know who killed Marnie because the truth will only bring more pain."

I was amazed. In a sharp tone, I said, "But her killer can't simply walk off into the sunset. The sooner he or she is apprehended, the sooner you can get on with your life."

"That sounds wonderful, but what about Marnie? What about her parents? How will they put their life back in order? Their daughter has been murdered. Their life will never be the same."

I nodded. "I know. But there has to be closure. It helps to know that the criminal will suffer for his crime."

Natalie's tone was edged with grief. "Suffer, how? By being put in prison? We have the death penalty here in Missouri. What if he's sentenced to die? Then two people will be gone." Her voice rose. "And for what? Why was Marnie killed? Why did she have to die?"

I didn't have the answers to Natalie's questions, so I kept still. She took a deep breath and tried to smile. "Sorry for that outburst, but I'm way beyond being stressed. I can't believe this is happening.

It's like some terrible nightmare that I can't shake."

"If you had to make a guess as to motive, why do you think Marnie was killed?"

"I haven't any idea."

"Did Marnie have a boyfriend? Did she date someone regularly?"

"She dated Eugene a few times, but I don't think it was serious."

Eugene? That was interesting. They would make a handsome couple. I glanced at Natalie. "You said 'dated.' Does that mean they'd stopped seeing each other?"

Natalie thought a moment. "I think so. There was a bit of tension between them." Seeing where my thoughts were headed, she quickly said, "But it wasn't anything serious. Eugene likes to play the field. He's a flirt. You've seen him in action. Marnie was smart. She would have figured him out."

"When I last spoke with Dan, he mentioned that Marnie was an asset to his work. Exactly what did she do?"

"My husband demands meticulous records." She shrugged. "Given his work, I can understand that, but I couldn't have done what Marnie did." Natalie twisted on the seat so she could look at me. "Do you understand hybridizing?"

"Generally. Crossing one plant with another."

Natalie made a face. "Later today when I check on Dan's orchids, remind me to give you a botany lesson." Soberly, she continued, "Marnie was a unique young woman. She came to us without any plant experience, but Dan was impressed with her willingness to learn. The Latin or scientific plant names didn't intimidate her. The tedious chore of recording data was a challenge. She was kind and generous." Natalie's voice broke. "She'd do anything for anyone."

It was time to change the subject. For the last half of the drive, I chattered about my garden, about work, about my father and DeeDee. When I pulled up my lane, there was a shiny green Dodge truck parked by the house. The vehicle was just like Bailey's old truck only a different color.

My heart raced as I led the way into the house. Sure enough, Bailey was in the library with my father, talking in low tones. When Natalie and I walked in, I caught the words "identify the body" and knew my father was telling Bailey about Marnie's murder.

"Hi, stranger," I said to Bailey.

"Hi yourself," he said giving me a slow smile. "Your father has been telling me —"

I quickly interrupted. "This is Natalie Parker. She was our hostess yesterday. Natalie, this is Bailey Monroe."

Bailey attempted to stand, but Natalie waved him back to his chair. "Stay put," she said as she crossed the floor. "It's good to meet you. Bretta has told me about you. How's the leg?"

While they chitchatted, I soaked up the sight of Bailey. It was wonderful to see him smile. To watch his eyes sparkle when he turned to me. His dark hair had been cut, and the silver threads were more prominent. His face was thinner, his body leaner. I longed to touch him, but couldn't bear the thought of him rebuffing me again.

I moved toward the door. "While you guys visit, I'll go pack a bag. I'm spending a night or two with Natalie."

Bailey said, "I'd like to speak with you, Bretta."

Natalie glanced at my father. "Why don't you give me a tour of the garden?"

Dad struggled to his feet. "I could use some fresh air if you don't mind the company of an old man."

Natalie took his arm, and they walked from the room. For a moment neither

Bailey nor I spoke. I cleared my throat. "Are you doing okay?"

"I'm fine." He stuck out his leg. "The cast came off last week. The muscles are weak, but I can navigate fine." He patted the cushion at his side. "Come sit with me."

I hesitated for a second, and then took the place next to him. Bailey said, "I owe you an explanation for my action the other night."

My cheeks burned. It had been humiliating to be caught spying, but it had hurt when Bailey had ignored my presence at the window. "I did a foolish thing," I said. "I'd rather not talk about it."

"We have to talk about it," said Bailey firmly. "My daughter, Jillian, and I have never had a very good relationship. Her mother's death ended what little tolerance she had for me."

I wanted to disagree. From what I'd witnessed, Jillian had guarded her father the way a bear would her cub, but I curbed my sarcasm. "What was the problem?"

"Jillian was conceived before Cheri, my wife, and I got married. I was on an undercover operation that had started to unravel. I couldn't leave my post, or four months of hard work would have gone down the drain.

"There was never any doubt in my mind that Cheri and I would get married. But I didn't finish the case until Cheri was nearly five months along. We quickly got married, but good intentions didn't change the date of our wedding or the date of Jillian's birth. She was a sharp kid and put two and two together.

"That discovery was made when she turned fifteen. But even before that, I was her least favorite person. I was gone most of the time she was growing up. When I was home, she looked upon me as an interloper who took too much of her mother's attention. As Jillian grew older, she resented how unhappy her mother was after I'd leave on assignment. When Cheri died, I barely made it home in time for the funeral."

"From what I saw, Jillian cares for you very much."

"My almost dying scared her. She says she doesn't want to be an orphan." Bailey grinned. "She's a very self-sufficient young woman, but it frightened her when she was faced with the fact that I might not always be around. Our time together these last few weeks was a special gift. I guarded it carefully, even excluding you. I'm sorry for that, but in order for me to get closer to my daughter, I had to keep you at arm's length."

"So you've worked through your problems with her?"

Bailey sighed. "Let's just say we've reached an understanding that somewhat eases my mind. But I want my relationship with Jillian to be stronger." He turned to face me. "I've made a decision, Bretta. I'm going away for a while."

My stomach constricted into a tight ball. "To be with Jillian?"

"Yes. She's getting married in a couple of months. Before she starts her new life, I want to know her better." He shook his head. "It's hard to imagine me as a grandpa, but there'll be grandchildren in the future. I want to be assured that I'll have a place in their lives."

I thought about the emptiness I'd felt when Bailey had been close and there was a chance I could see him. What would I do if he was miles away? I wanted to beg him to reconsider, but I didn't have that right, and I wouldn't have done it anyway.

I glanced at him. "I'm not happy about your decision, but my reason is selfish. I'll miss you."

Bailey picked up my hand and tenderly kissed it. "I'll miss you, too, but I won't be gone forever. A couple of months tops."

"Two months," I said softly. "Eight weeks. Approximately sixty-two days."

He chuckled and pulled me close so that my head rested against his chest. "Are you going to calculate hours and minutes, too?"

I sighed and snuggled closer. "At some point I might, but not now. This feels too nice." I raised my head and looked into his eyes. "Kiss me like you'll miss me," I whispered.

"My pleasure." Bailey's lips grazed mine before they settled in with a hunger that drove all thoughts out of my mind.

When the kiss ended, I was breathless. My smile trembled when I gazed up at him. "You *will* miss me."

"Did you have a doubt?"

"Yes, but not anymore."

His laughter rumbled deep in his chest. "Foolish woman." He nuzzled my ear. "If you need more convincing, I have a couple more tricks up my sleeve."

I turned and raised an eyebrow at him. "Are you sure those *tricks* are up your sleeve?"

Bailey threw back his head and hee-hawed. When he could speak, he said, "You, ma'am, are very observant, and absolutely correct." His expression grew somber as he studied my upturned face. "I love you," he said. "You know that, don't you?"

"Yes, but I like hearing it."

"You'll be careful while I'm gone."

"As careful as I ever am."

"I'm thinking about this current investigation. You're staying with Natalie for a few nights?"

I nodded. "If I'd known you were leaving, I probably wouldn't have agreed. I'd like to spend more time with you."

Bailey grimaced. "That's my new truck parked on your driveway. It's packed and ready to roll. I've asked DeeDee to give my house a thorough cleaning every week while I'm gone. She didn't want to take my money, but when I come home I want the house ready to live in."

"You're leaving right away?" I could hardly get the words past the lump in my throat.

"Yes. This is good-bye."

Tears welled up. "I hate good-byes."

Bailey tightened his arms around me. "But imagine what will happen when we say hello again in two months."

I squirmed around in his arms until I was pressed against his chest. I ran my hand over his cheek, down the side of his neck to the base of his throat where I felt the steady beat of his heart. My hand continued the journey across to his shoulder and down his muscular arm. When our hands met our fingers interlocked.

"We'll be like this?" I said.

Bailey didn't speak, but nodded slowly, his gaze on my face.

I took a shaky breath. "Two months, huh? Maybe I can lose those ten pounds I've been fighting, and I'll invest in a new nightgown."

"Don't waste your money," he said, running his hand over my hip, up my midriff to lay possessively against my breast. Before claiming my lips again, he whispered, "I don't want you to change one thing on this body while I'm gone."

Whispers in the foyer brought me back to reality.

"We c-can't go in t-there. They n-need this t-time t-together."

"I really should get back to the lodge."

"I'll handle this." In a loud voice, my father said, "And that was the garden, Mrs. Parker. It's coming along nicely, as you've just seen."

I moved reluctantly away from Bailey and smoothed my hair. My lips burned from the recent ravaging, but the sensation was pure bliss.

I called, "You guys don't have to stand around in the foyer. Come on in."

Like a herd of anxious gazelles, my father, Natalie, and DeeDee skittered through the doorway. I got up from the sofa but turned back to Bailey. "Go now, while I'm packing. We've said our good-byes. I don't want to watch you drive away."

He nodded and gave my hand a squeeze. "Fourteen hundred and eighty-eight hours, Bretta. I'm already counting."

With my throat tight and tears burning my eyes, I pulled my hand out of his. I walked from the room and didn't look back.

Chapter Six

The ride to the lodge was made in silence. After I'd told Natalie about Bailey's decision to visit Jillian for a couple of months, she'd patted my hand and summed up our present attitude. "Life sucks, don't it?" she said. "But the alternative is worse."

As we topped the bluff, Jacob was again sitting on the loading-dock steps. This time when I met his gaze, he hesitated for a second, and then he beckoned to me. I nodded and drove on by, parking by the front sidewalk. I took my suitcase out of the SUV and walked to the lodge. Deputy Whaler was stationed on the porch. While Natalie unlocked the front door, I asked, "Has it been a quiet day?"

"The phone's been ringing," he said, cocking his head toward the house. "If you've got an answering machine it should be loaded with messages."

Natalie pushed open the door just as the phone began to ring again. "That may be Dan," she said and hurried off.

I left my suitcase in the foyer. "Anything else going on?"

"Officials doing their job, ma'am. The kid that's staying over at the greenhouse has wandered around, but he's steered clear of the garden. Seems like an all right guy, kind of backward in some things."

"He's Amish."

"So I've heard. He doesn't dress like the Amish I've seen."

"I'd like to speak with him. Would that be all right?"

Jon nodded. "I have instructions from the sheriff that you, Bretta Solomon, can go wherever you please, with the exception of the gardens. If you'd care to go there, that's been approved, too, but I'm to accompany you."

I stared at him, taken totally by surprise. Finally I asked, "Are we talking about the same sheriff? The man I know as Sid Hancock? He's kind of short, has red hair, and usually scowls instead of smiles."

The deputy ducked his head to hide his grin. "That would be the one, Mrs. Solomon."

I shook my head. "I'm amazed, but I'll take Sid up on his generous offer. And I'm not interested in the garden." I shuddered. "I saw enough of it last night."

"I understand you ID'd the victim.

Pretty bad from what I hear. I was on traffic duty, so I didn't see the scene until the body had been removed."

I stepped off the porch. "*Gruesome* is the word that sticks in my mind. Are you the only officer on the estate?"

"For now. My shift is up at seven this evening. I'll be replaced with three deputies for the night hours. One is to be stationed here at the house; the other two will keep an eye on the business area and circulate in an unspecified patrol around the estate."

"Thanks," I said and this time I didn't tarry. Sid might have given me carte blanche, but he could revoke that privilege at any time.

I walked down the drive toward the loading dock, thinking about my relationship with Jacob's family. After my mother had passed away, I'd sold the farm to Evan and his wife, Cleome. They had seven children, and Jacob was the oldest.

Over the years, I'd visited with the Miller family. Evan and I'd discussed many topics, but we rarely talked about his Amish beliefs. That had changed when his brother, Isaac, was murdered. Evan had asked for my help in understanding the investigation that was conducted by the local law enforcement. He'd trusted me not to abuse our friendship, but trust is a fragile commodity during a murder inquiry. Prying questions had to be asked, and Evan and the rest of the Amish community hadn't taken the invasion of their privacy very well. Distrust, displeasure, and discrimination had hung like an angry cloud over the small town of Woodgrove, Missouri, home to more than fifty Amish families.

I hadn't been back to Woodgrove to visit the Millers since Isaac's murder had been solved. I'd had good intentions, but hadn't followed through with them. Finding Jacob here yesterday had been a surprise. I wondered what had happened to make him leave home and live among the English, which is what the Amish call anyone not of their faith.

Jacob straddled an ATV that was parked by the loading dock. The body of the four-wheeler was painted yellow; the leather seat was black. It looked like a giant bumblebee. When he saw me, he climbed reluctantly off the machine.

"Hi," he said in a dull tone. "I never realized how lonely Sundays can be. Jess was going to give me a riding lesson, but he didn't come out here today. I asked Eugene, but he's busy watering plants in the greenhouse."

I looked through the open loading-dock door. "Eugene is here?"

Jacob nodded. "He's in B greenhouse where the tropical plants are kept."

Not wanting Eugene to hear my conversation with Jacob, I said, "Let's move over to that tree where there's more shade." I led the way to the gigantic sycamore. A breeze stirred the leaves, but the air was hot and humid.

"I'd like to know why you've left home," I said.

"It is hard to explain to an outsider. Besides the Bible there are unwritten rules the Amish base their morals and way of life on. The Ordung are the unwritten rules of the church. *Rumschpringes* is recognized by the Ordung."

"*Rumschpringes?* Is that German?"

"Yes. Loosely translated it means 'time out' or 'running around.' Under the Ordung young men and women from the ages of sixteen to twenty can see what the outside world is like. This is their last opportunity before deciding to accept the Amish lifestyle. Many Amish go back east to Pennsylvania. There are stories of how they mix with the wrong kinds of people and use drugs and drink and party. I am not interested in shaming my family."

"Then Evan and Cleome approve of your present circumstances?"

Jacob smiled. "I did not say that. *Rumschpringes* is allowed, but not everyone practices it. I am the only one in our district who has left home to live among the English."

"What if you like this world? What if you decide never to go home?"

His smile disappeared. "There is that possibility, but we are not supposed to be prisoners. When someone accepts the Amish faith, he has come to that decision with his heart, as well as his soul. He is unwavering in his beliefs."

"Why did you choose to come here?"

Jacob hesitated, then said, "I have experience with plants. I'm accustomed to heat and hard work. I know how to use a shovel, and I can pull weeds. I would not have felt comfortable working in a hardware store or in a restaurant."

"And you knew no one when you applied for a job?"

Jacob's eyes clouded, and he stared into the distance. "No," he said softly. "I knew no one."

"You told me you'd only been here a week, and yet you and Marnie seemed to have had a close friendship."

Jacob shook his head as if clearing away an image. When he turned to me, his smile was gloomy. "Yes. I guess that's why I'm lonely. I won't see Marnie again."

"What did you and she talk about?"

Jacob chuckled. "I didn't do much talking. Marnie could talk all day. Harley said she jabbered like a parrot."

"On any particular subject?"

He shrugged. "No. She was looking forward to going to college this fall."

"What do you think happened? Why do you think she was killed?"

"I guess someone thought she was an inconvenience."

I frowned. "What do you mean? An inconvenience?"

"She must have been troublesome to the person who took her life."

"Do you have a reason for saying that?"

"Jess called Marnie pesky. Irma thought she was nosy. Marnie always had questions."

"What did Marnie ask Jess that annoyed him and made Irma think she was nosy?"

"Marnie was curious about everything. How many employees worked here at the greenhouse? How long people stayed, why they left? Was the water from the quarries more healthful for the plants than well water?"

There didn't seem to be anything unusual about those questions. When I've hired a new employee at the flower shop, I've been annoyed by questions about why I placed a flower in a specific spot or why I used that particular kind of greenery in a bouquet. I consider my work an art with intuition guiding my hand. I can't always explain why or how I do what I do. Had Marnie quizzed people because she was trying to learn or did she have another objective in mind?

I said, "Marnie told me you'd talked to her about your uncle's murder. How did that subject come up?"

"I don't remember. I got the feeling that she was looking for information, but she never told me what she wanted. We talked about things from my world and from hers. She admired my people and how their beliefs kept them unpretentious. She said that deception wasn't normally her way. To scheme felt wrong."

Scheme? That was interesting. I followed it up by asking, "Do you remember what you'd been talking about when she made that comment?"

"Dan had told her that there are orchid blooms that mimic a particular female insect. That way the bloom will appear attractive and will be pollinated and survive. I told Marnie I think human nature and Mother Nature have much in common. Deception is shared in both worlds. For plants this trickery is a marvel, but in humans it is sometimes wicked."

All along I'd thought Marnie had something specific in mind with this talk about questions and answers. Now I find that she'd also talked about deception and scheming. I looked at Jacob. "I don't suppose Marnie gave you any details about this scheme of hers?"

"No, and I didn't ask." He ducked his head. "We were just talking. I didn't know that it was important." He raised his head to meet my gaze. "I chose to leave my family and observe *Rumschpringes* so I could learn more about the entire world, not just the Amish way of life."

He gestured disparagingly. "But I'm like a newborn calf. I want to stand on my own two feet, but I keep stumbling. There were questions I could have asked, but I didn't. There were things I could have done, but I didn't."

"That's called hindsight, Jacob. We all wish we'd done things differently in our lives."

Overcome with emotion, he blinked his eyes, but the sheen of tears glistened. "A second chance is all I'm asking for. One more chance."

Puzzled, I asked, "To do what? Nothing will bring Marnie back."

Jacob dashed a hand across his eyes. "Marnie?" he said, sounding confused. "Yes. Of course. I know."

The poor guy was really broken up. I touched him lightly on the shoulder. "I'm sorry to keep pressing you to remember things, but I want Marnie's killer caught."

"I don't think I'm helping you."

I wanted to agree, but I pointed to Dan's laboratory instead. "Have you been in there?" I asked.

Jacob shook his head. "I've looked through the glass door. Orchids don't interest me. They're too — uh —" He lifted a shoulder. "I don't know what the word is."

"Alien?" I said. Seeing Jacob's baffled expression, I added, "Different, strange, or maybe weird."

"I don't like the words strange or weird. Different is a better description. It doesn't sound so judgmental." Jacob gestured to his T-shirt and shorts. "Dressed like this I can walk down any street in River City, and no one gives me a second glance. But if I were dressed in my Amish clothes, people would gawk, point, or say cruel things.

"Marnie said she liked me because I am open and truthful. She said she didn't want to be deceitful, but sometimes the end justified the means." Jacob's brow wrinkled in thought. "Marnie must have meant that if she did something wrong it would end in something right. But she is dead, and her killer is free." He held out his hands. "Where is the justice?"

I didn't have an answer — yet. But without hesitation, I assured Jacob that I was working on it. My statement amazed me. I never thought that I, Bretta Solomon, would get purposely involved in an investigation but apparently, DeeDee was right. My subconscious was always at work. I picked up information, stored away impressions, and listened to what people had to say.

At the moment, I was at a loss. No specific idea had presented itself. While I was thinking, Jacob said he was going for a walk down the drive to stretch his legs. I wasn't ready to go back to the lodge. Seeing the open loading-dock door, I decided to have a word with Eugene.

I went up the steps and into the main corridor of the greenhouse. It was hot outside but the ventilating fans created a strong current of air. I stopped and lifted the damp hair off my neck. My conversation with Jacob had left me uncomfortable. I couldn't put my finger on the reason, but something felt off. He'd answered my questions readily enough. When I'd asked why he'd come to work for Parker Greenhouse, his explanation had sounded rehearsed. I shrugged. Perhaps that's the reason he'd given to Evan and Cleome. And yet, something didn't feel right.

I smoothed my hair and walked down the corridor. My sneakers made a whisper of sound on the concrete floor. Passing an open door, I glanced in and then away. I took a couple more steps then stopped. A movement in the far corner had caught my attention.

On tiptoes, I retraced my way back to the doorway. The light was dim, the room in shadows. I saw an Amish straw hat lying on the cot. A stack of dark clothing was neatly folded on a chair. This had to be Jacob's room.

I stepped to the door, reached around the doorframe hoping to locate a light switch. My fingers found it, and I gave it a quick flip. The bare bulb illuminated unadorned walls, a battered chest of drawers, and Eugene squatted in front of a suitcase. At the moment his hands were motionless, but the rumpled contents of the suitcase gave testimony to the fact that he'd been rifling Jacob's personal possessions.

My tone was cynical. "Shame, shame. And on a Sunday, too. Didn't your mama teach you it's not polite to rip off others?"

Chapter Seven

Eugene jumped to his feet with a piece of paper grasped in his hand. When he saw my gaze fixed on it, he let it go. Like a glossy black-and-white butterfly it fluttered back into the open suitcase.

Flashing me a quick smile, he said, "Bretta, you know me better than that. I wouldn't rip anyone off, especially an Amish guy. What could he have that I'd want?"

"Nothing material, but I think you were upset by his friendship with Marnie."

Eugene's head snapped up, but his tone was smooth. "Friendship is the operative word. They were just friends. I have the proof right here."

He turned and picked up the paper he'd dropped. When he held it out to me, I saw a black-and-white photograph of a young Amish woman. Her dark hair was covered with a white cap, head tilted at a beguiling angle. Her eyes stared straight at me. Something about the photograph niggled at me. I made a move to take the picture, but Eugene pulled it away.

Snickering, he said, "Old Jake has himself a babe waiting at home. He wasn't interested in Marnie." He put the picture back in the suitcase and slammed the lid.

Softly, I said, "But you didn't know that until you found the picture."

"That doesn't matter. Marnie and I didn't have an exclusive arrangement."

"You dated her."

"We went out a few times."

"What did you expect to find among Jacob's belongings?"

Eugene shrugged. "I wanted to see that photo. He usually carries it with him. I've seen him staring at it, but he hasn't shown it to anyone."

"That's called privacy, Eugene." I waved a hand at the suitcase. "Apparently, a concept you've never learned."

Eugene hunted for the words to defend his action. He opened his mouth a couple of times, but when he couldn't come up with a plausible excuse, he said, "I have work to do." He would have gone on his way, but I wasn't finished with him.

"Just a minute," I said and waited for him to face me again. "Why do you think Marnie was murdered?"

Eugene gulped. "I don't know. She was

usually in control of most situations. She could work anyone around to her way of thinking."

"Could she work you?"

"Hell no. I'm my own man."

"So she couldn't work you." I paused then added quietly, "And she couldn't work the person who took her life."

Eugene's face paled. "You aren't thinking I killed her?"

"I'm not accusing you, Eugene. I'm stating a fact that you gave me yourself."

He took a step toward me. "How long have we known each other, Bretta? Four? Five years? Surely you can't believe that I'd murder anyone."

I edged my way to the door. "I wouldn't have thought you'd enter another person's room and search his property, but you did. Maybe you loved Marnie and the thought of her getting close to Jacob made you furious."

His reaction took me by surprise. He whipped out a hand and grabbed my arm. "I never killed her. I loved her. I never would have hurt her."

"Let go of me," I said, jerking my arm.

Natalie spoke from the doorway. "What's going on in here?"

Eugene dropped his hold on me and rearranged his expression. Like a chameleon, he reverted back to his normal ingratiating self. "I'm sorry, Bretta," he said in a contrite manner. Hanging his head, he mumbled, "I'm upset about Marnie's death. I lost my temper when you baited me." He turned to Natalie. "I know she's your friend and a good customer of the greenhouse, but I'm steering clear of her when she's in *detective mode*. I like the florist side better."

Eugene walked out of the room. Natalie stared after him and then turned back to me. "What in the world did you do to him?"

I rubbed my arm and shook my head. "Were you looking for me?"

Natalie studied me. When she saw I wasn't going to tell her anything more, she said, "I'm going to Dan's greenhouse. I thought you might like to tag along."

I glanced at the suitcase. I wanted another look at that picture, but after chastising Eugene for pawing around in Jacob's belongings, I couldn't very well do the same thing myself.

I followed Natalie down the loading-dock steps. We crossed the employees' parking lot, where five delivery trucks were parked as well as three vans with the

Parker Greenhouse name and logo stenciled on their sides.

Natalie opened the door to the orchid house. She led the way into a small antechamber that contained a sink, a trash can, and a shelf stacked with white paper gowns and footies for covering our shoes. Taped to the door in front of us was a big sign.

AUTHORIZED PERSONNEL ONLY
YOU ARE ABOUT TO ENTER
A STERILE ENVIRONMENT
PLEASE WASH HANDS
PLEASE COVER CLOTHING
AND SHOES
PLEASE KEEP INNER DOOR
CLOSED AT ALL TIMES

With our hands freshly washed and our shoes and clothes concealed under disposable coverings, we stepped into Dan's laboratory. The first thing I noticed was the change in temperature. The atmosphere was fresh and cool with air circulating among the plants.

"This is really nice," I said, raising my voice so Natalie could hear me over the fans. "It doesn't feel like other greenhouses I've been in."

"It isn't like other greenhouses because

orchids need a different climate. Dan is hand-pollinating the plants so all insects and birds have to be kept out. There can't be any unscreened openings. Intake vents pull the air from outside, filter and humidify it before releasing it in here."

The structure was approximately twenty by forty feet long. An open-weave cloth lay across the roof, blocking out some of the harsh August sun. The floor was cement with several drains. A wide bench ran down the middle with narrower benches on each side. Plants covered all the surfaces.

I'd expected fabulous blossoms in every size, shape, and color. A few cattleya were in bloom, as were phalaenopsis and some cymbidiums. The rest of the plants, which numbered around two hundred, were flowerless. The plants themselves were uninspiring with their pseudobulbs — thickened stems where water and food are stored, enabling the plant to survive periods of drought — resting above the soil. The thick-bladed leaves draped and drooped over the edges of the pots.

Natalie said, "Disappointing, isn't it?"

I nodded. "I thought there'd be more blooms."

"Sometimes there are, but many of these

plants are dormant. After they rest, they'll come into bloom again. When that happens, Dan will cover the flowers with drawstring pouches so he can control which bloom gets the pollen from his choice of plant."

I walked down the aisle, stopping when I came to the first section. A neatly printed sign said this genus was *Ophrys*. Reading tags I saw there were fifteen plants equally divided into three varieties: *O. holoserica, O. apifera,* and *O. insectifera*.

"Latin names," I said. "The O must mean the genus *Ophrys*."

"The second is the species," said Natalie. "*O. holoserica* is the late spider orchid. *O. apifera* is the bee orchid and *O. insectifera* is the fly orchid."

I grinned. "I'm impressed. For someone who doesn't care about this place, you seem to be knowledgeable."

"Dan loves orchids. He eats, talks, and breathes his work. I've picked up some facts by osmosis — I can't escape it."

I waved my hand at our surroundings. "What else do you know?"

Natalie shrugged. "Dan is breeding a plant he can sell through the greenhouses. Instead of huge blooms, he wants a compact plant with delicate sprays of flowers that have unique markings. He's working with several different families of orchids. They're all tagged and grouped. At first it was a hobby, and I could live with that. But his interest has grown until he's obsessed. He's finished pollinating this group of orchids, and now he's waiting for the seed to mature."

My knowledge of orchids concerned only the flower, having used them in weddings and corsages. But I'd lived on a farm and had watched my mother save marigold and zinnia seed from her garden plants. I cited the next stages. "Dan will collect the seed, germinate it, and grow the plants until they bloom. That's when he'll see if his cross was successful."

"That's right. Dan says it'll take from five to seven years before he'll know if the seed produces the kind of flower he's after. He could collect the seed and send it off to be germinated, but that would take part of the procedure out of his hands. He wants to be involved in all aspects — from the selection of the parent plants, to the breeding, the harvesting of seed, to the germination, to the final plant with blooms."

"I had no idea orchids were so slow-growing. Maybe that explains why the blossoms are expensive." I frowned and looked at the mature plants on the benches. "Doesn't he have any baby plants yet?"

Natalie pointed to the rear of the greenhouse. "They're called plantlets and are kept in a special room referred to as the nursery." She made a face.

I walked down the aisle to the two doors. One led into an office. The other was posted with another sign. This one was in Dan's own handwriting.

IF I AM NOT AT YOUR SIDE
DO NOT ENTER!
DAN PARKER

I cupped my hands to the glass and peered in. A four-foot-wide cabinet with a stainless steel worktable dominated the room. A manufacturer's tag mounted on an upper door said it was a Laminar Flow Cabinet. To the right was a table filled with glass flasks and illuminated by fluorescent lights. Each flask was labeled, but I couldn't make out the words. In some cases the flasks contained bits of green. I assumed this was the germinating orchid seed. It looked as if Dan was on his way to growing seedlings of his own making.

"What's going on in here?" I asked.

"That cabinet has an exhaust system that keeps unwanted particles out of the air. Orchid seedlings tend to get fungus. If that happens the whole batch has to be aborted."

I gave the seedlings another look before I turned away. I walked back down the greenhouse, reading labels, staring at the plants. "I'm impressed, Natalie. I think Dan's work is fascinating." I frowned. "It reminds me of something, but I can't think what." I shrugged. "Anyway, it's exciting. Dan could be on the threshold of hybridizing an entirely new species of plant."

"Yeah, I know." Her tone was glum.

"Why don't you like coming in here?"

Instead of answering me, she went back into the anteroom and removed her gown and footies. I followed, but I wasn't going to drop the subject. If this place was as important to Dan as Natalie said, then there had to be a good reason why she didn't like coming in here.

Once we were outside, I said, "Well? You've been behind Dan in everything he's done. When he first started the greenhouses, you worked next to him. You delivered plants, watered, fertilized, did whatever needed to be done. What is it about the orchids that has alienated you?"

"It isn't the plants. It's Dan. Like I said, he's become obsessed with this work." She stopped and took a deep breath. "You're right. I did work alongside him building this business, but now we have employees." Tears came to Natalie's eyes. "Maybe I'm jealous. I'm not needed."

I reached out to put my arm around her, but she stepped away. "I'm ready for a swim," she said. "Are you coming with me?"

I wiped the sweat off my brow. She didn't have to ask me twice.

Twenty minutes later I was drifting on a raft, cool as a cucumber, even though the hot sun felt brutal to my exposed skin. Natalie had turned on the gas grill. The smell of past cookouts rose in the air to mingle with the smell of chlorine. I was too tired for a workout, but Natalie was swimming laps. I watched her, marveling at the effortless way she glided through the water.

When she took a breather, I said, "This water feels heavenly."

She grabbed a raft and floated out to me. "While I was swimming laps, what were you thinking about?"

"Bailey. By now he's miles and miles away."

"Yeah. I miss Dan, too. There's something about being in the water that makes me yearn for a little belly rubbing."

"Natalie!" I laughed, splashing water at her. "I can't believe you said that."

She cupped a handful of water and let it trickle over her bare arm. "Don't you just love the feel of water on your skin?"

"Yeah, especially after a hot day like this." But she had reminded me of something. I lowered my voice. "Since we're divulging secrets, I've got one."

All ears, Natalie turned to me. "What's that?"

"You know how smooth and cool gelatin feels on your tongue? Well, I've always had this fantasy to romp in Jell-O."

Natalie's head shot up like a turtle's. "You've got to be kidding. It would be cold and slimy." She grew thoughtful. "What flavor?"

Carl had known that I dreamed about a raspberry romp, but I didn't share that element of my fantasy with Natalie. I giggled self-consciously. "Does it matter?"

We were laughing and splashing when tires crunched on the gravel. "Who's that?" I asked, peering at the fence.

"I'll go see." Natalie climbed out and slipped and slid across the tiles that surrounded the pool. Peeking through a crack in the boards, she said, "It's Uncle Donovan and Emily."

"I'm getting out," I said, already paddling for the ladder. "I look like hell in a swimming suit."

"They won't care," protested Natalie.

"Well, I do." I climbed out and wrapped a giant towel around my waist.

"The front door is locked," she said. "After I let them in, I'll bring back our steaks. While they cook, we can visit out here."

I was rubbing the moisture from my hair when Emily and Donovan came out the study doors. Yesterday when I'd seen Emily, she'd been a frazzled medic, tending minor injuries. Today she looked more like herself, with her dark hair swinging free about her shoulders. She wore a pair of white slacks and a red knit top.

While I'd caught a glimpse of Donovan on Saturday evening, I hadn't spoken with him in months. For sixty-two, he was a fine-looking man who fancied western wear. The price of his lizard-skin boots would have paid my electric bill for a month. He'd shed some pounds and toned his muscles. His hair was silver, his eyes a startling shade of blue. He was Natalie's blood kin, but there wasn't an iota of resemblance between them. He'd been the major investor when Dan had expanded the present greenhouse operation, and had accepted the position of vice president, in charge of whatever needed to be done.

"Bretta," he said, extending his hand. "I'm glad you're here with Natalie. I've been worried about her. I called several times today, but either no one answered or the line was busy. She tells me you're staying with her. That's a load off my mind."

I shook his hand and nodded. "It'll be a mini-vacation, swimming and eating Natalie's cooking."

Emily smiled. "I smelled the grill as we drove up. We're crashing your party."

Natalie came out the doors carrying a plate with two huge steaks. "We're hardly in the partying mood, Em."

Emily sighed. "I'm sorry. I didn't mean —" She stopped, unsure what to say.

To cover the awkward moment, I took her arm and moved over to a couple of chairs. "I heard your public service announcement on the radio last week."

She chuckled self-consciously. "It wasn't

my idea. I was nervous, but it came off pretty well. My supervisor thought I might reach more people if they heard my voice."

"You sounded very sympathetic. If I had a problem, I'd come to you."

Emily smiled. "Thanks. It's not easy educating the public. Men are the most difficult to persuade that they aren't invincible."

Emily was a counselor at the Spencer County Healthcare Center. I'd attended one of her seminars on lowering cholesterol. "What kind of questions do you get?"

She settled back in the chair and crossed her legs. "I got a real doozy last week. A woman said her herbalist had prescribed garlic tablets, but they made her breath stink. She didn't want to waste the pills, so she wondered if she could crush them and use them in her spaghetti sauce."

Emily paused for our laughter before continuing. "That was a silly example. Most of what I get is serious. The woman who's found a lump in her breast, but is afraid to have it checked. The man who loves his wife, but can't tell her he has an impotency problem. Most people are afraid or embarrassed to see their own doctor."

Donovan had come to stand behind

Emily. Placing his hands on her shoulders, he leaned down and brushed her cheek with his lips. Looking up at us, he said, "As you can see, my wife takes her work very seriously."

Emily frowned. "No more than you do. We're here because of *your* work."

I sensed a bit of tension between them and wondered if there was a power struggle going on as to whose job was more important. Emily was Donovan's second wife. His first wife had been a stay-at-home mom. He'd been a rodeo announcer, keeping long hours, traveling around the country. Left alone, Donovan's first wife had found she had more in common with her next-door neighbor, a house husband.

Natalie forked the slabs of meat, making them sizzle as fat dripped onto the hot coals. In a crabby tone, she said, "I suppose you're here to talk about Marnie. I'd hoped to have a nice quiet meal."

"We can have this discussion after you've eaten," said Donovan. "But we *will* have it."

She waved the long-handled fork. "Let's hear what you've got to say."

Donovan's eyes narrowed at her tone. "I'm not the enemy, Natalie. All this publicity about the greenhouse can't be good for business."

Her shoulders slumped. "I know, but what are we going to do about it?"

"That's why I'm here. Dan has all he can cope with in Oregon. It's up to you and me to make some decisions. What I propose is that we hire a private firm to investigate Marnie's murder."

I quickly spoke up. "But the sheriff is spearheading the case."

Donovan shrugged. "I see his campaign posters all over town. Is he giving his all to solving this murder? I don't think so. That's why I've contacted this new detective agency." He pulled a business card from his pocket. "I found this last night on the windshield of my car. An hour ago, I talked to the old gentleman. Hiring him seems a viable solution."

I closed my eyes wearily. Old gentleman, indeed. It could only be my father.

Chapter Eight

I didn't sleep well that night though my hostess had seen to my every need. I'd dined on grilled steak, a baked potato, and crisp salad followed by strawberry shortcake. My room was peaceful. The bed was comfortable, the sheets faintly scented with lavender. I had everything necessary for a restful night, but I couldn't sleep.

Knowing how I felt about his detective agency idea, my father hadn't put my name on his business cards. Donovan had been amazed to learn of my connection to the "old gentleman." He'd called my house, just moments after Natalie and I left, to make an appointment with my father at a local restaurant. They'd discussed the case, but not once had my father mentioned that I was his daughter.

When I enlightened Donovan about my father's omission, Donovan was annoyed. He wanted to be made aware of all facts, and if my father had neglected to mention this glaring detail, then perhaps he wasn't the man for the job.

Natalie had pointed out that I was already involved, and the subject was dropped. I knew my father would be crushed, but it was better to have his feelings hurt than for him to suffer physical pain because he'd gotten in over his head.

My thoughts kept me awake well into the wee hours before weariness kicked in and I slept. I don't set an alarm. My inner clock usually tells me when it's time to get up, but instead of waking at my regular hour, I dozed on. When I finally opened my eyes, bright sunshine highlighted the room.

A glance at the clock on the nightstand brought me out of bed in a hurry. Eight-thirty! The flower shop opened at nine, and I still had to dress and make the twenty-minute drive into River City.

Grumbling under my breath, I jumped into a green split skirt, added a white top, and slipped my feet into a pair of white sandals. As I combed my hair I went into the hall and dialed the shop. After three rings, Lois picked up the receiver.

"The Flower Shop," she said in a nasal tone.

"Hi. It's me. Sounds like you still have a sinus problem."

"It's getting better. At least I can stand up without getting dizzy."

"I'm gonna be late. I overslept."

"Looks like a quiet day, so take your time. From what I read in yesterday's paper, you had a tragic experience on Saturday. Are you okay?"

"I'm fine. I'll fill you in when I get to the shop. See you as soon as I can."

I hung up and went into the bathroom to finish getting ready. Fifteen minutes later, I was perfumed, powdered, and prepared for my workday. I galloped down the stairs with my handbag flopping against my hip.

Taking a moment, I stuck my head around the kitchen doorway. Natalie was seated at the table picking at a fried egg. She looked like hell. Her hair was matted on one side. She hadn't dressed but wore an old nightgown that had been washed so many times the print was faded and the lace frayed at the neckline.

"I'm late," I said. "I have to go."

Natalie frowned. "Since you weren't up at the crack of dawn, I thought you were going to spend the day with me."

"I can't. I have to get to work. But I'll be back after five. Okay?"

Dispirited, she nodded and bent over her plate.

"I'm sorry," I said. "But you said you would be okay during the day."

She glanced up and gave me a weak grin. "Go. See you later."

I hesitated for another second, then sprinted for the front door. I felt guilty for leaving her, but there wasn't anything I could do. Once I got to the flower shop and saw how the day might go, I could possibly leave early, but I didn't tell Natalie that. No sense getting her hopes up.

I stepped outside where the air was already hot and humid. I got in my SUV and fired up the engine. Driving down the lane, I saw a couple of deputies having coffee. I waved and zoomed by.

There was no need to speed, since Lois had the flower shop covered, but I didn't waste time on the trip into town. I'm a creature of habit. I like to be at work early so I can enjoy a cup of coffee and ease into the day. Today my routine had been disturbed, and I was out of sorts.

Coming up behind a slow-moving vehicle, I swung out to pass. A car was headed my way. I had plenty of time to get back into my lane, but the experience left me huddled behind the steering wheel, my hands shaking.

"Slow down," I said under my breath. "Relax."

Just to prove I could deviate from my routine without going manic, I decided to stop for doughnuts. Merry's Delights was located eight blocks from the flower shop and made fantastic apple fritters. I rarely indulged, but this morning I had the urge to sink my teeth into a confection dredged in cinnamon and gooey icing. No slots were available out front, so I parked in the alley. I walked around the building and met Irma coming out of Merry's front door.

She hefted a big pastry box when she saw me. "I left you a few goodies inside, but not many. I figure morale will be low this morning at the greenhouse. Maybe something special for break will help raise spirits."

Irma had dark circles under her eyes, and her hair didn't have its usual crested wave of bangs.

She would have walked on to her car, but I touched her lightly on the arm. "Food is a panacea for all that ails," I said. "I'm here for the same reason, but I don't think doughnuts will erase the murder from either of our minds. Marnie was a sweet young lady, but she was curious, asking questions all the time. Did you notice that about her?"

A wary look crossed Irma's face. "I heard you were staying with Natalie. With your reputation, I told Har—" She stopped and quickly amended, "I told Harman, my — uh — cat that you'd be nosing around."

I raised an eyebrow. "Your *cat* is interested in what I do?" I shook my head. "I'd more likely say it was Harley." Putting a note of understanding in my voice, I said, "It's only natural that two . . . uh . . . co-workers would discuss what happened. What was your conclusion?"

Irma's cheeks were red and her tone flustered. "I was told by the sheriff not to discuss the case, but I keep thinking that maybe Marnie had a stalker." She looked up and down the street. In an undertone, she added, "You didn't hear that from me and if you say I said it, I'll deny it." She marched off and got into her car.

Astonished, I watched Irma drive off. A stalker? I thought of Eugene and his quick temper. I'd never seen that side of him. Uneasy with my thoughts, I walked into Merry's. The place was hopping with morning coffee drinkers and people searching for a sugar rush to jump-start their bodies. I stood in line, but my lust for sweets was gone.

Had someone been bothering Marnie?

Why hadn't Sid said anything about that? Did he even know? When it was my turn, I made my choices and returned to my vehicle carrying a bag of assorted goodies.

I was only eight blocks from the flower shop. With traffic heavy, I decided to use the alley instead of getting back on the street. It wasn't a scenic route by any means. Delivery trucks had broken up the asphalt, leaving potholes that slowed me down. Trash cans and Dumpsters hadn't been emptied yet. The smelly debris added to the sinister aspect of the unkempt, weed-infested lane.

A block from my shop, an old lady hobbled toward me, taking more than her fair share of the confined space. I pulled over as far as I could. The woman's head was down. Her scuffed boots shuffled the dirt in a listless manner. Her hair was wispy and gray. She was of average height but as plump as a toad, her bulk draped in a floral-printed muumuu.

In my red SUV, I wasn't difficult to see, but she kept her gaze on the ground. I had gotten over as far as I could and had come to a full stop. If she didn't look up soon, she'd ram her nose into the hood of my car. I figured it would startle her, but I tapped my horn gently. The sound didn't phase her. She plodded on a course that would surely bring her injury.

I put the gearshift into park and stepped out. "Ma'am," I called. "Hello!"

She was perhaps twenty feet from me. At the sound of my voice, she stopped. Slowly she raised her head. Startled, I sucked in a breath. Her face was covered with warts. Her nose hooked like the beak of a bird. Her eyes were sunk deep in their sockets and barely visible.

I was ashamed to stare, but then it occurred to me that no one could be this hideous. She limped to the side of the alley and flung out her arm, indicating that I was to pass. I got back into my vehicle and closed the door. I engaged the transmission and let the engine idle me forward.

As I passed her, I glanced out my window. From this vantage point, I saw I'd been looking at a rubber mask. She raised a large hand that was covered with a white glove smeared with a reddish brown stain. In a playful manner she twiddled her fingers at me, then spun on her heel. I twisted around in my seat and watched her flee down the alley like a bat out of hell. In a few seconds she was out of sight.

Spooked, I gripped the steering wheel and stomped on the gas pedal. I slowed down only when I came to my parking space at the back of the flower shop. I slid to a stop and killed the engine. Grabbing the bag of pastry, I leaped out and ran up the steps. Breathing hard I flung open the back door and slammed it, twisting the lock for good measure. I took a deep breath to steady my nerves then headed for the workroom.

"You guys won't believe what just happened," I said coming through the doorway. My voice dwindled away. Lois, my designer, and Lew, my deliveryman, stood at the front counter. They both turned and stared at me. Their faces were pale, their eyes wide with shock.

I put the bag of doughnuts on a table. "What's wrong?"

In unison they pointed to the front of the store. From here I had an unhindered view of the front showroom. My shop is narrow but deep, the entry door squarely in the middle with a display window on each side. Both plate-glass panels were shattered. A crowd had gathered on the sidewalk.

On wobbly legs I made the journey past the worktables, past the counter, past the front cooler. I stopped about midway down the room. "Have you called the police?" I asked.

Lois said, "Yes. They're sending someone immediately."

I nodded and looked over the destruction. Two bricks lay on the floor, their reddish brown color almost blending with the carpet. I stared at the bricks for a moment then went to a worktable and grabbed a white towel.

"What are you doing?" asked Lois.

Lew chimed in. "Shouldn't you leave things alone until the police arrive?"

"I'm not going to disturb anything," I said. I bent down and rubbed the white cloth across the surface of the brick. I stood up and turned the cloth toward the light.

The residue was an exact match to the smear of color on the old woman's white gloves. Remembering how fast she'd run away, I knew she hadn't been old, and who's to say she was even female? Under that garb she could have been anyone.

A lump of fear twisted my gut as I revised my thoughts — not just anyone. The need for a head-to-toe disguise meant that I'd recognize the person who'd done this. In fact, chances were I'd probably talked to him or her in the last couple days.

It was after two in the afternoon before the excitement tapered off. I had to deal with the law, my insurance company, and a glass installation business that couldn't get to my windows for another day. This delay initiated the need for a repairman to nail sheets of plywood over the gaping holes, which in turn meant that we had to post a sign outside that said: YES! WE ARE OPEN FOR BUSINESS!

The broken glass was picked up, the carpet vacuumed. Silk arrangements and plants were examined for shards. My back-to-school window decorations had been obliterated. I'd fashioned an apple, the size of a bushel basket, out of Styrofoam packing peanuts squashed into a trash bag, and covered it with crushed red velvet material. Splinters of glass had sliced the velvet fabric, allowing the peanuts to slither from the slits like white maggots feasting on a piece of decayed fruit. My display had taken a day to construct. It took two minutes to toss into the trash.

Besides the work, we had well-meaning neighbors dropping by to empathize and bemoan the destructiveness of people in our small corner of the world. It all took time and energy, commodities I was lacking. My employees and I kept up a brave front, but by midafternoon we were drained.

I put a final piece of fern in the vase of roses I'd designed. "This order doesn't have to be delivered immediately," I said. "Let's take a break."

"I'm ready," said Lois. She pulled up a stool and sat down. "I'm pooped."

Usually she kept her neat appearance through any and all situations, but not today. Her dark hair hung across her damp forehead in limp strands. Her cheek had a smudge of dirt, and her blouse had come untucked from the waistband of her slacks. Tenderly, she rubbed the Band-Aid on her index finger.

I nodded to the injury. "Are you sure it's okay? Do you need to see a doctor?"

"No. I was just careless." She raised her husky voice. "Hey, Lew, we're taking a break. How about getting us a couple cans of soda out of the cooler?"

"Be right there," he called. "I've got to wash up."

I looked at the grime on my hands and sighed. "I should, too, but I don't have the energy to move."

Lois nodded. "It's been one helluva day. According to Josh, who has the video store next door, the old woman who tossed the bricks really had a pitching arm. She sent those chucks of clay hurling — *Wham!*

Front and center on each of those windows. I didn't see anything, but it sounded like someone had fired a gun. I rolled under the table. I thought we were under attack."

Lew came into the workroom with three cans of soda. He put one in front of each of us. "We *were* under attack," he said, pulling up a stool.

Like actors in a commercial, we settled back and popped the tabs on our sodas. With choreographed precision, we tipped the cans to our lips and took long, satisfying drinks.

Lois put her can down and burped. "Boy, that hit the spot," she said, wiping the moisture from her lips onto the back of her hand.

Lew's expression showed his disgust. He'd worked just as hard as Lois and I, but his necktie was straight, his shirt snowy white, his trousers neatly creased. "You are so crude," he said.

Lois narrowed her eyes and took a big gulp of her drink. This time she belched long and loud. "Now *that's* crude," she said.

Lew was straitlaced and very proper. Lois loved to irritate and provoke him. I usually ignored them, but this time I shook my head. "Come on, guys. Cut it out."

"He started it," said Lois, eyeing Lew expectantly.

In a haughty tone, he said, "I will not lower myself to your level." He turned to me. "I think we need to address our present situation, boss."

I shrugged. "What's to discuss? The glass will be replaced tomorrow. Until then there's nothing to do. I wondered what I could give myself for my birthday. Guess I'll pay the insurance deductible and call it a fine celebration."

"Not a fun gift, Bretta," said Lois. "You need to splurge. Treat yourself to something special. There's a new massage parlor down on Dover. Why don't you —"

Lew stood up in such a tizzy he knocked over his stool. Waving his hands, he said, "Rubber masks. Bricks through windows. Hijinks, low blows, and dirty tricks. When I came to work here, I thought my job would be delivering flowers. Not ducking projectiles."

Lois scoffed. "You weren't even close to getting cold-cocked."

"It's the principle. I shouldn't have to wonder what's going to happen next." Lew stared at me. "I read about that woman who was murdered Saturday at the

Parkers'. Considering this morning's event, I have to assume you're involved up to your eyebrows, which in turn means that I am, too."

Lew's face was red. Beads of moisture glistened on his balding head. I didn't particularly like him, but he was a good employee. He knew River City people and the streets where they lived. In a pinch he could wrap a plant, and his florist bows were well crafted. But if he was unhappy working here, I wasn't going to beg him to stay. It would be an inconvenience to replace him, but I didn't want anyone, especially an employee, dictating how I spent my free time.

I set the stool back on its legs. "I have talked to a few people about Marnie's murder. But just so you'll know, I've done it with the sheriff's approval."

Lew snorted. "I find that difficult to believe."

Lois nodded to the front door. "Ask him yourself."

The front doorbell jingled. Lew whipped around to watch Sid enter the store. While the sheriff surveyed the damage to my shop, Lew turned back to me. "You saw him coming into the shop."

"Yes. But that doesn't change the truth. I have his approval."

Sid joined us, declined a stool, and leaned against the table. "Never a dull moment, huh?" he said to me. "Thought I'd stop by and bring you up to speed on what the investigating officer found out."

"Let me guess," I said. "He discovered the wig, mask, and clothes discarded in the alley. Nothing remarkable about them so there are no leads as to who it was."

"That about sums it up except the wig and mask haven't been found. Whatever you've been doing, Bretta, has touched a nerve. I'd tell you to stop, but as long as you're careful, you just might flush out the guilty party. In the meantime, I've got my men checking to see who was absent from the greenhouses this morning."

"Speaking of which, Irma, the greenhouse bookkeeper, told me she thinks Marnie might have had a stalker."

Sid jerked back in surprise. "That's the first I've heard of it." He shook his head. "I don't need more crap. I've got all I can do to investigate what's already been disclosed." Abruptly, he turned to Lois and flashed her a winsome smile. "How are you? How's your family?"

She blinked. "Well . . . uh . . . I'm fine. They're fine."

Sid turned to Lew. His tone was solicitous as he asked, "And you, sir? I hope your mother's health is good."

Lew mumbled a reply, but I could see he was mulling over Sid's courteous demeanor. Suddenly Lew's spine grew rigid. His skin flushed a rosier pink. "Bretta," said Lew. "Sheriff Hancock is using you."

I nodded in a resigned fashion. "Yeah. That's the general consensus."

Lew shook his head in disbelief. "I can't believe you'd allow such a thing." He grabbed the vase of roses off my worktable. "Political claptrap. Campaign twaddle. Bah! I'm out of here. This place reeks of insincerity and hypocrisy."

"But you *will* be back tomorrow?" I asked.

"Yes," Lew said piously. "Someone has to lend a touch of sanity to this loony bin."

He slammed the back door just as my father marched in the front. Sid pushed away from the table. "Well," he said, "here comes my cue to take a hike."

The two men met as they rounded the front counter. Neither spoke. Neither acknowledged the other in any way, shape, or form. Under my breath I said, "Damn, I wish I could get away with that."

"What?" said Lois.

"Just go on about my business, pretending neither man exists."

"If you'd been on the ball, you could have slipped out the back door."

"Too late now," I muttered. Pasting a smile on my face, I said, "Hi, Dad. What brings you downtown?"

"I was at the diner and heard about your busted front windows. I came over to see if you were all right."

I held up my hands. "I'm fine," I said. "Not a scratch on me."

I might as well have saved my breath. My father was determined to deliver a lecture charged with warnings, but cleverly wrapped in a tender, loving package of concern. He settled himself on the stool next to me. His tone was soothing, his words gentle, but I zoned out.

Instead, I thought about Natalie's pool. The aquamarine water could be addictive. It was a delight to think about that silky water waiting for me at the end of this horrendous day. Maybe I should consider a swimming pool for my own personal use. I had the perfect spot for it. The more I thought about the idea the better I liked it. Forget the peonies, petunias, poppies, and pansies. Make way for a swimming pool. I'd call it therapy — a necessity for my mental health.

Dad was saying, "— thought I might have an active part in the case, but the man I talked to changed his mind. He didn't give a reason when he called, but I'm taking it in stride. The way I see it —"

I stifled a sigh and wondered what Natalie had planned for dinner. Maybe I should call her and tell her I'd bring takeout. No, she liked to cook and it would keep her busy. Chances were she was already in the process of creating some divine dish. I loved her creamy chicken enchiladas, especially if she accompanied it with guacamole dip.

The pitch of my father's voice alerted me he was winding down. I opened my ears and heard him say, "— her idea to go undercover. She starts out there tomorrow."

Bewildered, I said, "I've missed something. Repeat that last part."

My father spoke slowly and patiently. "She applied for a job at Parker Greenhouse and was hired. She starts tomorrow."

I had to ask, though I knew the answer. I licked my lips. "Dad, who are you talking about?"

"Why DeeDee, of course. She's going undercover at the greenhouse. We have it all planned out."

Chapter Nine

It was after five o'clock, and DeeDee and I were seated at my kitchen table. The discussion had been one-sided, and as far as I was concerned that's the way it would stay.

Leaning forward, I lightly touched her hand. "The word *forbid* is normally not in my vocabulary, DeeDee. I don't like hearing it so I try not to use it in reference to others. However, in this instance, I have to *forbid* you from doing this ridiculous stunt. It's dangerous. It's unnecessary. It's foolhardy."

She blinked rapidly, and I softened my voice. "I do admire the fact that you drove out to the greenhouse and applied for a job." I gave her a quick smile. "I just hope it wasn't because you're unhappy here."

"This is my h-home," she said slowly. "But I t-think I can h-help you."

"I don't need help because I'm not doing anything."

DeeDee grimaced. "I k-know better than t-that."

"All right. I am doing a little detecting,

but I could stop immediately and it wouldn't make any difference to the investigation. Sid and his deputies are on the job, and they're working day and night to find Marnie's killer. My involvement is superficial. Yours should be nonexistent. Understand?"

DeeDee's chin came up. "Give me s-some credit. I know my capabilities. I'm not a d-detective, but I d-do have e-ears." Her tone was earnest. "No one at t-the greenhouse k-knows me. I'm s-simply a young w-woman who stutters." Her lips turned down at the corners. "It's irritating but just because I can't s-speak quick and s-sure, people think I'm slow. That my b-brain is defective."

"I have never thought that, and you know it."

"With you at the P-Parker house, I don't h-have anything to do. Albert says —"

I rolled my eyes. "I can just imagine what Albert says, but that don't make it right." I glanced at the clock above the refrigerator. "I have to go. I guess I won't forbid you from going to work at the greenhouses, but I'm seriously asking you not to do it."

I waited, but DeeDee didn't comment either way. She walked me to the front door. I sensed she was trying to come up with some argument to sway me, but I couldn't think of anything she might say that would make a difference. I knew she desperately wanted to do this, but if anything happened to her, I'd never forgive myself, especially if I'd given her permission.

I turned, and her face lit with expectation that perhaps I'd changed my mind. Again, I dashed her hopes. "I'm sorry, DeeDee, I know you're disappointed, but this is best."

I glanced past her into the library and saw spools of purple and lavender crepe paper stacked on the coffee table. "What's that for?" I asked.

DeeDee looked behind her. She turned back to me and stared me straight in the eye. "My mother asked m-me to m-make some crepe p-paper roses."

Yeah, right. My birthday was a few days away. My favorite colors were purple and lavender. I felt sure DeeDee was feeding me a line, but I played along. "Really?" I said. "I didn't know you had that talent."

Her gaze was unwavering. "Would y-you like me to m-make you one?"

"I'm tempted, but I need to go. Natalie is expecting me." I took three steps toward the front door, and then pivoted on my toe. DeeDee had wilted with what I took to be relief that I'd left the subject of the crepe paper. Once I faced her again, she squared her slim shoulders and raised her eyebrows inquiringly.

"D-did you f-forget s-something?" she asked.

I grinned. "You're good, sweetie. In fact, you probably could pull off this undercover gig, but it's more dangerous than fibbing to me about crepe-paper roses." I pointed to the oak trim. "Don't use thumbtacks when you hang the streamers. Holes in the woodwork would not please this birthday girl."

Chuckling at the astonished expression on DeeDee's face, I left my house and headed for Natalie's.

A different officer prowled the front drive when I parked at the lodge. I waved to him and went up the steps to the door. I didn't have a key but when I tried the knob, the door was unlocked. I stepped into the foyer and called, "Natalie? It's Bretta. Where are you?"

"I'm in the study."

I hurried down the hall and stopped in the doorway. This was Dan's room and lacked Natalie's extravagant use of color. The walls were painted a soft cream and were covered with pecan-wood bookshelves. The carpet was a gentle blue. Floor-to-ceiling windows looked out on the fenced pool. Longingly, I gave it a hard stare before turning to Natalie. She sat at Dan's desk, reading from a stack of manila folders. I frowned. "Why didn't you have the door locked? I could have rung the bell."

She looked up. "Or I could give you a key."

"That's not necessary." I didn't plan to be here long enough to need a key. Changing the subject, I said, "What's that smell?" I wrinkled my nose. "Is something burning?"

Natalie sighed. "Not anymore. I scorched dinner, and I don't feel like tackling another meal. How about I fix us a bologna sandwich? We can eat it out by the pool."

My spirits drooped. I'd hoped for something tasty. Bologna slapped on a slice of bread didn't fill the bill, but I wasn't going to grumble.

"That's fine with me," I said. "What are you doing?"

"I started out looking through Dan's

desk for any bills that might get overlooked while he's away." A furrow creased her forehead. "In the bottom drawer I found this stack of old personnel files."

"You sound surprised."

Natalie shrugged. "Current employee records are kept in Irma's office. I assume they're still there. But this stack encompasses the last three years, and they're for employees who aren't on our payroll anymore." She gestured to the stack that was about ten inches thick. "Can you believe we've had this many greenhouse employees in the past thirty-six months? Are we that hard to get along with?"

I laughed. "I doubt it. I've gone through plenty of new people myself at the flower shop. It isn't easy finding the right person for the job." I leaned over her shoulder and thumbed the tabs thoughtfully. Jacob had said Marnie had asked about employees — how long they stayed, why they'd left. I said, "Why do you think Dan brought these files to the house?"

"I don't know unless he was thinking of contacting someone to see if they'd like to come back to work for us." After a moment, she shook her head. "But I don't understand why he'd do that. We have new people apply for work all the time."

"When did he bring them in?"

Natalie shrugged. "I can't be sure, but I think it was Friday evening. He was in here reading when I told him goodnight and I went off to bed." She stared up at me. "Why? Is that important?"

"I'm not sure, but when I spoke to Marnie in the garden, she mentioned that she needed to come to Dan's study and look over some papers. I think you should call Dan and ask him why he —"

"No. Tomorrow is his mother's funeral. I can't bother him with this." Natalie studied the files. "Since Dan brought them to the house, that could mean he didn't want anyone to know he was interested in them." She looked at me. "Maybe we'd better skip dinner and do some reading."

My stomach ached with hunger. I knew I'd never be able to concentrate without some food. I suggested we eat and read at the same time. Natalie agreed. It didn't take us long to put together our sandwiches.

In ten minutes we were back in Dan's study with plates and glasses of iced tea. Natalie sat at Dan's desk. I moved some gardening books off a table and pulled up a chair. We divided the stack of files in half. I felt a twinge of guilt as we commenced to snoop into the private lives of past Parker employees.

Parker Greenhouse requested the usual information on their job application forms — name, address, phone, and social security number. There were questions concerning medication, back problems, tolerance of heat, past experience, and a place for the names and addresses of three character references.

An hour later, I was none the wiser. I leaned back and stretched. "I don't know about you, but I'm stumped. You've employed old men, young men, old women, and young women. Some are college educated, while others didn't graduate high school. When I compare dates of employment with dates of departure, I see several people didn't stay very long."

"That happens frequently. People think they want to work with plants, but they don't realize the job is strenuous. In the long run, they'd rather flip a burger at the local fast-food restaurant than lug plants, especially when you factor in the summer heat. Most people don't like to sweat."

I could relate to that. "I've noticed that when summer help is hired, it's usually college students. Is there a reason?"

Natalie nodded. "They have plans to go

back to school and we need extra hands and strong backs during the summer growing season. It works out fairly well. They don't have to be trained or experienced. We put them to work weeding, toting, mowing, and such. Marnie fell into that category. She wanted short-term employment."

Natalie's eyes grew round at what she'd said. "Oh, dear, I didn't mean —"

I nodded. "I know what you meant. In my half of the stack it seems like young women were hired more often than young men."

Natalie turned her stack so she could read the names on the tabs. Finally, she said, "I don't think that's intentional. Uncle Donovan does most of the hiring. Jess has input if the person is to work in the greenhouses. Harley has his say when the help is for the gardens."

I chuckled. "I saw Harley and Irma in a hot clench yesterday in the garden. Are they dating?"

Natalie's lips thinned into a grim line. "I hope not. Irma's married, though she's far from happy. Her husband, Larry, has cheated on her at least twice. This last woman had his baby." She sighed deeply. "Irma and Larry have three children of their own. I think this other woman is taking Larry to court so she can get child support out of him. Irma says they're already strapped for money. I feel sorry for her, and I imagine Harley feels the same way. He was probably offering her some friendly comfort."

I remembered how Irma had caressed Harley's brawny back and drew my own conclusion as to what I'd witnessed. But I kept my thoughts to myself. Instead, I said, "Going back to these files, the facts speak for themselves. More women were hired than men."

Natalie only shrugged and picked up another file. I separated my stack into two piles — males in one, females in another. The females outnumbered the males almost three to one. I pushed the male files aside and categorized the female files by age. The oldest woman was in her forties. The youngest had just turned nineteen when she'd been hired, but she'd quit after two weeks. I made a note of the name.

"Do you remember a Dixie Ragsford?" I asked.

Natalie smiled. "A lovely young woman and very ambitious. Had plans to go to Nashville and be the next country western singing sensation."

"Did she make it?"

Natalie grimaced. "I don't know. Once they leave our employment we rarely hear from them again."

I pulled another file off the female pile. "What about Carmen Martinez?"

"She went to work at Kmart. I saw her just last week."

"How about Shannon Plummer? She left after two weeks."

Natalie thought for a moment. "I don't remember her. What are you looking for, Bretta?" She tossed the file she'd been reading onto the desk. "In fact, what are *we* doing? I've been through this stack again and again, but I haven't seen anything unique or mystifying. And I'm not sure I'd recognize it even if I saw it."

"Call Dan," I said softly. "Tell him you found the personnel files and wondered if you needed to do something with them." I could see she was thinking about it, but knew better than to push the issue.

After a few minutes, Natalie picked up the phone and pressed a series of numbers. I wasn't going to leave the room, but I traded Natalie's stack of files for mine. Bending over the first one, I pretended to read.

Behind me, Natalie said, "Hi, sweetheart. It's good to hear your voice. Are you doing okay? I'm all right. I haven't heard yet when Marnie's funeral service will be. Yes. I'll send flowers. I called to see if I needed to do something with those personnel files in your desk. What?"

The note of astonishment in Natalie's voice caused me to swivel around. Natalie kept her eyes on me, as she said, "*Marnie* asked you to bring those files to the house."

"Why?" I said softly.

Natalie nodded once, twice, three times. "All right. Okay. Okay." Softly, she whispered, "I love you, too," and hung up.

"Well," I said as soon as the receiver was back in its cradle. "What did he say?"

"Thursday Marnie asked him if she could see these files. When he wanted to know the reason, she wouldn't give him an answer. On Friday, she asked him again, but this time she told him that a friend had worked here, but had disappeared three months ago."

"Disappeared from where?"

"Dan didn't get all the particulars. Marnie was upset. She kept saying she'd let her down, whoever she was. Dan is upset with himself for not thinking about these files sooner. He wants me to turn them over to the sheriff immediately."

"Did Dan know this friend's name?"

"Paige Cooper."

"Cooper?" I repeated. I'd missed that file, and then realized Natalie had the first part of the alphabet. I'd had the tail end. I flipped through her stack and found it. I read over the information. Paige Cooper. She was nineteen years old and a high school graduate. I recognized the address as being on the lower-income side of River City. Paige had listed her mother as next of kin and to be notified in case of an emergency. Last job before coming to work at Parker Greenhouse was at a convenience store.

"Did you find anything?" asked Natalie.

"Not much." I turned the paper over. Last day of employment was two weeks after she'd started to work.

I studied the papers, wondering why Marnie had requested to see employee files for the last three years. If she'd wanted the names of Paige's coworkers, she'd have asked for only last year's data. What was she looking for?

Paige had come to work a year ago last August. Two weeks later she had given notice that she was leaving. I had to assume that Paige had been fine until she'd disappeared three months ago.

Had Marnie hired on at Parker Greenhouse to look for information on Paige's disappearance? What had she learned that would make her think something here at the greenhouse could shed light on her missing friend?

Chapter Ten

Sid had to be made aware of the files. I wasn't going to wait until morning to notify him of this latest development. I called his office, figuring he was slumped at his desk, examining reports, but was told Sheriff Hancock was at home. As I dialed his number, I decided he'd probably needed a change of scenery and had taken his work home with him.

Sid answered after the second ring. "Sheriff Hancock. What's going on?"

"Hi, Sid. This is Bretta. If you've got a minute, I'd like to —"

His impatient sigh whistled in my ear. "I'm ready to walk out the door. I have to be at a political rally in twenty minutes."

I bit my lip. I'd been off the mark. So much for Sid being slumped at his desk examining reports. "I think this is important," I said. "I've just found out that Marnie asked Dan if she could look over the greenhouse's personnel files for the last three years."

"Where are you going with this? Cut to the bottom line."

Rapidly, I said, "Marnie's friend, Paige Cooper, worked at Parker Greenhouse last August. After two weeks she quit. Three months ago, she disappeared. I think that's why Marnie came to work here. She was looking for information on her friend."

Silence greeted my jumble of words. Finally, Sid said, "I want your formal statement on the present murder. You can give it when you bring me those files tomorrow. As for this Cooper woman, I remember something about the case, but I need to refresh my memory. Good-bye."

He hung up before I could say another word. I was irritated. Maybe Dad and Donovan were right. Perhaps Sid was so intent on winning the election that he wasn't being thorough on this murder.

A half hour later, Natalie lost interest and went up to shower and watch television. I hardly noticed when she left the study. I was like a hound with his snout to the trail. I had to see where the scent took me. I started all over again by making comparisons. I looked for other employees who'd been hired at the same time as Paige. I found three. They were men, ranging in age from eighteen to fifty-two. Next I checked character references to see if any of the employees listed the same sources. No match.

Tapping my forehead, I murmured, "Why did Marnie want to see these files? What did she hope to find?"

Going back to the dates, I checked to see how many employees had left after only two weeks. When I'd finished I had three files — Paige Cooper. Dixie Ragsford. Shannon Plummer. One file per year. I straightened the stack and pushed it aside to make way for an in-depth look at these three folders. All three were young — Paige and Dixie had been nineteen. Shannon had been twenty. All were from River City.

Time slipped away as I went over each file again and again. I kept shuffling them, trying to find similarities, but my brain was too tired to think. I looked at the clock and gasped. I'd been at this for hours and still wasn't certain about anything.

My next step was to contact each woman on my list, but it was too late for that tonight. I'd have to wait until tomorrow. What I needed was a list of addresses and phone numbers. I picked up a pencil, but didn't have the energy to begin.

I stood up and pushed the rest of the folders into a tidy stack. Should I put them in the desk drawer? My hands grew still. Natalie had surprised an intruder the morning after Marnie's murder. Had someone come into the lodge looking for these files?

To be on the safe side, I decided to take them upstairs with me. I flipped off the light, glanced out the front window, and saw the deputies patrolling the grounds. Breathing a sigh of relief, I took my weary body off to bed.

Early the next morning, I stopped by the flower shop to make photocopies of Paige's, Dixie's, and Shannon's files. I started the coffee brewing and then drove to Sid's office. River City's administrative buildings were located in a quadrangle that covered four city blocks. The sheriff's department, library, post office, and city hall encircled the Spencer County courthouse — an imposing three-story limestone structure. With so many offices concentrated in one area, parking is often at a premium. At this early hour, I had my pick of slots and pulled into one. Sid's designated space was empty.

The woman at the front desk told me he was at a Sunrise Optimist Club meeting, delivering a campaign speech, but he had left instructions concerning my arrival. I had experience giving statements and was quick and concise. After the paper work was completed, I handed over the files and received a note from Sid. It was to the point: *Bretta, back off this Cooper woman until I've reviewed the facts. Sid.*

Fine, but he hadn't said I couldn't pursue other leads. At the flower shop I poured a cup of coffee and took it into my office. I tried the phone numbers that Dixie and Shannon had used on their application form. Both had been disconnected. Next I tried the numbers listed under character references. Out of six, only one person answered, and she'd never heard of Shannon Plummer.

Undaunted, I pulled my copy of the River City Residential Directory from the shelf. I labored at cross-referencing the addresses from the applications to people who lived on that same street. Next I narrowed these down to next door neighbors. I heard Lois and Lew come into work and called hello, but I kept compiling addresses. It was a tedious process, but after an hour I leaned back and studied the list.

The phone rang. I heard Lois answer and call to me. "It's Natalie, Bretta. She wants to speak with you."

I picked up the extension in my office. "Hello."

"You left early this morning so I didn't have a chance to remind you that I want to send a bouquet of flowers to Marnie's funeral service."

"Has her body been released from the coroner's office?"

"Yes. From what I understand her family will be making funeral arrangements sometime today. Fix a nice bouquet, but don't be too extravagant. I think there's going to be a memorial, and I want to donate to it as well."

"I'll take care of it."

"I see the files are gone. You've taken them to the sheriff?"

"Yes. That's why I left the lodge early."

"Did you learn anything more after I went upstairs last night?"

I picked up my list. "Do these names mean anything to you? Paige Cooper, Dixie Ragsford, and Shannon Plummer?"

"I told you about Dixie and her ambition to be a country-music singer. From what Dan said, Paige was Marnie's friend. But I don't remember Shannon Plummer."

Disappointed but not surprised, I said, "Okay, but call me if you think of something." I started to caution Natalie not to say anything about the files or mention the names, but she'd already hung up.

I went back to my list of addresses. Since I was hoping for a good gossip with a nosy neighbor, I didn't think a phone call would reap any rich rewards. What this situation called for was the personal touch with an added bit of incentive. From my point of view that meant I needed to arrive bearing a gift or bribe if that turned out to be the case. Either way, I figured a single red rose wrapped in florist tissue would enhance my chances of getting the conversational ball rolling.

Now that I had a plan I was ready for action. I passed through the workroom on my way to the back cooler. After choosing several perfect red roses, I came back to my table and prepped the flowers. As was our custom any rose that left my shop had to be wired and the stem end placed in a water tube.

When I went to the cabinet to get the waxed green tissue, Lois said, "Did Natalie give you a flower order?"

"Yes. I'll dictate it to you while I do these roses." I proceeded to give her the information, concerning the bouquet for Marnie's service. "You'll have to check with the funeral home later today to see when the service is." I glanced around the shop. "Where's Lew?"

"On deliveries. He'll be back shortly."

"That's good. Since we aren't busy, I'm going to be gone for a while."

"Do I dare ask who you're giving the roses to?"

"No one person." I gave Lois a quick grin. "I'm spreading the joy around."

Lois cocked an eyebrow. "In exchange for what?"

While I wrapped the roses, I gave her a quick account of my intentions, and how I'd come to this plan, and why I felt it was necessary. "Those personnel files are important, I'm just not sure why or which ones. I'm starting with Dixie's and Shannon's, because Sid has warned me off of Paige's. I picked these ladies because they left Parker Greenhouse two weeks after they started work and because they're all about the same age."

Lois frowned. "Why is that important?"

"I don't know that it is, but it's something they all three had in common." Quickly, I amended, "All four if I count Marnie's age, too."

My summary coincided with my task. I finished both and stood the roses upright in a plastic container. "So," I asked, "what's your opinion? Do you think I'm on to something?"

Her tone was droll. "Yeah. A collision course with a killer."

I shook my head. "I don't think so. Usually I go to the people directly involved, but this time I'm taking my inquiry away from the main suspects. I'm approaching the motive for Marnie's murder from a totally different angle, looking for background information." I picked up the roses, my purse, and a clipboard before I headed for the back door.

"Hey!" called Lois. "When will you be back?"

"Noon should give me plenty of time," I said, closing the door.

I'd decided to start with Dixie Ragsford. As I drove to the first address on my list for her, I thought about my cover story for asking questions. The truth is always a first option, but that often leads to a lengthy explanation as to why I'm involved. Keeping it simple, I decided to say there could be back pay due Dixie for overtime at the greenhouse. Money always got people's attention and it would be a way to introduce the subject of the greenhouse. Seemed feasible.

Fifteen minutes later, I'd located the

house, which sat midway on the block. It was well kept and had been newly sided with white vinyl. The harsh sun had burned the close-clipped lawn to prickly stubble. It crunched under foot as I crossed a patch to the front door.

I looked for a doorbell, but didn't find one. I rapped on the aluminum storm door. I had Dixie's application form attached to the clipboard. I had the rose in hand. Putting a smile on my lips, I was ready. I waited. Inside the house I heard movement — creaky floorboards. Brisk steps made the windows jiggle in their frames. Finally, the interior door swung open.

My gaze had been straight ahead. I had to tilt my head down to meet the stare of the tiny woman standing in the doorway. She couldn't have been more than five feet tall. Piercing blue eyes studied me. Her gray hair was brushed back from her face and anchored tightly to her scalp with rhinestone combs. She wore a floral-printed house dress covered with an apron like my mother used to wear. It had deep pockets and was edged with rickrack, a trim I hadn't seen in years.

"Yes?" she said. "I don't buy from door-to-door salesmen or women, for that matter."

"I'm not selling anything. I'm sorry to bother you, but I need information on" — I glanced at the clipboard — "a Dixie Ragsford. She worked at Parker Greenhouse two years ago and because of a bookkeeping error, she might be due some back pay. I tried the phone number on her application form but it isn't in service." I flashed a winsome smile and held out the rose. "This is for your trouble, Mrs. Hinkle."

"Well, you've got the right place," she said, eyeing the rose. "But you've got the wrong person. I'm Mrs. Jamison. I keep house for Mr. Hinkle. His wife passed away about six months ago. He's bedridden. Can't do a thing for himself."

I offered the rose again, and this time she opened the door and took it. I said, "Could you ask him if he remembers Dixie Ragsford?"

"He might. His mind is sharp, but his body's about done for." She shook her head. "Sad. He lies there and thinks about all the things he used to do." She sniffed the rose. "Nice," she murmured. "If you'll wait here, I'll go ask him about this woman. What was her name again?"

I repeated it and watched the door swing shut. I had little hope for any useful information, but there was always a chance. Five minutes passed and then ten. It was hot on the stoop. Beads of perspiration trickled down my back. Wistfully, I looked at my SUV. I'd left the engine running and the AC on. It was too tempting. I was turning to go when I heard footsteps from within the house.

This time when the door opened my smile had melted, quivering at the edges. The housekeeper took one look at me and said, "You spend most of your time inside, don't you? This heat really gets to a person who's used to air-conditioning."

"It's plenty warm today."

She chuckled. "That's an understatement. It's hotter than hell, but Missouri's like that — always extremes. Tomorrow we might need our long underwear, but I doubt it."

She hunched her shoulders and spread out her hands. "Well, I've got some bad news. Mr. Hinkle remembers this Dixie. In fact that's what took so long. He remembered all sorts of things. One thought brought up another and another and another until I almost lost track of what you'd asked in the first place. Her father was a large animal veterinarian. Dixie used to accompany him when he went on medical calls. He died a couple years ago when he was gored by a bull. Her mother remarried and moved away. I tried to tell Harry Hinkle that you wanted information on Dixie, not the family, but once he gets to reminiscing, he dredges up stuff that's no use to anyone."

"That's all good to know, but did he say anything about Dixie?"

Mrs. Jamison pursed her lips. "I guess you could say Dixie lives in River City. Given her circumstances, I'd more say she exists here. Harry Hinkle says Dixie was depressed when she came home and tried to commit suicide. He says it was before his Ava got sick because she went to the hospital to visit her, and she's still there."

I was confused. "Ava?"

"Good gracious, no. Ava was Harry Hinkle's wife. That poor woman is dead and buried. It's Dixie who's in the hospital. She's a mental patient out at that place on the edge of town. You know the one. It has the big black fence around it."

"Coventry Acres?" I asked.

"That's it. That's the one. Harry Hinkle says that when Ava came back from visiting Dixie, she told him she'd never go again. It was too upsetting. Of course by that time the cancer had gotten a grip on her liver. She couldn't do much going even if she'd wanted to."

"I appreciate all this information," I said. I went down the steps and edged my way toward my vehicle.

Mrs. Jamison kept talking. "Harry Hinkle says Dixie used to sing. That's what she wanted to do — be a famous singer. He says she went to work at a greenhouse to get money for a bus ticket to Nashville. As far as he knows she never went to Nashville, but she did go up north. She came back to River City with a bunch of cash, but her father was dead and her spirit was broken. Harry Hinkle says Dixie had lost her ambition to be a singer and her will to live. That's when she tried to kill herself."

When Mrs. Jamison paused to take a breath, I quickly said, "You and Mr. Hinkle have been a big help. Thanks again."

Cold air enveloped me once I was behind the steering wheel. I backed out of the Hinkle drive and headed south. Three blocks later, I reached over and turned the AC down. My skin was hot, but inside I was cold. My condition had nothing to do with the temperature, but everything to do with what Mrs. Jamison had told me.

Paige had disappeared. Marnie had been

murdered. Dixie had suffered a mental breakdown. Before I looked up anyone connected with Shannon Plummer, I had to see Dixie for myself. My next stop was Coventry Acres' psychiatric ward.

Chapter Eleven

The black wrought-iron fence that encircled Coventry Acres was impressive. It seemed to stretch forever. The facility was one level and was built of red brick with white trim. Old trees had been preserved during the construction process. The leafy branches framed the building giving it a sheltered, protected air.

I parked in the visitor's lot and entered the main door through an atrium. Monstrous rubber trees and speckled dieffenbachia grew in redwood tubs. A blooming jasmine plant perfumed the air.

I filled my nose with the sweet scent, preparing myself for the coming odor of captive people in a confined area. Once I was in the main lobby, I took a tentative breath. Not bad. Smelled like nutmeg and cloves. I proceeded to the desk where two ladies were having an animated conversation.

"I'll take Tom Selleck over Mel Gibson any day," said the older of the two. She had curly hair and a nice smile.

"But it was a good movie," persisted the younger. She had eight earrings curving the edge of her right lobe. "At least the plot made sense, and the acting was believable."

"I suppose, but I get tired of all the special effects. Cars blowing up. Bodies strewn around. I like a good old-fashioned love story." She turned to me and flashed her pearly whites. "Hi. What can I do for you?"

I showed her a rose. "I was hoping I could visit Dixie Ragsford."

She raised an eyebrow. "Really? Our singer rarely gets visitors. Let me check with the wing supervisor." She picked up the phone and poked a couple numbers. Her voice was low, and the conversation was short.

She turned back to me and smiled again. "It's a go. Marilyn is sending you an escort."

Surprised, I asked, "Do I need one?" I was thinking bodyguard.

The younger woman giggled. "I know what's on your mind, but you'll be fine. The only danger here is getting lost. Dixie is on D-wing. For a first-time visitor the corridors can be confusing."

I nodded and turned to the older

woman. "You called Dixie 'our singer.' Does that mean she performs?"

"She croons to her dolls."

"Will I be able to talk with her?"

"You can talk all you like, but she won't answer. She doesn't speak. She just sings."

"And rocks," added the younger woman. "She rocks in her chair and sings to her dolls."

I was digesting this bit of information when a young woman hurried toward me. "Are you Dixie's visitor?" she asked breathlessly.

"Yes," I said. "My name's Bretta Solomon."

"I'm Judy." She looked at the rose in my hand. "If that flower has a wire, you'll have to remove it."

I quickly pulled the wire off and wound it into a tight ball. Looking around for a place to put it, I finally stuffed it down in my purse. "Now can I see Dixie?" I asked.

Judy nodded. "If you'll come with me."

I thanked the ladies behind the reception desk, and then galloped after Judy, who loped down a corridor. "Why the rush?" I asked when I'd caught up to her.

She slowed her pace and grinned. "Sorry. These endless halls do it to me. I feel like Alice in Wonderland in the tunnel.

I want to get to the end as soon as possible."

Now that we were going at a slower pace, I looked through some of the open doors. The rooms were bright with sunlight. The walls painted muted beige with warm undertones. Oak veneer furniture and overstuffed upholstered chairs added a homey atmosphere. Patients/residents sat at windows or gazed at television sets. Most were old, some in wheelchairs.

Judy said, "This is the assisted living wing. B-wing is the infirm, most of whom are bedridden. C-wing is our new Alzheimer's unit. We're headed for D-wing. It's been known as psychiatric care, but the powers-that-be are now referring to it as BHU — Behavioral Unit, which doesn't have a stigma attached."

"Do you take care of Dixie?" I asked.

"Yes. I have all summer, but next week is my last. I'm enrolled in nursing school. I'll miss my patients, but I'll be back to visit. This summer job has shown me that I'm not going into geriatric or psychiatric care. Too depressing. I'm thinking about obstetrics or pediatrics. I can't decide."

I studied the young woman at my side. Her figure was plump. She used little if any makeup. I liked her fresh clean looks. "Tell me about Dixie," I said.

Judy glanced at me. "I feel sorry for her. She's a talented lady, but little good it'll do her. Her voice is that of a mature woman, but her mind is childlike."

"Will she acknowledge that I'm in the room?"

"No."

"Does she follow what you tell her to do?"

"If I say it's time for her bath, she'll undress. If I say it's time to get up, she'll put on the clothes I've laid out for her."

"Does she ask for anything? A book or magazine? A piece of candy?"

"No."

"But she sings?"

"Oh yes."

"Does she do requests?"

Judy stopped in the middle of the corridor. "What's that supposed to mean?"

"I wasn't being flippant. I wondered if Dixie might respond to something besides her expected daily routine."

Frowning, Judy said, "I've worked here all summer and you've never visited Dixie. I know you told me your name, but exactly why are you here?"

I didn't know how to answer. I wasn't

going to get into the whole story but even part of it sounded strange. My silence didn't help matters.

Judy stalked off, saying over her shoulder, "I think you need to speak to my supervisor before I take you to Dixie."

"No, please, I'll try to explain." Judy stopped and waited. "I was hoping Dixie might be able to clear up a mystery for me. Perhaps you read in the newspaper about the woman who was murdered over the weekend?"

Judy nodded. "Outside of town at that greenhouse. But what does that have to do with Dixie?"

"Dixie used to work there."

Judy shrugged. "She's been here for over two years. What could she know about something that took place recently?"

"I'm not sure, but her name came up on a job application form. I've been doing some investigating on my own."

Judy's eyes widened. "Oh. Bretta Solomon. Now I know why that name sounded familiar. I've read about your amateur detecting. You're a florist, too."

I felt my cheeks redden. "I'm a florist first, but yes, I do some sleuthing on the side."

"I still don't understand what you think

Dixie can tell you, but come on."

"If it will ease your mind, you can stay in the room with us."

"I planned on that. Dixie is a special lady. I don't want anyone or thing to upset her."

"Is there any hope that she'll get better? That she'll resume a normal life?"

"I'm not a doctor, but I doubt it. I've read her case history and it's sad. She was gone from River City for about six months. When she came back, her father, whom she adored, had died. Her mother had a new boyfriend and was about to remarry. Dixie went into a deep depression and tried to take her life. She was hospitalized, but slipped into a catatonic state. She stayed that way for almost a year. Last Christmas someone wheeled her into the activity room for a program. The music reached her. She began to sing. She underwent another evaluation, but other than being able to sing, there hasn't been a change in her condition."

"What kind of music does she prefer?"

"All kinds, but mostly country. Sometimes she'll sing 'Amazing Grace.' When she does, we all get chills. It'll bring tears to your eyes." Judy turned a corner and unlocked a door. "This is D-wing."

I hesitated before I stepped over the threshold. Judy smiled. "Don't let the locked door bother you. It's here for the safety of our patients, some of whom like to wander. On D-wing the people are docile. We aren't licensed for violent cases."

I nodded and followed Judy down a narrower hall. All the doors were open and showed rooms that were small and sparse. Where the other area had been furnished with wood furniture and upholstered chairs, here it was metal twin bedsteads and night stands. I gestured to a room. "The decorator must have skipped this section."

Judy shrugged. "Most of these patients don't know where they are, let alone what kind of furniture they're sitting on. Besides, the state picks up the tab for their care. That doesn't include frills. Our patients are kept clean and medicated, entertained if they're interested. But most of all they're safe, from the general public as well as themselves."

We turned another corner and Judy stopped at an open door. "Here we are," she said softly. She walked into the room. In a kind voice, she said, "Hey, Dixie honey, you have a visitor. This is Bretta Solomon. Can you tell her hello?"

The young woman sitting in the rocking chair didn't respond. Judy spoke as she crossed the floor. "I told her how wonderful you sing. Can you give us a chorus or two?" No answer. Judy patted Dixie's hand and motioned for me to come forward.

I approached the young woman slowly. Light from an uncovered window played across her face. Her eyes were open but vacant. Her lips were tipped up in a slight smile. In her arms she cradled a rag doll, its face was pressed against her breast. She patted the doll's bottom, keeping time with the tempo of the rocking chair. She wore her long dark hair loose around her slim shoulders. She was dressed in faded blue jeans and a pink T-shirt. Her feet were covered with a pair of fuzzy pink slippers.

Following Judy's hand gestures, I walked around in front of Dixie and leaned against the window frame. She looked normal if you discounted the expressionless eyes. I had to clear away the lump from my throat before I could speak.

"I'm . . . uh . . . pleased to meet you, Dixie. I have something for you. It's a rose. Do you like flowers?"

No answer.

I laid the rose on the windowsill. "I see

you have a doll. I used to have one that was dressed just like yours. Only my doll's dress was red. You must like pink. Is it your favorite color?" I didn't expect a reply, but continued talking quietly. "My mother made all my doll clothes. I'm not very handy with a needle and thread." I talked about nothing for a few more minutes, then said, "You and I have several friends in common. Do you remember Dan and Natalie Parker? Or Jess, Harley, Irma, Donovan, or Eugene?" I paused after each name but there wasn't any response, not even a flicker of an eyelash.

I looked at Judy and shrugged. "I guess I'd better go." I leaned forward and touched Dixie's hand. "It was nice meeting you. Perhaps I'll come again. Would you like that?" Nothing. This time I couldn't keep the tears from filling my eyes.

Abruptly, Dixie stopped rocking. She didn't look at me, but held out her doll. I glanced at Judy for instructions.

She smiled. "Dixie offers her doll when she likes someone. Apparently, she likes you. You may hold her doll for a few minutes, but you have to give her back. Isn't that right, Dixie?"

"Thank you," I said, taking the doll. As I turned the lump of stuffing around I saw it didn't have a face. I ran a fingertip over the puckered material where the button eyes had been removed. "For safety reasons?" I asked, thinking about the wire I'd removed from the rose.

Judy quietly explained, "No. Dixie doesn't want faces on her dolls." She pointed to three more sitting on the bed. "Several of the nurses have given her dolls, but Dixie plucks at the thread until it unravels and the features are gone. We've tried plastic dolls with fancy dresses and lifelike hair, but she hides them under her bed."

I couldn't control a shiver. "Why?" I wondered aloud.

Before Judy could speak, Dixie grabbed the doll out of my hands. She tucked it protectively against her breast. Softly, she sang, *"Amazing Grace how sweet thou art —"*

I listened until she started the third verse then slowly walked out of the room.

Once I was in my SUV, I wiped my eyes. Dixie's voice was just as melodious as I'd been led to believe. Her talent was there for anyone to hear, but her mind had locked away any chance she had of being a star — or even having a normal life. It was pitiful and so incredibly sad.

I pushed thoughts of Dixie's present situation away and concentrated on how she fit into this case — if there was a connection. Judy had said Dixie had been gone from River City for about six months. I assumed that was after she'd quit her job at the greenhouse. Harry Hinkle had told Mrs. Jamison that Dixie had been depressed when she came home. Judy had said that Dixie came home, discovered her father was dead and her mother was about to remarry. Judy had said Dixie went into a depression and had tried to take her life. Which tale was true? Was it important that Dixie was depressed when she got home or depressed when she learned the sad fate of her family?

I picked up the clipboard and removed Dixie's job application form and replaced it with Shannon Plummer's. What would I find out about her? I took a shaky breath and drove out of Coventry Acres. I had three possible addresses for information concerning Shannon, all neighbors. They all were located in River City's elegant subdivision, Lakeview Estates.

It was a fifteen-minute drive to the suburb and another five minutes down a newly backtopped private road. Soybean and cornfields lay on my right. Off to my left was a valley with the Ozark Mountains in the distance. This abrupt change from flat cropland to ridges and bluffs and valleys was always a surprise. I'm accustomed to Missouri's unique countryside, but it never ceased to amaze me how a few miles changed the landscape.

August was a dry, brittle month. Underbrush puts up a courageous fight for moisture, but it's the trees that are the winners. They sap any available water, and the lesser vegetation turns brown and dies.

I knew I was getting close to Lakeview Estates. The roadside ditches were neatly mowed, and the view was more accessible. Fifteen years ago the parcel of land had been developed by a group of men who'd seen beyond the scrawny trees and eroded topsoil. They'd visualized a ten-acre lake embellished with stately homes. A dream is a dream until money comes into play. The realization of those men's fantasy was awe inspiring.

I passed under the arched entryway. On my right was a slab of granite engraved in flowing script, LAKEVIEW ESTATES. Prime building locations were at the water's edge. Once that area had filled up, more houses were built, encircling the lake like enlarging ripples cast from a stone. The streets were named after the developers' family members. I was looking for Alberta Avenue.

I turned off Bethany onto Alberta and drove slowly, looking at the house numbers. I was in the third tier of homes; the first tier closest to the lake. I had three addresses to choose from, so I picked the biggest and showiest home. I pulled into a drive that was so wide I could have made a three-point turn in a Winnebago.

I grabbed a rose and my clipboard and walked up a winding sidewalk to a house that gave the illusion of being constructed with more glass than stone. Its angles and the forty-five-degree slope to the roof would have been a builder's nightmare. The grass was the shade of green usually associated with spring. Sprinkler heads were sunk in the ground at regular intervals.

This time there was a doorbell. At my touch the chimes played a musical tune. I had no indication that anyone was around. No sound of occupancy. No creaky floorboards. No jiggling windows. The woman simply appeared at the glass door.

Poof! Human being.

And a fine specimen she was. I could see nearly every inch of her smooth, tanned skin. She was dressed in a skimpy lime green bathing suit. Her hair was dark blond and pulled into a ponytail on top of her head. Wispy curls framed her face and softened her features. Her nose was a little too short. Her eyes were a little too big. But I was nitpicking. The woman was gorgeous.

"May I help you?" she asked politely.

I had my clipboard with Shannon Plummer's job application on top. I had the red rose in hand. I smiled. "I hope so. I'm looking for Shannon Plummer."

Her green eyes crinkled with humor. "I haven't heard that name in a while. Why do you want her?"

I was here to get information not give it. Besides, anyone who lived in this area wouldn't be impressed by my cover story of back pay. "Do you know her?" I asked.

"Sure." She gave a throaty chuckle. "You could say we're inseparable."

I thought that over, then said, "Are you Shannon?"

"Very good, but I haven't been a Plummer for almost two years. I'm a Taylor now." She opened the door wider. "Come in. It's too hot to talk out here."

I stepped onto a white marble floor that made me want to pull off my shoes so I could cool my hot feet on the smooth stone. The walls were white accentuated with hammered-brass trim. A fountain bubbled merrily off to my right. On my left was a six-foot piece of sculpture made from twisted copper water pipes. Solder marks brazed the metal and had been used to attach couplings that jutted out at odd angles. Suspended from the center of tangled pipes was a grimy wrench.

Shannon followed my gaze and laughed. "Pretty cool, huh? My husband presented me with that gift last year on our first anniversary. It's supposed to personify my maiden name."

Plummer. Cute. I said, "When you have children how will you keep them from climbing on it? It looks like a jungle gym."

Her friendly smile cooled. "They'll treat my property with respect."

Sure they will, I thought to myself. Out loud, I said, "This is a beautiful home. You used to live next door?"

She relaxed. "Yes. Riley, my husband, is ten years older than I am, but I've adored him from the moment my family and I moved here. Riley was a sober, bookish type of guy." She waved a hand. "I tried never to open a textbook. I didn't dream that he'd loved me, but things work out if they're meant to be. He and I were made for each other."

I murmured something that sounded like "how nice."

"Why were you looking for me?" she asked.

Turning to the business at hand, I moved the clipboard so she could see the job application form. Holding out the rose, I said, "I wanted to talk to you about the time you worked for Parker Greenhouse."

By degrees Shannon's refined poise disintegrated. The warmth and confidence drained away, leaving her face ashen. She flinched as if I'd pinched her. Hoarsely, she whispered, "Who are you? Why are you here?"

"As I said, I'm —"

"Get out of my house." She stumbled past me and pushed open the door. "Go now!"

"But I just wanted to know —"

She grabbed a vase off a side table and raised it threateningly.

I didn't hesitate. I dropped the rose and ran for the door. Glancing back, I saw Shannon glaring at me. The fear that radiated from her eyes was confusing, but her rage spurred me on to my car. I hopped in and tore out of that driveway. I almost made it to the entryway before I had to pull over. My hands were shaking so badly I couldn't keep them on the steering wheel.

I leaned back in my seat and closed my eyes. If I stretched my compassionate nature, I could accept Shannon's anger. No one wants a stranger poking around in her past. It was the fear that puzzled me. Why was she afraid? And of what?

I jumped in alarm as fingers pecked on the glass at my side. Jerking around I saw a man standing outside my SUV. His face was unfamiliar, but his eyes held concern.

"Are you all right?" he shouted.

I pushed a button and the glass slid down. "I'm fine. Probably got too hot."

He nodded. "It can happen mighty quick with this heat. I won't bother you, but if you need a drink of water, I live right over there." He pointed to a house. "My name is Cordell. Max Cordell. Come on over and sit a spell. Martha'll have the air cranked up. Once I get inside, I'll have to wear a sweater." He grimaced. "Damned hot flashes. She should've been done with them years ago."

Detecting is taking advantage of whatever presents itself. Max wasn't on my list, but he was handy. I said, "If you have a minute I'd like to ask you about one of your neighbors — Shannon Plummer Taylor."

"I'm acquainted with her and her husband. Fine couple. They're of a different generation than me. I knew her parents better. Wayne and Alice were good neighbors."

I'd learned when I questioned someone cold it often helped to insert a few facts. I sounded convincing and knew more than I did. "I just came from a visit with Shannon," I said. "I dropped in unannounced, and she was busy. She seemed rather high-strung. Is she okay?"

Max shrugged. "Far as I know. She can be touchy and moody, but so is my wife. I wouldn't think anything about it."

I waved my hand at our surroundings. "I know she used to live here with her parents. Where are they now?"

"Jamaica. They sold their house when Shannon got married."

Based on Max having said that Shannon could be touchy and moody, I said, "She's different than I remembered."

"Were you one of her teachers?"

That sounded reasonable. I felt like a heel for lying, but I nodded.

Max said, "She was quite a handful, but

I probably don't have to tell you that since you had her in class. Shannon didn't want to go to college. Didn't want to get a job. All she wanted to do was run around. Wayne finally put his foot down. He told her if she wanted her name kept in his will, she'd find a vocation and do it fast. He'd been a stockbroker, so I assume a large inheritance was involved. Shannon amazed everyone when she took a job at a greenhouse. She wasn't exactly the outdoors type unless you count lying in the sun by a pool. She worked for about two weeks at this greenhouse and then she was transferred up north."

Mrs. Jamison had said Dixie had gone up north. I hadn't thought the place overly important until Max tossed out this hunk of news. Who had transferred Shannon up north? Parker Greenhouse didn't have an affiliate anywhere. Thinking Shannon had changed jobs and gone to another greenhouse, I asked, "Do you remember the name of the business?"

"Parker Greenhouse. They had a murder up there this past weekend. Bad situation, all this killing and such. I don't want to go off my place, but that doesn't necessarily keep a person safe."

I was confused and wasn't sure what to

ask next, but Max was still talking.

"— Shannon packed her bags and told her family she didn't want them to visit her. She said she'd write or call if she wasn't too busy. She was determined to be totally on her own." He scratched his head. "She must have done well. When she came home, she was driving a fancy car. According to my wife's coffee klatch, Shannon also had a healthy bank balance. Her father was impressed. In fact everyone around here was. Shannon had grown up and settled down."

"She'd changed after this trip up north?"

He looked at me quizzically. "You noticed it yourself. Look at the man she married. I've heard rumors that Riley Taylor plans to run for state representative in a few years. He needs a wife like Shannon. She'll be an asset to him and his campaign and her money won't hurt."

I thanked Max and assured him I was feeling fine. I pulled away from the curb and out the entrance of Lakeview Estates. As I left the subdivision behind, I shook my head, wondering about Max's remark that Shannon could be an asset to her politician husband. A young woman didn't break all ties with her family and move away without a good reason. Max's talk of a new car and a healthy bank account coincided with what Mrs. Jamison had said about Dixie. She'd said Dixie had come home with a "bunch of cash."

I shook my head. Talk of a large sum of money was always suspicious. I'd be willing to bet the copper water pipes in my house that Shannon Plummer Taylor's past couldn't stand up to the probing of a dirty campaign. I didn't have the resources offered by an opposing political party intent on finding a scandalous morsel, but I did have Sid.

Chapter Twelve

I made it back to the flower shop by noon, but just barely. My reception was chilly, but my mind was on the conversation I planned to have with Sid. Lois had four orders, and I helped her get them ready for Lew to deliver. With everything under control, I waved good-bye and drove to the sheriff's office.

I found Sid at his desk, munching on a tuna sandwich. I hadn't had lunch, but the sight of soggy bread and limp lettuce didn't whet my appetite. I gave him a detailed account of what I'd discovered about Dixie and Shannon, but I made it clear that I hadn't asked any questions about Paige Cooper.

"So what do you want me to do?" Sid asked in an irritated tone.

Really ticked off, I took a deep breath. I let it out softly. "For starters, I thought you might do a background check."

Sid pushed the last of his sandwich into his mouth and studied the notes he'd made while I talked. "On this Shannon woman?" he mumbled. He swallowed the wad of bread, chasing it with a gulp of coffee. "Why? Just because she worked at Parker Greenhouse three years ago?" He squinted and brought his notes closer. "Dixie Ragsford, two years ago. Paige Cooper, one year ago." He looked at me. "Where's their connection to the here and now?"

"Like I told you, Marnie and Paige were —"

"Yeah, yeah. Marnie was a friend of Paige's. I'm not seeing a pattern. I'm not seeing a motive, and I sure as hell don't see the killer's identity."

I kept my temper, but I nearly curled my toes through the soles of my shoes. With feigned patience, I asked, "Would you rather I kept these thoughts to myself?"

Sid leaned back in his chair and scowled. "Damned tempting offer, but I can't say for sure you aren't on to something." He sighed, then asked, "Where do you think this is headed?"

I raised my eyebrows. "What? The investigation?"

"Hell no. Looking into this Shannon's background."

"You said there isn't a pattern, but I see one. Four young women worked at Parker Greenhouse. Three of them left after only two weeks. One disappeared. One tried to commit suicide and was placed in a psychiatric ward. One seemed afraid of her past. And one was murdered."

In a mocking tone, Sid asked, "All because they worked for your *good* friends?"

I shifted uncomfortably in my chair. Since I didn't have an answer to his question, I voiced my own. "Why did these women go away? Where did they go? How does the money figure in? Why didn't Paige return?"

He leaned back and rubbed his eyes. After a moment, he stared at me. "Right now my only concern is the present murder. If we drag in this other stuff, we could spend valuable time chasing down details that might not pan out."

"That's possible, but maybe if we dig —"

Sid snorted a laugh. "We? Judas Priest! I'm not sure I can handle that."

"Then don't," I said, coming out of my chair. I wanted to stalk from the room, slamming the door after me, but I had one more question. "Have you done any more checking on Paige Cooper's disappearance?"

"I don't see the relevance."

"So you haven't checked?"

"I didn't say that."

I could have ground my teeth into tiny

nubs, but I kept my cool. "Are you *saying* anything?"

Sid heaved a sigh that fluttered the papers on his desk. He leaned forward and picked up his notebook. "I haven't talked personally to Mrs. Cooper, but I did look through the missing person report."

Flipping pages, he found what he wanted. "Here's what the original report states. According to the mother, her daughter worked at Parker for two weeks, then transferred to another greenhouse operation up north. She received letters regularly from her daughter until about three months ago. Officer Jon Whaler took the call about the missing young woman. He went out to the greenhouse and talked to Jess McFinney. The upshot of that conversation was that there couldn't have been a transfer. Parker Greenhouse isn't associated with another business."

Sid glanced up at me. "Deputy Whaler read the letters that Mrs. Cooper had received from her daughter. The return address was a P.O. Box in Frankfurt, Minnesota. Nothing in those letters remotely suggested foul play or gave him another lead to pursue. He called — uh —" Sid stopped to study his notes. He nodded. "Yeah. Here it is. Deputy Whaler called

Frankfurt and talked to the sheriff up there. He in turn went to a couple of area greenhouses and checked, but found no record of Paige Cooper having ever worked at either place. Whaler asked the sheriff to check the post-office box. No leads there. The box was under Paige's name, and the rent paid for a year. Deputy Whaler marked the Cooper case open but unresolved. His personal opinion was that she'd taken off."

"Why? She thought enough of her mother to write to her, even though she was lying about her situation. Why just disappear without a word?"

Sid closed his notebook. "Lord, Bretta, I don't know. Why does anyone do anything? If everyone toed the line, I'd be out of a job."

The muscles in his throat constricted as he swallowed. When he spoke his tone was more amicable. "About those — uh — Parker Greenhouse personnel files. I haven't given them my professional assessment, but I plan on doing that immediately."

"Are you thinking I'm on to something?" I couldn't hide my smile.

Sid saw it and glowered. "Get out," he said, but his tone was only mildly aggressive. "You've disrupted my work long enough."

"I'd like to speak to Mrs. Cooper. Is that okay?"

Instead of answering, Sid scribbled something on a piece of paper, then pushed it toward me. "Take it," he said.

I crossed to the desk and picked up the scrap of paper. It was Mrs. Cooper's address. I didn't tell him I'd made a copy of Paige's file, which included her home address. Tucking the paper into my purse, I asked, "Since you gave me the address, does that mean I have your blessing?"

The heat that flared in Sid's eyes sent me scuttling out the door.

I had to pass the front of my flower shop on the way to Mrs. Cooper's home. I was happy to see the new plate-glass windows were in the process of being installed. A flash of guilt made me ease off the accelerator. I was spending too much time away from my business. I glimpsed Lois inside the shop, talking to one of the workmen. That should have been my job, but here I was, tracking leads on a murder case.

Slowly, I drove on. I could leave the entire investigation in Sid's hands, but I didn't want to back off. I was involved this time because of Sid. I wanted to help him win his reelection. I owed the man. He'd been a good friend to my husband, Carl, but that was just part of the reason. When I got right down to the bedrock of my intentions, I loved pitting my brain against corruption. But I didn't like putting my life and those I loved in jeopardy.

Like I'd told Lois, I was tackling this investigation in a different way. In the past, I'd gone directly to the suspects, asking questions, probing, and prompting a response. While I'd made headway, I'd also captured the attention of the killer, which had resulted in some scary close calls. The Parker Greenhouse personnel files had given me another avenue for seeking the truth. I had a gut feeling I was on to something. I just wasn't sure what.

Since I was in a reflecting mode, I acknowledged that I also had a point to prove to Sid. This time I wanted to show him that I could be an asset during an investigation, not a hindrance. Of course, that remained to be seen. And even if I made that point and came up with something Sid deemed valuable, that didn't mean he'd give me credit.

I turned the corner onto the street where Mrs. Cooper lived and watched for street numbers. I found the house and turned into the drive, parking next to a ramp that sloped gently up to the front door. The house was shabby. White paint curled like decorative fringe from the siding. A curtain flickered at one of the front windows. I quickly climbed out and headed up the ramp. The door opened before I could give it a tap.

The woman sat in a wheelchair and was a bundle of bones wrapped in a red-plaid-blanket cocoon. Her hands were those of an old woman, her fingers like claws. But her face, while thin and hollowed, was youthful. Her eyes were a warm shade of blue. Her brown hair had a few silver strands.

"Mrs. Cooper?" I asked.

"Yes. Is this about Paige?" Her voice was shrill with suppressed excitement. "Has she been found?"

Slowly, I shook my head. Mrs. Cooper's blue eyes went misty. A shudder passed over her emaciated body. Listlessly, she said, "I don't get any company, so when I saw you, I jumped to that conclusion."

"I'm sorry," I said. "I've come to ask about your daughter, but if you'd rather not talk, I understand."

"No. No. I have to talk about her." Mrs. Cooper squeezed her eyes shut and whispered, "If I talk about her, then she *has* to be alive." Her eyes flew open. "Can you understand that?"

"Yes," I said.

Mrs. Cooper wheeled her chair away from the door. "Come in. You'll find it uncomfortable in here, but I have to stay warm or my rheumatoid arthritis makes it too difficult to move."

She rolled over bare floors to a place near the front window. I could see from the worn varnish on the boards that this was where she spent much of her time. Near her was a table covered with newspapers, a can of soda, and a jar of Starlight Mints. I sat on a threadbare chair and tried not to stare. The room was nearly devoid of furniture. Off to my left was the kitchen. Down a short hallway I could see light coming through three open doors. I took them to be bedrooms and the bathroom. A television set was on, but the sound had been turned down. Above the console was a collage of pictures.

"That's my Paige," said Mrs. Cooper proudly. "Go look, if you'd like. I've dedicated that wall to my daughter."

I got up and went to the shrine. The photos were amateur shots encased in cheap gold plastic frames. The pictures were in chronological order. Paige in diapers, toddling toward a sandbox. Her first birthday. Her first day of school. I skimmed over these photos and turned to another set, which I assumed was when she'd entered junior high. Her hair was limp, her gaze shy. She was tall, thin, and gangly. When I came to her high school graduation pictures, I found that Paige had changed very little. Her face had filled out some, but her gaze was just as bashful. It was as if she hadn't the confidence to stare into the camera's eye.

This thought made me pause. Something connected with staring straight into a camera's lens. I frowned but couldn't come up with an answer. I shrugged and looked at the final photo of Paige in a cream sheath dress. The neutral shade did nothing to enhance her drab coloring. Her hair had been coaxed into a slight curl. Her eyes shone. Her lips were tipped up in an expectant smile. Knowing I had to make a comment, I pointed to the last photo. "She looks very nice here. I can sense she's excited about something."

Mrs. Cooper sighed softly. "I keep thinking I should take that picture down. That was the beginning of this nightmare."

I went back to my chair and sat down. A small fan oscillated, but stirred only hot air. Mrs. Cooper huddled under her blanket like it was the middle of January. Sweat had soaked my thin cotton shirt.

I said, "So there isn't any misunderstanding, I'm not with the police, but I do have Sheriff Hancock's okay to be here. My name is Bretta Solomon. I'm a friend of Dan and Natalie Parker. I was at the greenhouses when Marnie Frazier was murdered. I have some experience in solving mysteries, and I'm working on an angle in conjunction with Marnie's death. That angle is your daughter. I'd like some information about her, if you feel like talking."

"If it will help find my daughter, I'll tell you anything and everything. Ask me whatever you want."

"I'd rather you tell me the events that led up to Paige's disappearance."

Mrs. Cooper leaned back and winced with pain. "All right. I can do that. I've gone over and over it in my mind until I've refined it down to the bare facts."

"Facts are always best, but if you have personal observations, I'd like to hear them, too."

"Then I'll start with my explanation as to why Paige is gone. I think she's being kept from me against her will. If she could, she'd be in touch. She would call or write or come see me. But in order for you to believe that, you have to understand the kind of woman Paige is, and the kind of relationship my daughter and I have."

"That's what I want to hear," I said, encouraging her.

At this point, Mrs. Cooper needed nothing more from me. She talked for the next half hour on Paige's kindness, thoughtfulness, and generosity. All these attributes were illustrated with anecdotes, some of which dated back to Paige's childhood. None were relevant to what I wanted. Twice I tried to redirect Mrs. Cooper's rambling, but she wouldn't be stopped. I finally gave up and simply nodded at the appropriate spots.

"Usually Paige listened to me," said Mrs. Cooper, "but on the subject of this party, she was adamant that she would attend." Mrs. Cooper pointed to the photo of Paige dressed in the cream-colored dress. "I took that picture before she left. I had a bad feeling about that evening from the beginning. She wasn't the partying type, but she'd made Virgil's acquaintance at that convenience store where she'd worked. We scraped up the money for a new dress. She fussed over her makeup and hair for hours."

Mrs. Cooper rubbed her hands and flinched. "I realize that young men these days don't come to the door for their dates, but to sit out front and honk the horn? He upset me to no end. Paige gave me a kiss and rushed out. I tried to wait up for her, but I fell asleep. I'm not sure what time she got home, but it was well after three in the morning. She slept in the next day. When she finally came out of her room, I knew something was terribly wrong, but she wouldn't talk."

Tears came to Mrs. Cooper's eyes. "When I kept asking her questions, Paige finally admitted there was a problem, but as an adult she would handle it."

Mrs. Cooper took a piece of the plaid blanket in her gnarled hands. "I left her alone. As the days went on she seemed to be doing better, but I wasn't. I had a reaction to some new medicine and had to go into the hospital for a couple of weeks. The doctor wanted my progress closely monitored. Paige came to see me, but we didn't have any private time. I got out of the hospital and our life was almost the same as it had been before she went to that party. Then one day she told me she was changing jobs and going to work at a greenhouse. She worked there for two weeks, then said she was being transferred up north."

"She used that term, 'transferred'?"

"Yes. I understand now that wasn't the case, but that's what she told me. I didn't like the idea of her going off, but she was excited. She said that when she got back, she'd have saved money, and we'd move out of this old house into one that was better equipped to handle my disability."

"So money was the incentive?"

Reluctantly, Mrs. Cooper said, "I suppose, but I keep thinking about that party. She changed after that night."

"How much time passed between the party and her story about being transferred?"

She thought for a moment. "About two months."

"Did she give you a date as to when she would return from this other job?"

"No, not before she left, but in her last letter, she said she would be home soon."

"Would you let me read her letters?"

Mrs. Cooper didn't hesitate. "Yes. I think they're important. They'll give you an insight into Paige's personality. You'll be able to see for yourself that she is a thoughtful, loving daughter. She would never go away and not contact me. Never!"

I assumed she'd have to wheel herself into another room to get the letters, but Mrs. Cooper simply reached out a hand and moved aside the newspapers from the tabletop. She picked up a bundle tied with a frayed pink ribbon.

Caressing the top envelope, she said, "I imagine you'd like to take them with you." She licked her lips and took a shaky breath. "And that will be fine, if you swear I'll get them back."

I agreed, took the parcel, and placed it on my lap. "Where does Marnie fit into all of this?" I asked.

Mrs. Cooper's face crumpled. She bowed her head and cried softly. I started out of my chair to offer her comfort, but she waved me to stay seated. She took a couple of breaths and finally said, "I'm sorry, but I feel responsible. I was desperate for help."She stopped to swallow a sob. "I called Marnie because she was Paige's friend."

"Was Marnie at this party?"

Mrs. Cooper shook her head. "No. She wasn't acquainted with any of those young people. After Paige disappeared, Marnie tried to talk to this Virgil, but he scared her. He came on to her. Marnie wouldn't tell me what he said, but I think he was very crude to her." She mopped the tears from her cheeks. "I just don't understand why Paige was attracted to him."

I didn't say it, but I figured he was the first and only man who'd shown Paige any attention. "What did you hope Marnie could do, taking a job at the greenhouse?"

A spark of anger suddenly shone in Mrs. Cooper's eyes. She thumped her thighs and said, "I'm so useless. I can't do anything without help. I try not to ask. I try to be self-sufficient, but I thought Marnie could be my legs and eyes."

"What was the plan?"

"I'd tried numerous phone calls to the greenhouse, but no one could or would answer my questions. So I knew a direct approach would be senseless. Ordinarily, I don't resort to subterfuge, but in this case I didn't hesitate. Marnie was to snoop. She was a smart young woman. I left the details up to her. The last time I saw her was two days before she was killed. She was feeling pressed for time. She would be leaving for college in a few weeks, and she hadn't discovered anything. Everyone at the greenhouse was friendly and nice. She didn't feel any hostile 'vibes,' as she called them. She especially liked and trusted Dan Parker. Before she left that last time, we decided she should take him into her confidence. Tell him she was looking for information about Paige."

"She did that. She asked to see the personnel files for the last three years."

Mrs. Cooper frowned. "Personnel files? Why would she want to see them? She knew everything there was to know about Paige."

"I think she discovered some facts that made her want to review the other employees' records."

Mrs. Cooper stared at the floor and murmured, "I wonder what it was." She sat quietly for a moment, then turned a direct gaze on me. "You said you're a friend of Dan Parker, so I'm assuming you trust him. If we discount him as a suspect, then who else knew Marnie asked for those files?"

My smile was grim. "Mrs. Cooper, never think that you are useless. That's an excellent question, and I intend to find the answer."

Chapter Thirteen

The facts were piling up. At the core of the case were three women who'd worked at Parker Greenhouse, but had left after two weeks. Money was involved. Was it from a payoff? And for what?

All this thinking and traveling had made me hungry. I pulled into a fast-food restaurant. I knew I'd made a bad choice, but I hadn't eaten all day. I ordered a roast beef sandwich with horseradish sauce, but I skipped the French fries. No sense going completely off my diet. I wolfed down the sandwich as I drove across town. I wanted to buzz on out to the greenhouse, but I couldn't in good conscience do that until I'd dropped by the flower shop. I knew I was in trouble when Lew greeted me with a glare.

"Well, look who's here," he said sarcastically. "It's our phantom employer. Have you dropped in to design and depart like you did earlier?"

I ignored him. "The windows look wonderful. Thanks for putting in a temporary display, Lois. The fall colors were a good choice. We'll skip another back-to-school theme."

She didn't say a word, but kept poking yellow and white daisies into the bouquet she was designing.

Hoping to elicit a response, I directed a question to her. "Is everything okay?"

Lois lifted a shoulder. Her answer was delivered in a cool tone. "It's been a day of complaints. Mrs. Gamble called. She wants to know what she can do to keep her neighbor's dog from peeing on her tropical hibiscus."

"Mothballs," I said.

"That's what I suggested. About an hour ago, Irene Putney called. Her dozen roses didn't last but a day."

"A day? That's strange. A flower doesn't die that quickly. I wonder what happened."

"I asked and found out the old gal put about fifteen aspirins in the water. It seems a garden club member told her that aspirins would make the roses last longer."

Annoyed, I said, "Maybe one, but never fifteen. What did you tell her?"

"That roses rarely get migraines."

I chuckled. "Cute."

Lois didn't crack a smile. "Irene didn't think so. I had Lew take her another bouquet as part of your good-business policy, but I told her she'd have to do a program for her gardening club on drug abuse among flowers."

"And?"

Lois made a face. "She agreed if I'd help her come up with more fallacies. At the moment nothing comes to mind."

I offered, "I'll help you do some research."

Lois gave me a hard look. "Are you sure you have the time?"

I dropped my gaze to the bouquet of daisies. It was lopsided, which told me more than her tone. Lois's bouquets were always symmetrical. I was in deep do-do, and it was time to make amends. There was only one alternative. I had to involve my employees in the investigation.

Dragging out a stepstool, I sat down and leaned my elbows on the worktable. "I need help," I said. "You've both been my sounding boards in the past. I want you to listen to what I've discovered and help me make sense of it."

Lew snorted his disgust.

Lois rolled her eyes heavenward, as if to say, *Here we go again*.

I ignored them and gave an exaggerated sigh of relief. "Thanks, guys," I said. "I knew I could count on the two of you."

Resigned, Lois said, "Whether I listen to you or not, the pay is still the same. Besides, whatever you have to say will surely be more interesting than hearing about Lew's corns."

"I don't have corns," said Lew. "These new shoes have rubbed the skin raw on my big toe."

Lois grimaced. "The subject of blisters and corns is very titillating." She nodded to me. "Go ahead, Bretta, see if you can top that. I'm listening."

Lew eased his foot out of his shoe. "Me, too," he grumbled. "Maybe if I concentrate on something else, I'll forget the pain."

My audience could hardly be described as receptive, but at least they'd stopped giving me the cold shoulder about my extended absence from the shop.

To grab their attention, I began, "Once upon a time there were four women who worked for Parker Greenhouse. Their names were Shannon, Dixie, Paige, and Marnie."

"Once upon a time?" said Lew.

"You mentioned those names earlier," said Lois.

I pointed to her. "Very good. You *are* listening."

Lew said, "What about me? The 'once upon a time' line threw me, but I'm up to speed now."

That was debatable, but I pushed on. "Three years ago, Shannon worked at Parker Greenhouse for two weeks, told people she'd been transferred up north, went away for a while, then came back driving a new car and sporting a healthy bank account.

"Two years ago, Dixie worked at Parker Greenhouse for two weeks, went away up north for a while, and came back with 'a bunch of cash.' She discovered that her father had passed away and her mother was about to remarry. She was depressed and tried to take her life. She now resides at Coventry Acres in the psychiatric ward.

"One year ago, Paige worked at Parker Greenhouse for two weeks, said she'd been transferred up north. Before Paige went away she told her mother that when she returned she'd have money, but Paige *never* came back.

"Two months ago, Marnie went to work for Parker Greenhouse, hoping to discover what had happened to her friend Paige. Marnie was murdered."

Lew's mouth hung open.

Lois leaned weakly against the table.

"Good heavens above! What kind of mess have you uncovered?"

Having caught their interest I went on to describe my meetings with Shannon, Dixie, and Mrs. Cooper. I ended by saying, "Each person has touched me in a different way. Dixie's singing voice was sensational, but watching her croon to that faceless rag doll was heartbreaking."

I stopped and thought about the rag dolls sitting on Dixie's bed. I murmured, "Why doesn't she want those dolls to have features?" Giving myself a shake, I spoke up. "Mrs. Cooper seems able to cope with being in a wheelchair, but her daughter's disappearance has compounded her pain."

Lois said, "What's going on out at the greenhouse?"

"I haven't any idea. You know how I feel about Natalie and Dan. I'd trust them with my life."

Lew said, "Which you very well may be doing since you're staying out there."

"Dan isn't at the lodge — he's still in Oregon. Regardless of that fact, I don't think the danger comes from him, and especially not Natalie." I shook my head. "Help me out, guys. Toss out some possibilities. Stimulate my brain. I've been running around gathering information. Now I need to put it into theory, but I don't know where to start."

Lois said, "Give me a minute." She stared at her arrangement, as if seeing it for the first time. Making a face, she adjusted some of the daisies until the bouquet was perfect. She tied a yellow bow to the handle, priced the arrangement and took it to the front cooler for sale.

When she came back to the worktable, she gave me a fierce glare. "Don't think I don't know why you've told Lew and me this tale," she said. Her lips tipped up in a smile. "Congratulations. It worked. I can see why you've been neglecting the shop. If I were honest, I'd admit you haven't been missed. Lew and I can handle the work, so keep on digging. You'll get to the bottom of this mystery sooner or later."

I ran my hands through my hair. "But I don't want sooner or later. I want now. Don't either of you have any thoughts?"

Lew said, "You kept saying 'up north.' Where up north? Northern Missouri? Michigan? Canada? Where?"

"Frankfurt, Minnesota," I said. I pulled the packet of letters from my purse. "Mrs. Cooper gave me Paige's letters." I untied the pink ribbon and fanned the envelopes on my worktable. "Why don't you guys help me out by reading some of these? Three pairs of eyes are better than one. You might see something that I might miss."

Eagerly, they picked a couple of letters and started to read. After a moment, Lew said, "Paige is extremely homesick. Listen to this: 'I'm saving my money, Mom, so I don't go out often. I miss you more than I ever thought possible. I wish for many things, but most of all, I wish I could see you again.' " Lew sighed. "That's sad."

Lois looked up. "Paige was working. I wonder why she didn't make a few friends?"

I said, "Too shy is my guess. I don't think she made friends readily."

Lois said, "Listen to this: 'At least I don't have to brave the icy roads. The weather is mild without any snow.' " She frowned. "This was written on December the eighteenth. I can't imagine Minnesota without snow at that time of year."

Lew said, "We had a mild winter last year. Maybe Frankfurt did, too."

Lois's eyes sparkled. "I know how we can find out." She hopped down from her stool and went to the florist directory we kept by the phone. "I'll just call up a Frankfurt florist and ask about last year's weather. The eighteenth is close enough to Christmas, I'm sure she'll remember." She flipped the pages. "Frankfurt has three flower shops. I'm calling this one," she said. "I like the name, Always in Bloom." She made a note of the number and dialed.

Interested in the outcome of this conversation, I put down my letter.

"Good afternoon," said Lois. "I work in a Missouri flower shop, and I was wondering if you could recall the kind of weather you had last December. I'm thinking around the eighteenth." Lois listened a moment. "No. No. Not at all. This isn't a complaint about an order." She nodded. "Really? There was that much snow? And the wind chill made it necessary to cover all the poinsettias that were delivered."

Lois chitchatted a few more minutes with the Minnesota florist before she hung up. "Well," she said, facing us with her hands on her hips. "What do you guys make of that?"

Lew shrugged. "I'm not going to say Paige lied. Perhaps she knew her mother would worry if she thought Paige was driving on icy roads."

"That's a possibility," I said, but I didn't believe it. I went back to reading my letters. I didn't find anything that suggested any new thoughts. But in a letter Paige had written in January, she again mentioned the warm winter.

Once we'd finished reading, I asked, "Did these letters stimulate any new ideas?"

Lois said, "I don't think Paige was in Minnesota."

Lew said, "I think Paige is a considerate daughter who didn't want to worry her mother."

Lois snorted. "You and I couldn't agree on nothing."

"We can't agree on anything," said Lew in a weary voice.

Lois narrowed her eyes at Lew before turning to me. "You mentioned something earlier that caught my attention. I got the feeling that you were upset by the fact that Dixie's rag doll was faceless. Why does that bother you?"

"I don't know."

She pointed to a glass case where we kept stuffed animals that were for sale. "In that last shipment we got four dolls that you'd ordered. None of them have faces. They're dressed in Amish clothing. You thought they were cute."

Slowly, I walked over to the case and

stared at the dolls. All wore little white caps over hair made of black yarn. White aprons covered dark blue dresses. The faces were smooth, unadorned fabric.

I slid the case door open and reached inside. Taking out one of the dolls, I hugged her tight against my chest. My lips felt wooden as I said, "Did I mention that Evan Miller's son, Jacob, is working out at Parker Greenhouse?"

Lois spoke from behind me. "Evan Miller, the Amish man?"

I nodded. "Did I mention that Dixie's father was a veterinarian? That he specialized in large animals?" I didn't wait for an answer. "Did I mention that he often took Dixie with him when he went on medical calls?"

I turned to face Lew and Lois. "I think Jacob knew Dixie from when she came with her father to treat Evan's livestock."

Lew spoke with skepticism. "But Bretta, surely there are other veterinarians in River City who doctor Amish animals. What are the odds that Jacob knew Dixie?"

I countered, "What are the odds that an Amish man would go to work at Parker Greenhouse where Dixie had worked? What are the odds that this same Amish man would have in his possession a photograph that could be Dixie dressed in Amish clothes?"

Lois gasped. "You saw this picture?"

I nodded. "On Sunday, the day after Marnie's murder. I didn't get the opportunity to study the photo, but I saw the dark dress covered with an apron, the dark hair covered with the white cap."

I stared at the doll in my hands. Grimly, I said, "I've been such a dope."

"Aren't you being rather hard on yourself?" asked Lois. "There wasn't any reason for you to suspect that Jacob had a connection with anyone who'd worked for Parker Greenhouse."

"That's true, but the moment I saw that photo of an Amish woman I should have been alerted that something wasn't right."

In perfect unison, Lois and Lew asked, "Why?"

"Amish don't have their pictures taken, and they most definitely don't pose, staring straight into the camera."

Lew said, "You're exactly right, Bretta. 'Thou shalt not make to thyself a graven image.' "

I nodded. "The Amish consider posing for photographs to be an unacceptable act of pride. That picture wasn't of a true Amish woman, but the coloring, the shape of the face, could very well be Dixie Ragsford."

Chapter Fourteen

My plan to involve Lois and Lew in the investigation had worked so well they all but gave me the bum's rush out the back door. My crew of two sternly informed me they could handle the flower shop until I brought this mystery to a conclusion. All they asked was that I keep them posted on any and all developments.

With these instructions in mind, I drove to the greenhouses. I arrived just as the employees were taking their three o'clock break. Some of the workers were outside having a smoke. Others were in the lounge, indulging in brownies artistically arranged on a plate rimmed with a platinum ring. Hmm — my dishes at home carried this very same design.

My gaze circled the room until I found her. DeeDee was slouched in a chair, all wide-eyed and guilty looking. It appeared that she'd put in a hard day. Her blue T-shirt was sweat stained. Her curly dark hair had lost its bounce, hanging in clumps around her ears. Many times I'd come into the kitchen to find her slaving away over a hot stove. Pots would be steaming, the contents boiling, but I'd never seen her as wrung-out as she was at this moment.

A speck of pity touched my heart, but it was gone before I could identify it. She'd brought this on herself. I had plenty to say to her, but to the room in general, I said, "Looks like I'm just in time."

"Help yourself," said Irma, dabbing a smear of chocolate from her chin. "I'm not staying. I have to get back to my bookkeeping duties, but when I heard there were homemade brownies in here, I had to stop by for a treat."

"They look luscious," I said. I picked up the biggest square on the plate — my plate — and took a bite. I chewed blissfully. When I could speak, I said, "My housekeeper oversees my diet. She *never* fixes me anything like this."

Irma said, "You can thank our newest employee. DeeDee, this is Bretta Solomon. Bretta is a greenhouse customer and a good friend of Dan and Natalie Parker. Bretta, this is DeeDee Henry. DeeDee is helping us for a few weeks until we get caught up with some work, and then she's off to cooking school."

"Cooking school?" I said, raising an eyebrow. "If these brownies are any indication, I'd say you have a wonderful future ahead of you."

DeeDee ducked her head and murmured, "T-Thank y-you, m-ma'am."

Irma leaned close. "Jess says she's a quick learner and a hard worker, but she stutters and is very shy."

I glanced at DeeDee and saw her cheeks redden. She'd heard Irma's comment. Before I could think of a way to ease DeeDee's embarrassment, the young woman next to her stumbled to her feet. Her face was pale. She clutched her stomach and gagged.

"Sorry," she gasped. "Don't feel well." She staggered out of the lounge and into the bathroom. The door slammed shut.

"What's wrong with her?" I asked.

"Food poisoning?" suggested a woman. Everyone laughed. Three people reached for another brownie.

A man with crumbs on his shirt said, "If that's the case, at least we'll die happy."

"No, seriously," I said. "She looked very ill."

Irma shrugged. "We get this every summer. Someone gets too hot and spends more time in the bathroom than she does potting cuttings." Unconcerned, Irma walked out.

The man with the crumb-covered shirt smirked. "Ah, the shortcomings of the weaker sex . . ."

This bigoted remark opened a loud discussion. No one paid any attention when the young woman came out of the bathroom and sat down next to DeeDee. Amazed, I watched this formerly ailing woman pick up a brownie and eat every morsel. She topped it off with a candy bar from her purse.

DeeDee noted my interest. She frowned, stared at the door I'd entered, and then back at me. I could take a hint. Aware that she was watching, I picked up another brownie. It was a defiant act on my part. DeeDee would never bake this kind of snack at home. She knew I couldn't leave them alone, and I knew each bite inflated the fat cells on my butt. I ate the brownie anyway, sauntering out of the lounge and into the corridor.

Eugene was at the order desk, making calls to customers, taking their orders for delivery tomorrow. Jess and Natalie were talking over by the door that led out onto the loading dock.

I walked up to them and heard Jess say, "Put that bunch of puffers and hackers in house B with the tropical plants. All this second-hand cigarette smoke might kill off those aphids that have moved in on the bougainvillea."

"Would that really work?" I asked.

Natalie turned. "I thought that was your SUV parked outside. You're home early."

Jess said, "In answer to your question, Bretta, probably not. There used to be an insecticide on the market called Black Leaf 40. It contained nicotine concentrate — tobacco juice. We mixed it with water and sprayed infected plants. It was an excellent pesticide but the government banned it several years ago." Jess cracked a snide smile. "Figure that one out. We can't control pests, but pests can control the government. Tobacco is big business."

"But you use other insecticides?"

Jess nodded. "I'd rather not, but we have to. The very conditions that make plants grow — high humidity and heat — also makes the bugs proliferate." He frowned at me. "Why all the questions?"

"While I was in the lounge, one of the girls got sick. I was just wondering if she was exposed to some chemical —"

Jess held up his hand. "You can stop right there. All kinds of government agencies would be on my ass if I didn't follow strict precautions. If the woman got sick it wasn't because of any insecticide used on this property. You can be damned sure of that." He turned on his heel and stalked off.

I grinned sheepishly at Natalie. "Guess he set me straight. I wasn't accusing anyone of anything. I was just —"

"— fishing for information?" said Natalie. "It's a wonder you have any friends at all. You seem to antagonize people with your questions."

"Only if they have something to hide."

"And you think Jess does?"

Aware of Eugene sitting close by, I said softly, "At this point I'm not sure of anything." I studied Natalie. Her face was flushed and her eyes sparkled. "What's going on with you?" I asked.

Natalie could hardly speak for smiling. "Dan's coming home tomorrow."

"Well, that's good news. No wonder you look as if you've won the lottery."

A shadow passed over her face. "His mother's funeral was this afternoon. He's been through so much. I hate that he's coming home to more sadness."

"What sadness?" said Donovan, coming up behind us. "Are you talking about Marnie's death? Has there been any new evidence?"

Natalie looked at me, and I shook my head. "Nothing that I've heard," I said. "But Sid is working night and day. He's made her murder top priority."

"As well he should if he wants to get re-elected," said Donovan.

Natalie said, "Maybe those old personnel files we found in Dan's desk will help."

Donovan sighed. "So that's where they are. Irma's been squawking all morning about those missing files. She went to the cabinet to put away some folders and found the slot empty. She wanted to call in the deputies patrolling outside, but I told her there was a logical explanation. A thief wouldn't come in here and carry out employee records." He frowned. "I wonder why Dan wanted them?"

I knew without a doubt that Natalie was about to blab. I tried to stop her with a nudge, but she drew an audience with her opening remark. "Marnie's murder is just the tip of the iceberg."

Jess, pushing a cartload of plants, stopped to listen. Irma came out of her office and Eugene left off making phone calls so he could hear what Natalie was saying.

"Bretta would have told this more professionally," Natalie said, casting me a smile. “But she’s too modest. She’s the one who noticed that we’ve had several employees who work for a couple of weeks then go away. One of the women has disappeared.” She thought a moment then said, “Her name was Paige.” She looked around the circle of faces. “That’s why Marnie came to work here. She was friends with Paige and was trying to figure out what might have happened to her.”

The air crackled with tension. This was the very situation I’d been avoiding — confronting the suspects with information. While Natalie talked about Marnie’s generous nature, I glanced at Irma. Why had she been upset that the files were missing? Why call it to everyone’s attention? Unless she knew that once they were discovered to be gone, she’d be held accountable because they’d been stored in her office.

I turned so I could see Eugene. His eyes were narrowed. His handsome face seemed carved of stone. By his own admission he’d loved Marnie. Was her death a crime of passion? A quarrel between lovers?

Jess and Donovan took care of the hiring and firing of employees. Out of the corner of my eye, I watched them. Was Jess’s interest casual? Should I discount Donovan as a suspect simply because he was Natalie’s uncle?

Was I making too much of the information I'd gleaned from the files? Mentally, I gave myself a shake. No. I was on the right trail, but Natalie had alerted my prey. With each word, Natalie placed me in more danger.

A cold fist closed over my heart when she said, "Shannon Plummer. Dixie Ragsford. Paige Cooper. Those are the names of the employees. Do any of you remember them?" Trying to jog their collective memories, she added, "I think Shannon worked here three years ago."

Donovan's gaze danced lightly across my face. "Natalie, I can see from Bretta's stricken expression that what you've told us wasn't necessarily meant for our ears."

Natalie swung around to stare at me. "I don't care what the sheriff says, Bretta. We can trust these guys. Besides, surely the more people who know what you're looking for, the more chances you'll have of learning the facts. Isn't that how sleuthing works?"

I cleared my throat. "Sometimes."

A sly laugh sounded from behind me. I turned. Harley leaned against a wall. He nodded politely, but his tone was cold. "But it's never a good idea to tip your hand, is it, Mrs. Solomon?"

I licked my dry lips. "I prefer to keep some information to myself."

Harley smoothed his Fu Manchu mustache. "Or be more selective as to who you confide in." He waved his arm to include Irma, Eugene, Jess, and Donovan. "My guess is we're the last people you'd have shared that information with, but you don't know us like Natalie does."

My irritation flared. "Are you saying that just because you work together, your lives are open? You each know all there is to know about the others?"

Harley clamped his lips shut, but Irma said, "Here at Parker Greenhouse we're a family. We care about each other."

"Oh, really. Did you care enough about the young women Natalie mentioned to find out why they left after only two weeks?"

Irma frowned. "Two weeks is hardly long enough to establish a relationship. You have no idea how many people come to work here and leave. We can't follow up on all of them."

"Perhaps, you're right," I said, lifting my chin. "But while they were here, did you try to get to know them? What if I told you that Paige's mother is in a wheelchair? Since her daughter's disappearance she's alone with her pain and heartache. When I mentioned Parker Greenhouse to Shannon Plummer she became edgy and excitable." I stared at the faces around me. Softly, I asked, "I wonder why? Did you know that Dixie tried to kill herself and is living at Coventry Acres in a psychiatric ward?"

A strangled cry punctuated my final words. I jerked around. There was Jacob, his face contorted with anger. I started toward him, but he waved me away.

When he spoke his voice was as cold as death. "Why would you spread such vicious lies about my . . . about Dixie?"

Chapter Fifteen

I went to Jacob and tried to take his arm, but his hostility toward me was red hot. In a gentle tone, I bribed him. "I'll tell you Dixie's story if you'll come with me." He hesitated for a moment, then stalked ahead of me out the loading dock doorway and down the steps. He waited for me on the drive.

I wanted privacy, so I led the way to the gardens. I told Deputy Swanson, who was on duty at the entrance, that Jacob and I needed to talk. He agreed to let us in if we stayed away from the crime scene. He also said he would have to follow us at a discreet distance. I told him that was understood.

The three of us entered the garden with Deputy Swanson about twenty feet behind us. It was late afternoon, and the sun was scorching. There wasn't a breeze to evaporate the droplets of perspiration that gathered on our skin. I kept waiting for Jacob to speak, but he was silent. I hoped he was corralling his scattered thoughts, so that he could speak coherently when we finally had a dialogue going.

We took the path away from the stone cornucopia, passing the Garden of Contemplation. It would have been a nice place to stop, but the sun bearing down on the gravel sent out endless waves of heat. Turning back to Deputy Swanson, I called, "Let's head for the Moon Bridge and the waterfalls. It should be cooler there."

He wiped his brow and nodded.

We plodded on in silence. I sneaked a peek at Jacob. His eyes were on the path. His mouth set in grim lines.

I touched his arm, but he drew away. "I'm sorry, Jacob," I said. "I would never have been so blunt about Dixie's condition if I'd known you were close by. I was trying to raise some moral consciousness among those people, not to hurt you."

"You said she tried to kill herself? Why?"

"From what I understand, while Dixie was gone, her father was gored by a bull and died. When Dixie came home she found her mother about to remarry. Dixie was depressed, and she tried to take her own life." Again I wondered if this was the sequence of events or if Dixie had come home depressed. This was bugging me, but I didn't know where to find the answer.

Jacob said, "You must have the Dixie I know confused with someone else. My Dixie would never do harm to herself."

"It has to be the same woman, Jacob. The father of the Dixie I met was a veterinarian. She often went with him on his medical calls." From the paleness of Jacob's face, I knew I'd finally convinced him we were speaking of the same young woman.

At the foot of the Moon Bridge, I said, "Let's cross over and sit on that stone bench by the waterfall." Without a word, he did as I directed.

Deputy Swanson was as good as his word and stayed behind us. His presence made me feel secure, while the distance allowed Jacob the freedom to vent his emotions, which seemed to have been bottled up inside of him for a long, long time.

Once we were seated Jacob started to talk, rapidly, his tone filled with passion. "I was sixteen when I met Dixie. Her father came out to our house to treat one of our milk cows. I'd never seen anyone like Dixie, so lovely, so gentle. That old cow was a mean critter, but Dixie stood next to her and sang. I didn't understand all the words, but Dixie's voice was as smooth as cream."

Jacob pulled the photograph from his pocket. Up close, I immediately recognized Dixie dressed in Amish clothing. Softly, Jacob said, "That first moment when I set eyes on her, I knew I was in love. She was three years older than me. She was English. She was book smart and talented, but I loved her."

He touched the picture with a fingertip. His voice trembled as he said, "And the amazing part was that she loved me, too. The next day she drove out to the house. She told my father she was checking on the cow, but I knew she'd come to see me. Before she left we agreed to meet that evening on the gravel road that backs our farm."

"Down by the creek?" I said, knowing the place all too well.

Jacob nodded. "We met under that old oak tree, fitting our bodies between the exposed roots, snuggling in the moonlight. For two weeks she drove out from town every night so we could be together. Then she stopped coming to see me. I went to the creek each evening, but she never came again."

He glanced at me. "The pain in my heart was almost more than I could bear. I didn't know what to do. When I was in

Woodgrove, I used a pay phone and tried to call her home, but she wasn't there. My family doesn't shop in River City, so I couldn't go to the address of her father. I buried my pain and tried to forget her, but I would think of her often. The days slipped into months before I got a letter."

"Did you notice where it was mailed from?"

"Of course. I memorized everything about that piece of paper. She wasn't in Missouri, but in Frankfurt, Minnesota. When I was at the library I looked it up on the map. So many miles away, but when I held that letter in my hands, I felt as if she was at my side."

"What was she doing in Minnesota?"

Eagerly, Jacob turned to me. "I can recite the contents of her letter if you are interested."

My heart ached for this young man. Such love and devotion and it was going nowhere. But I could tell he wanted to say the words that were imprinted on his soul. "Yes," I said. "I'd like to hear her letter."

Jacob licked his lips and closed his eyes. "My darling, Jacob. I miss you more than I can possibly say. You are my friend and lover rolled into one fine man. It is hard to find the words to write what I want to tell you. If you were here, I'd sing of my love. But if you were beside me, there would be no need for words or songs."

Jacob's voice broke, but he kept quoting. "I went to work at Parker Greenhouse, but they transferred me up north. The river is close to my cabin. A spring keeps me in comforts that I need, but you do without."

I frowned. Jacob must not have memorized that sentence correctly. It didn't make sense, but I didn't interrupt.

Jacob continued, "Before I left Missouri, I had this picture taken. I wanted you to see that I *could* be an Amish wife you would be proud of, even though you've said we can never marry. I wish I had your sensible, insightful character, but I feel only with my heart, which is broken. Perhaps that explains why I'm giving away the last link I have to you. If I were whole, I might do things differently. I pledge you my eternal love, Dixie."

In my mind I pictured the woman I'd met at Coventry Acres. I tried to compare that person to the author of the letter Jacob had recited to me. The two images seemed incompatible. Yet the Dixie I'd physically faced was a mere shell of a woman; there wasn't enough substance to draw an understanding of the Dixie Ragsford Jacob had loved.

I would have liked to ask questions about what an Amish man and a wannabe country music singer had in common. It sounded as if they'd discussed the future. How had they understood each other's hopes and dreams when they were worlds apart? Surely they knew their relationship wasn't going anywhere?

While those lines of inquiry might have satisfied my curiosity, they had nothing to do with Marnie's murder. Keeping Sid's remark about the "here and now" uppermost in mind, I asked, "Why did you take a job at Parker Greenhouse?"

"I am moving to Illinois to work in a cabinet shop and to find a wife. Before I left Missouri, I had to see this place. It was the last location I knew Dixie had been except for the cabin she mentioned. I do not know where that is. The envelope only said Frankfurt, Minnesota, and a post office box number."

Jacob glanced at me. "What I told you about *Rumschpringes* was true. I have left home to decide if I want to take my Amish vows. But in my heart if I'd found Dixie at Parker Greenhouse, I'd have gone anywhere with her."

"Did you have reason to think she would be here?"

"No, but I hoped."

"Have you told anyone here about Dixie?"

"No. No one."

"What about Marnie?"

"I didn't talk about Dixie by name. Marnie asked if I'd been in love. I told her I used to know a woman who'd worked here a couple years ago. She'd gone out of my life but not out of my heart. Marnie understood. She said Eugene wanted her to be his special girl, but she wasn't interested. She said she'd never been in love, but Eugene wasn't her idea of the perfect man."

"Did Marnie question you about Dixie?"

"She asked if I'd seen or talked with her since she'd left here. I said I'd gotten a letter from her when she was transferred up north."

My heart skipped a beat. This had to be the clue that had made Marnie ask to see the personnel files. "What did Marnie say when you mentioned that?"

"I don't think she said anything. We dropped the subject."

"Did you know Marnie came to work here because she was looking for another woman who'd been transferred up north?"

"No. Not till I heard you say so at the greenhouses a while ago."

Switching back to the contents of the letter, I asked, "What did Dixie mean when she said she was 'giving away the last link I have to you'?"

His brow wrinkled. "I've thought about that many times, but I don't know what she was talking about."

"Did you give her a necklace, a trinket, some gift?"

"Nothing."

Deputy Swanson's radio squawked. I glanced over and saw he'd sidled closer. He had a pen in hand and his notebook open. It was obvious he'd been listening and taking notes. At first I was irritated, but then I relaxed. At least I wouldn't have to update Sid on this new information.

The deputy gave me a sly grin, then turned to speak into his walkie-talkie. His body stiffened. He listened intently. All I could hear was Swanson's crisp reply. "Yes, sir. Yes, sir. She's right here. Got it." He crossed to us and said, "Let's go."

"What's wrong?" I asked as we were herded over the Moon Bridge and down the path to the lodge driveway.

The deputy's voice was disapproving. "I

was told by the sheriff that if you asked I was to tell what we know so far."

"Well?" I said. "I'm asking."

Swanson heaved a sigh. "A woman was attacked in Lakeview Estates with a pipe wrench. She sustained massive head injuries. Her husband found her body in the foyer of their home. She died on the way to the hospital without regaining consciousness."

I stopped on the path and whispered, "Shannon Plummer Taylor?"

Swanson's eyes widened. "Yes, ma'am. Looks like the sheriff was right."

Shannon dead? I pictured her as I'd last seen her, eyes filled with fear, her beautiful face distorted with anger. I swallowed the lump in my throat. Absently, I asked, "What do you mean, it looks like the sheriff was right?"

"He said I wouldn't have to supply the name of the victim. You'd know."

Yeah, I knew plenty. I knew that just a short time ago I'd stood among the suspects and said that Shannon was edgy when I'd mentioned Parker Greenhouse. I might as well have said, "Killer, go get her before she spills everything she knows."

My frustration and anger grew as we strode along the path. By the time we got to the entrance into the gardens I was seething. "We have to make sure everyone is on the premises," I said sharply. "If someone is missing they'd better have a damned fine alibi."

The deputy's lips twitched. "Yes, ma'am! Except that's already being handled. Here comes Deputy Carter with that information."

The man was young and cocky, sauntering along like he had all day. He motioned to his fellow officer to step away from us so they could have a private chat. I wasn't having any of that. I was overstepping boundaries right and left, but the fact that Shannon had been murdered drove protocol out of my head.

"Are they all here?" I demanded.

Carter looked at me as if I'd sprouted horns and a forked tail, which wasn't far from wrong. I was feeling as mean as the devil. When Carter didn't answer, I turned an evil glare on him. "Did you *personally* see Eugene, Jess, Irma, Donovan, Harley and — uh — Natalie here on these grounds or at the greenhouse?"

The younger officer looked to the older one for guidance. Swanson shrugged. "The sheriff says to tell Mrs. Solomon whatever she wants to know."

Uncertain, Carter, said, "All are accounted for except for Harley. He's gone to the bus station to pick up some freight."

In a no-nonsense tone, I asked, "How long has he been gone?"

Deputy Carter shuffled his feet. It was obvious he didn't like answering a civilian's questions. Reluctantly, he said, "About thirty minutes."

I made some fast calculations. "If he's been gone thirty minutes, he should be arriving shortly, unless he made a detour to Lakeview Estates. Is there any way you can check to see if he's at the bus station?"

Carter rolled his eyes and didn't answer. Swanson's lips twitched with suppressed amusement. "It's being done, Mrs. Solomon. An officer has already been dispatched to that location. I think *we* have things under control."

Instead of taking offense at his smug tone, I only felt relief. Let these officers think what they wanted. I didn't care as long as the murderer was caught before he killed — "Dixie!" I said in a strangled tone. "If the killer is tying up loose ends, he may go after her, too."

"Who is Dixie?" asked Carter.

Jacob grabbed my arm. "Do you think she is in danger?"

I patted his hand. "I don't know." To

Carter, I said, "There isn't time to explain. Get Sid on that radio. I have to talk to him." Both men stared at me but neither moved. I lowered a fierce glare on Swanson. "My involvement in this case is unique, but there it is. Why question it? I want to talk to Sid."

Swanson put the walkie-talkie to his lips. I didn't hear what he said, but after a moment, he handed me the radio. Unaccustomed to using the apparatus, I shouted, "This is Bretta, Sid. I'm worried about Dixie Ragsford's safety. She's at Coventry Acres, remember?"

"You don't have to scream," said Sid. "We stopped using tin cans and string last week. I can hear you just fine."

I lowered my voice, but anxiety kept my tone high-pitched. "I think Dixie needs protection. Can you send someone out there? Someone who knows the situation and can be on his toes?"

Sid's tone was as dry as lint. "Will I do?"

Chapter Sixteen

Jacob begged the deputies to take him to Coventry Acres so he could be with Dixie. When his request was denied, he didn't argue, but walked away. Sid pulled Swanson off guard duty and sent him to the crime scene at Lakeview Estates. Deputy Carter was miffed at having to stick around when the action was elsewhere.

I hung around the loading dock waiting for DeeDee to get off work. I felt as if a shadow had crept across my life, eclipsing the sunlight. Shannon was dead. Jacob's spirits were crushed, while Mrs. Cooper kept a vigilant watch by her front window in hopes that her daughter would return. I was pretty sure that wasn't going to happen.

I glanced at my watch. It was almost twenty minutes before DeeDee would be leaving. I couldn't stand still. I walked past the loading dock, down the length of the greenhouses and across the employees' parking lot. The clank of metal on metal drew me down steps to a concrete pad. Jess had the door open to the pump house and was hammering on a motor.

"Damned piece of junk," he said.

"Trouble?" I asked.

He looked over his shoulder. "I told Dan two weeks ago we needed to replace pump number five, but he said to hold out until it wouldn't pull water. Well, that's happened." He glanced at his watch. "It's too late today to go into town and buy another. I have plants wilting in F, G, and H greenhouses. I'll have to hook up to another pump, which will take time and put added strain on that motor."

I walked around the wooden structure and gazed at the landscape. It had been years since limestone had been quarried from this land, but the excavation had left its mark. The mined pit had filled with water and dominated the immediate view. It covered more than an acre and was crystal clear, reflecting the sky's azure blue color. Deep ruts bore testimony that heavily laden trucks had once carried cargo from the quarry's rim. A piece of an old conveyor lay abandoned, choked in weeds.

When I lifted my gaze beyond the lake, a curtain of vegetation shielded the remaining property. Sumac, buck brush, wild elderberry, and blackberry briars grew in a snarl beneath the canopy of trees. The thicket was a natural border, barring humans from trespassing.

Jess had come out of the pump house to stand next to me. I nodded to the view. "When I'm on top of the bluff with its manicured lawns and cultivated gardens, I forget how wild the rest of the property is."

With the toe of his work shoe, Jess nudged a tendril of Virginia creeper that had eased its way onto the concrete pad. "We might forget, but Mother Nature hasn't. She's always looking for ways to reclaim her domain. We have to keep a constant vigil if we want to maintain control."

He picked up his tools and sighed. "Some days it don't seem worth the trouble. We're standing on a thousand acres of brush, weeds, and trees. When the Osage River overflows its banks during the rainy season, the valleys flood, leaving behind trash and silt."

Jess turned away and headed up the steps. I followed, listening to him talk. "About eight years ago, some man came around selling aerial photographs that he'd taken of this place. Dan bought one and hung it in his study. The picture shows five more quarries filled with water. A couple old shacks his great-grandfather used when he was hunting. But none of it is easy to get to unless you hanker for bugs and briars."

Jess stopped on the parking lot to gaze around him. "With its family history every inch should be well tended. If it belonged to me, I'd hire a bulldozer so I could make the whole damned place accessible, not just this corner."

Embarrassed, he glanced at me. "Don't think I'm being critical of Dan. He's a good man. He built this profitable business on nothing but a piece of land and the desire to succeed. I admire that." He ran a hand over his sweaty face. "I'd better get busy. I've got plants wilting." He walked away.

I looked off into the distance but saw nothing except trees and more trees. What lay beyond them? Jess had said five water pits and a couple of hunting shacks. My eyes narrowed thoughtfully. But Dixie, Shannon, and Paige had gone "up north."

A car's engine roared to life on the employees' parking lot. The workers were leaving. I arrived at the loading dock just as DeeDee came out the door. She was listening to the young woman who'd been sitting next to her in the break room. The woman didn't look sick now. Her expression was animated. Her eyes sparkled as she waved her hands, illustrating some point she was trying to make.

DeeDee nodded and smiled until she caught sight of me. I watched her sneak a quick peek at her car in the parking lot. She took a couple of steps in that direction before I called, "Miss, I was wondering if I could have that recipe for brownies? They were fabulous."

DeeDee stopped and summoned up a tight smile. Her companion said, "I'll see you tomorrow." She walked to the parking lot, digging in her handbag. She pulled out a couple of crackers and popped one into her mouth. She was a slender woman but had the makings of a paunch.

"Your new friend seems to have gotten over her sick spell," I said.

"Alicia h-has an u-ulcer. S-She has to w-watch what s-she e-eats."

I wanted to say she *watched* the food as it disappeared down her gullet, but I refrained. Alicia's stomach woes were the least of my worries. Aware of people moving around us, I said softly, "We need to talk, but this isn't the place. I'll call you later. You *will* be home?"

DeeDee's eyes widened as she looked

past me. "N-Natalie!" she said under her breath. "I-I have to go or s-she'll r-recognize m-me."

"That doesn't matter. Your undercover work is over." I took a step toward DeeDee. I was going to tell her there had been another murder, that it was too dangerous for her to keep up this charade, but she scampered to her car.

Thoroughly exasperated, I turned and saw Natalie gazing after DeeDee. Catching my eye, Natalie said, "That looked like the young woman —"

Conscious of the other workers leaving, I hastily said, "Yes, that's the woman who brought the fabulous brownies. I asked for the recipe and she said she'd bring it to work tomorrow." If I had my way, DeeDee wouldn't show up for work. But for safety's sake, I didn't want her associated with me.

Using a diverting tactic, I said, "So, what's on for tonight? Have you scorched another meal for our supper? Or are we having bologna sandwiches again?"

Pride in her cooking skills brought Natalie's chin up. "As it so happens," she said. "I've fixed us a fine meal, and it's even low-cal."

"Great," I said, trying for some enthusiasm. It didn't happen. I wanted to stuff my face with something gooey concocted from cheese or chocolate or whipped cream. If nuts or caramel or a flaky crust were included on the menu then so much the better.

Natalie frowned. "I thought you'd be happy with low-cal. Aren't you dieting?"

"I guess, but I was hoping to eat at least one of your famous dishes while I was here. With Dan coming home tomorrow, I'll be leaving."

Natalie's face lit up. "Tomorrow. I can hardly wait." Her shoulders slumped. "Which means his orchids had better be in excellent condition. I'm on my way over to his greenhouse to check on them. You want to come with me before we go up to the house?"

"Yeah. Sure," I muttered, falling into step next to her. I wasn't in the mood for the orchid house. I was hungry.

"What's wrong?" said Natalie giving me a sidelong glance. "You surely can't be upset over a low-cal meal. I saw you talking with those deputies and one of them left. Has there been a new development in Marnie's death?"

"Yes, but I can't talk about it. Sid asked me not to say anything."

"You talked to Sid?" When I nodded,

Natalie said, "No wonder you look out of sorts. Will it put a smile on your face if I tell you we're having blueberry cheesecake for dessert?"

I grimaced. "I guess a single ray of sunshine is better than none."

"Don't be a gloomy Gus, Bretta. Let's celebrate. Dan is coming home."

"Yeah. Celebrate."

Natalie's voice was sharp. "I'm upset about Marnie's death, too, but for tonight, can't we leave the investigation in the authorities' expert hands?"

I heaved a sigh. "All right," I said but I didn't sound happy about it.

"You have a birthday coming up in a few days, right?"

I gave Natalie a hard stare. I wasn't the only one capable of diverting attention. I said, "You know my birthday is tomorrow."

"What's on your wish list?"

"I can't have what I want."

Natalie stopped at the door of the orchid house and cocked an eyebrow at me. "And what would that be?"

"Bailey. He's gone, and he hasn't called me once."

"Maybe he's waiting until tomorrow so he can give you his best wishes."

"He may not know it's my birthday."

Natalie held open the door to the lab. As I walked past her, she said, "He's a government agent. He knows."

Following her lead, I picked up a paper gown and shoved my arms into the sleeves. "Ex-agent, and he may very well exit my life."

She shook her head at my moroseness but didn't comment until we'd finished covering our clothes and shoes. "We'll discuss Bailey later," she said. "Right now, I have to check the temperature and humidity in the nursery. While I'm here, Dan wants me to examine the seedpods on the *Oncidium lanceanum*."

I chuckled. "That sounds like a disease. What are you looking for?"

"Dan says that by now the seedpods should be expanding if his hand pollination was a success."

"Where are these plants? I'd like to see them."

She waved toward a bench on the right. "They're the ones in the middle."

Natalie hurried across the concrete floor to the back of the greenhouse. I stepped over to the bench of orchids. Everything was precisely labeled and it was easy to spot the specimen Dan was interested in.

The *O. lanceanum* was a striking plant.

The leaves were twenty inches long and four inches wide. They were stiff and erect and mottled with brown. The foot-tall flower stem had produced some small yellow flowers spotted with reddish brown and sporting a purplish rose lip. I leaned close and inspected the plants. I didn't have a clue as to what I was looking for on this orchid.

"Are they swollen?" asked Natalie, coming up behind me.

I shrugged. "I could whip these few blossoms into a gorgeous bouquet, but I wouldn't know an orchid seed pod if it reached out and nipped me on the nose."

Natalie pulled the plant closer. "See? This is the column." With gentle fingers she touched what I'd have called the stem. "All the reproductive parts of the flower are located here," she said. "The column contains the stigma, which receives the pollen, and the anther cap, which holds it." Her fingers moved down the column. "This is the ovary."

"It's called an ovary?"

"Yes. It's just below the flower and resembles a flower stalk. It contains the ovules, which contains the embryo sac. If Dan's hand pollination has worked, the ovary will be plump with seeds."

I leaned my head close to hers so I could have a look. "Was he successful?"

"I'm not an expert, but it looks like it's expanding."

"How did he pollinate it?"

"He uses an artist's brush and tranfers the pollen — powdered male-sex cells — from the anther of the stamen of the flower to the upper tip of the pistil. If fertilization is completed, the ovary will develop seeds." She took a step back from the plant and sighed. "When I talk to him later, I'll tell him the seeds are forming."

Without thinking, I said, "He should be one proud papa."

Natalie's smile was sad. "That's exactly how he'll feel." She waved her hand to our surroundings. "Remember, I told you that I was jealous of this place. I said it was because Dan spends so much time here. Actually, I'm jealous of these plants because they have the capacity to reproduce. Dan and I have a wonderful marriage, but to create a child together is a lifelong link we'll never have."

"At least you have each other," I said quietly.

"I know." Natalie touched my hand. "When Carl died, I couldn't begin to comprehend your pain. Don't you ever wish you'd had a child with him?"

My heart lurched painfully in my chest. I didn't want to have this conversation, but Natalie expected a reply. "Of course," I said, "but the time never seemed right. The years just slipped away." Tears filled my eyes, and I whispered, "I didn't know our life would be disrupted in the worst possible way."

Natalie shook my arm. "But it isn't too late, Bretta. You could still have a baby."

My tears were forgotten. "Are you nuts? I'm too old, too cranky, and too alone."

Natalie sighed. "I suppose you're right." She swiveled around on her toes. "Everywhere I look I see phases of reproduction." She turned and pointed across the greenhouse. "Dan calls that bench of plants his virgins in waiting. They haven't been pollinated." She pointed again. "That bench he's labeled menopausal because they're past their prime." She turned back to the bench next to us. "This one is the maternity ward." She jerked her head. "Back there is the nursery."

I knew what Natalie was getting at. Unable to conceive, she found it painful and frustrating to be in here among plants that were capable of achieving what she could not. I also knew that if I prolonged this conversation, we'd both become depressed. I pretended to miss her point. "They're just plants," I said. Immediately, I saw I'd made a wrong decision to treat this conversation lightly.

A spasm of irritation crossed Natalie's face. "You don't understand. Let's get out of here," she said as she led the way to the door. She jerked the paper covering from her clothes. "I need comfort food. I wish now I'd made beef stroganoff with lots of sour cream and Parmesan cheese." She removed the footies from her sneakers and added, "But I've got that cheesecake. I think I'll start with dessert and forget the chef salad. It's too damned healthy."

I took a final look around the greenhouse. An uneasy feeling had settled in the pit of my stomach. I couldn't put my finger on the reason, but I didn't think it had anything to do with Natalie's exasperation with me.

Annoyed with myself, I followed Natalie up the driveway. How in heaven's name did I think I could possibly comprehend a killer's motives, when I couldn't interpret my own body's signal that something wasn't right?

Was it the plants? Did Dan's orchids play a part in Marnie's death?

A glimmer of a concept flickered in my mind. Natalie had said a baby was a lifelong link. *I'm giving away the last link I have to you,* Dixie had said to Jacob. Unbidden Carl's face flashed into my mind. His expression was sad. His lips turned down. Was he disappointed? Why? Did he know about —

I recoiled from the image and my thoughts. Stepping up my pace, I caught up to Natalie and said the first thing that popped into my mind. "I'm thinking about having a swimming pool put in my garden."

She turned her head and stared at me. "I'm thinking cheesecake."

Chapter Seventeen

Natalie was as good as her word. She lit into the blueberry cheesecake, cutting a huge wedge for herself. She was in a mood. I tried to introduce a variety of topics to discuss, but nothing seemed to improve her disposition.

After picking and poking at a second helping of cheesecake, Natalie pushed the saucer aside and dished up a bowl of chef's salad. In a whiny tone, she said, "I detest black olives. Why did I put them in here?" She glared across the table at me. "It's because you like them. Now I'm going to have to pick them out."

I made a face. "Jeez, Natalie. If you want me to leave just say so. It's a good thing Dan is coming home tomorrow. Another day together under the same roof and you and I won't be speaking."

"That isn't true," she snapped. "I just don't like black olives. I was trying to make something that would please you." She closed her eyes and took a deep breath. When she opened her eyes, her voice was calmer. "I'm being ridiculous. Dan's laboratory does that to me. It brings out feelings I can't always handle. I wish you could —"

The phone rang. "Maybe that's Dan," said Natalie. She jumped up and scurried out of the room. There was a phone on the wall by the refrigerator, but apparently, Natalie wanted privacy. A few minutes later, she stepped to the door. She seemed flustered. "I'm going to be awhile. Why don't you go ahead and finish eating?"

"Is it Dan?"

She frowned. "Uh . . . no, it isn't Dan." She turned and walked back to the study.

"That's odd," I said under my breath. But then Natalie had been acting strangely since we'd visited Dan's orchid house. She'd said that his greenhouse brought out feelings she couldn't always handle.

I hoped when Natalie got off the phone, she'd be in a better mood. I had finished reading Paige's letters. I wanted to make a trip into River City to give them back to Mrs. Cooper, if she didn't mind the company. While I was there I thought I might ask her a few more questions.

While Natalie was in the study, I put the food in the refrigerator, loaded the dishwasher, and spiffed up the kitchen. When I finished, Natalie was still on the phone.

When . . . if . . . she ever got off the line, I wanted to call Mrs. Cooper. I glanced at the clock. Natalie had been on the phone for over thirty minutes. I slammed a cabinet door. Why didn't she hang up? Who was she talking to? And why was it necessary to gab this long?

I stared at the cabinet door I'd slammed. What was wrong with me? Was it anxiety? About what? I could pass this time in a productive manner. I tried to sort out the facts of the case but my brain refused to focus on Dixie, Shannon, Paige, or Marnie. Maybe I should call Sid and see if he'd learned anything about Shannon's murder. Why couldn't I concentrate? Why was I restless?

I was pacing the floor when Natalie breezed into the kitchen. "What a wonderful, wonderful day." She whirled around the room. "I think I'll make cinnamon rolls to celebrate."

"What are you celebrating?"

She giggled. "Life, and my husband's homecoming." She assembled the ingredients she would need for the cinnamon rolls. She opened the upper cabinet doors and gazed at a top shelf. "Would you hand me that crock, Bretta? A double batch is called for, and I need that big bowl."

Several inches taller, I rose up on my tiptoes and hauled the container down. I set it on the counter and turned to watch Natalie.

She floated around the kitchen as if on winged feet. "I'll need raisins, pecans, and lots of brown sugar." She glanced at me. "Do you want to help me —"

I shook my head emphatically. "Nope. I'm calling home to see if everything's all right."

She nodded and studied the pantry shelves. "Where are those raisins? I know I had —"

I hurried from the kitchen. I was never in the mood to cook, least of all tonight. I went into Dan's study and sat down behind his desk. I reached for the phone, but it rang before I could pick it up.

"I've got it," I shouted to Natalie.

She yelled back, "Unless that's Dan, I'm too busy to talk. Take a message, and I'll call back later."

"Okay," I bellowed. A house this size gave the old vocal cords a workout. I picked up the receiver. "Hello," I said. "This is Bretta."

"Hi, Bretta," said Donovan. "Dinner over?"

"Yes, and the dirty dishes are washing."

"I tried to call earlier, but the line was busy."

"Natalie was talking to someone. She won't say who it was but apparently it was good news."

"Maybe it was Dan."

"No. It wasn't him. I don't know what's going on, but her mood is so much better than it was before the call, I'm leaving it at that."

"Dan's still coming home tomorrow?"

"Yes. Natalie's in the process of making cinnamon rolls for his homecoming."

Donovan chuckled. "That's a good sign. Do you think she'd mind if Emily and I came out?"

"I'm sure she wouldn't. You want me to ask her?"

Donovan paused. "No. I think we'll drive on out."

"Is there a problem?"

"No. Actually, I need to catch up on some paperwork, and I thought I'd get more done if Emily was visiting with Natalie instead of waiting impatiently for me at home."

"Come ahead. There's blueberry cheesecake left from dinner."

"That's incentive enough right there," he

said. "I'll see you shortly."

Since I didn't plan on being here when Donovan arrived, I decided now might be my only opportunity to make an inquiry or two. Taking a deep breath, I said, "Before you hang up, can I ask you something?"

"Of course."

"I know you heard everything that Natalie said in the greenhouses this afternoon, but I want to clear up a couple of questions." Quickly, I outlined what I'd found in the personnel files and gave him a more in-depth account of my information on Dixie. I also told him about meeting Mrs. Cooper, Paige's mother.

As I talked, I spun my chair around and spotted a Rand McNally road atlas on the bookcase. I pulled it out and flipped the pages to the back section where it listed United States counties, cities, and towns.

In my ear Donovan chuckled. "You've been busy. So now that I have the background, I assume you're ready to pick my brain."

"What I want to know is, why do these young women go to work at Parker Greenhouse for two weeks and then tell their family they've been 'transferred' up north?"

"I don't know, Bretta. We don't have a

facility anywhere but here."

"But why would they each tell the same story?"

Donovan heaved a sigh. "Can't this wait until I get out there?"

"I suppose, but if you have an opinion, I'd like to hear it now."

"I don't. In fact, I'm sorry to say I don't remember these young women. The names are familiar, but I can't put a face to any of them. That makes it impossible to guess why they'd do or say anything."

"But doesn't it seem odd that they'd come here and work two weeks then leave?"

"Not at all. We have a large turnover of employees. Greenhouse work is hot and dirty. We rarely take time to smell the flowers."

While Donovan elaborated on the preconceived notion people had about working at a greenhouse, I ran my finger down the listing of cities and towns for a place called Frankfurt, Minnesota. I found it — population 3,000. I searched for the thin blue line that would denote the river Dixie had mentioned in her letter to Jacob.

Using my fingernail I measured off the mileage scale and saw the nearest river was eighty miles away from Frankfurt. But

Dixie had written Jacob that she was in a cabin by the river. If she was in a cabin in Frankfurt, Minnesota, where was the river?

At the end of Donovan's spiel, he said, "I'm concerned with this 'transferred up north' story. Seems like Jess mentioned something about being questioned by a deputy a few months ago, but I can't remember what it was about. If need be we can call him."

I mumbled something, said good-bye, and hung up.

Before the phone could ring again, I picked it up and quickly touched my home phone numbers. It rang three times before DeeDee answered.

"Hi," I said. "I guess you know why I've called."

"You s-said you w-would."

"You can't come to work out here tomorrow, DeeDee. It's too dangerous."

"It doesn't seem r-right that t-two of us n-not s-show up for work."

I didn't understand. "Two of you?"

"Alicia j-just called. She's b-been transferred up n-north."

I stiffened. "How long has she worked at the greenhouse?"

"Only a week. She k-knew this advance w-was c-coming, but she t-thought it wouldn't be for a-another week."

"Did she say who told her she was being transferred?"

"No. We d-didn't talk long. S-she had to p-pack, but s-she wanted to t-tell m-me good-bye."

My heart leaped with excitement. "When is she leaving?"

"S-she's being p-picked up at n-nine o'clock. Why a-all the q-questions?"

I glanced at my watch. It was almost eight-thirty. "DeeDee, what's Alicia's address?"

"I don't know."

Impatiently, I demanded, "What's her phone number?"

Paper rustled, and DeeDee said, "555-2833. Bretta, you're s-scaring me. What's g-going on?"

"I gotta go," I said and hit the disconnect button. When I got a dial tone, I punched in the numbers DeeDee had given me. It rang several times before a man answered. I asked for Alicia.

Without covering the receiver, he roared, "Alicia! Get your butt down here. Someone wants to talk to you. I ain't your damned answering service, girl. My beer's getting hot, and I've missed the first part of the news."

I cringed at the man's malicious tone. A minute passed, and then two before I heard a breathless "Hello" in my ear.

"Alicia? This is Bretta Solomon. I met you today at the greenhouse."

"Yes, ma'am. I can't talk now, I'm —"

I forced myself to speak calmly. "Alicia, I've heard you're leaving. Please, don't go until I've talked to you."

"Don't go?" she said in surprise. "But why?"

"When your ride comes, stall for time until I get there. What's your address?"

"I can't —"

Almost sure she would respond to a blustery command, I said, "Alicia, what is your address?"

I heard her gulp. "8112 East Florence."

I softened my tone. "Please stay there until I arrive, honey. This is very important."

I hung up the phone and started out of Dan's study. As I reached for the light switch, I saw the aerial photo of the Parker estate hanging by the door. A thin line like a vein traced a path across the corner of the picture. Leaning close I saw that it was the Osage River. The photo was only twelve by fourteen and sturdily framed in oak. On impulse, I reached up and took it down. Tucking it under my arm, I raced down the hall.

Grabbing my purse off the sofa, I called, "Natalie, I have to leave. Donovan and Emily are on their way out here to keep you company. I'll be back later." I didn't wait to hear her response.

I hopped in my SUV and carefully laid the picture on the seat next to the clipboard with my copies of the job applications. As I drove down the lane, there wasn't any sign of the deputy, but a patrol car was parked beside the entrance into the garden. I probably should have stopped and told him where I was going, but by the time I explained, Alicia would be gone.

I kept my window down. The rush of night air made me feel as if I was making better time. I turned on the radio and let the music drift around me. I should have asked Alicia point-blank who had called her. Had I handled this wrong? Maybe, but it was possible that I could discover who was picking Alicia up — if I got there in time.

I pressed on the gas and watched the needle climb. Glancing at the picture, I wished I could study it while I drove. This whole Frankfurt, Minnesota, business didn't make sense. Just because Frankfurt,

Minnesota, had been the return address on the letters written by Paige and Dixie, that didn't prove either woman had been in that town. Last December, Frankfurt had snow and a bitter wind chill, but Paige had called the winter mild. I was sure Paige hadn't been where she said, but why lie?

Mail could have been collected from the women and sent to someone in Frankfurt to mail, just as the mail in the post-office box could have been collected and sent to someone in River City. It made sense, especially when I factored in the consideration that there wasn't a river near Frankfurt, but there was a river very close to the greenhouse.

Suddenly I didn't want to keep Alicia from leaving, but it was crucial that I be at the East Florence address before she left. If I could follow the vehicle she got into —

I entered the River City outskirts and kept up my speed. The quickest way to East Florence was to travel down Bodine, hang a left on Brunswick, and stay on that main thoroughfare until I came to Pittman Road. I would have more four-way stops, but I could roll through them. I slowed my speed. I didn't want a cop to stop me. Time was running out. It was only a few minutes until nine.

It seemed to take forever, but finally I turned onto East Florence Street. I was in the six thousands. The address I wanted was two more blocks east. I traveled another block and peered ahead. A pair of brake lights flared red. I saw them flicker, once, twice, and a third time. The driver was impatiently pumping the pedal. I slowed to a crawl, pulled over, and parked. I snapped off my headlights to make it look as if I'd just gotten home. Down the street, I saw Alicia come out of a house. She scanned the block. I saw her hesitate, then walk slowly toward the van.

I'd had my eyes on her, but now I gave the vehicle a quick look. With the help of a street lamp I read the words in block print across the back doors — Parker Greenhouse. My lips dipped down in a frown. The passenger door swung open. The interior lights came on, but the seats had tall backs, and I couldn't get a glimpse of the driver.

With another look around, Alicia tossed in her suitcase. I could tell she was talking to whoever was inside. I saw her nod and step up into the van. The door swung shut. A rush of adrenaline shot through my body.

I didn't have a clue how to tail a suspect.

I was determined, though, and hoped that would offset my shortcomings. I waited until the van was about a block down the street before I pulled out of my parking spot. I didn't flip on my headlights but kept up a steady pace. When the van turned left and was out of sight, I put on my lights.

I made the turn and caught my breath. Where was the van? Good Lord, had I lost it already? The air in my lungs whooshed out in a mighty sigh of relief. No. There it was, just up ahead. I dropped back about half a block. We were still in the residential section of town, and the van was easy to keep in sight.

I glanced out my window long enough to get my bearings. A neighborhood grocery store sat on the corner. Next to it was a tire company, followed by a tavern with a neon sign advertising Bud Lite on tap. I grinned when I saw the insurance office. That's where I paid my premiums. I was on State Street, which intersected with Independence Avenue. If the van hung a right, I had a good idea which route we'd be taking.

Up ahead, the van's right blinker winked at me. I chuckled. "Thanks for the tip," I said quietly. We were headed out of town, going south, not north. It looked like our destination was the grand and glorious Ozarks. My heart beat a fast pace. The very direction from which I'd just come.

If I was correct, at the next intersection the van would turn left. That street would lead to the on-ramp that circled River City. Once on this route, we'd have smooth sailing until we reached the interstate. That's when I'd have to be alert. Traffic would be heavier, more cars to interfere with my keeping the van in sight. But I had a few minutes to collect myself before I had to deal with that problem — if the van turned left.

"Hot damn," I said, as the vehicle ahead of me made the turn.

I'd been hunched over the steering wheel, every muscle charged for action. Now I relaxed, but kept my gaze on that van. From behind me a truck's headlights glared in my rearview mirror and were distracting. I quickly adjusted the mirror and then glanced back to the road. From a side street, a car pulled out in front of me. I slammed on the brakes and wrenched the steering wheel hard to the right. I missed the car, but gave it a blast with my horn.

My heart was pounding. "Damned fool," I said under my breath. I leaned forward, peering through the windshield. The Parker van was still ahead of me. Its speed was steady, not too fast and not too slow.

I was about half a block behind it. I closed the gap. Soon we'd be at the interstate. Out my open window I could hear the steady *zip, zip, zip* of heavy traffic. I was so confident that the van would take the on-ramp, I flipped on my blinker to throw off any suspicion that he was being followed. For good measure, I moved into the turn lane.

Being overly confident is great if you're right. It's a real downer if you're proved wrong. The van zoomed past the on-ramp, under the overpass, and kept going. By the time I realized I'd made a mistake, it was too late to get out of the turn lane.

A blue truck whizzed by. I gave its driver an envious glance then did a double take. My father raised his hand. Forming an O with his thumb and index finger, he told me he had events under control.

I was struck speechless, if you discounted my string of profanity. I gritted my teeth in frustration. Why couldn't my father go meekly into retirement? Why did he have to meddle?

Like father like daughter, was my immediate thought.

I checked my rearview mirror. Cars were lined up behind me. Cars were in front of me. The light was red, and the van was disappearing with my aged father in hot pursuit. There was no time to wait for the light to change to green.

I stuck my head out the window to see how much room I had to maneuver the SUV. Not much. The guy behind me honked when I put the gearshift into reverse. I backed up an inch at a time. He honked again.

"Leave me alone," I muttered. "I've got enough problems." I put the gearshift into drive and pulled forward. I just might make it. I nudged the gas pedal and cranked the front tires until the power-steering motor squealed. I edged out of the lane with barely an inch to spare between my bumper and the car in front of me. I took off, leaving a stripe of black rubber on the pavement.

For the next mile I scanned the road, but I saw nothing. I topped a hill and glimpsed tiny pinpricks of red in the distance. Were they the taillights of my father's truck or the van? Afraid to assume anything but with no other recourse, I sped toward them, closing the breach.

A few miles later, I identified the van's

boxy shape puttering along at a mere thirty miles an hour. I didn't question why it was going slow, but I did question the whereabouts of my father. I hadn't passed another vehicle by the side of the road. Where was he?

Playing the part of an impatient driver, I swung into the passing lane, then faked uncertainty and pulled back behind the van. Without warning the blacktop ended. The chassis of the SUV *whooped* as it dropped off the smooth road onto gravel. My tires picked up loose rocks and flung them against the undercarriage. The racket was deafening.

I put up my window and slowed down. The dust was thick and made driving as hazardous as navigating through fog. The van's taillights were blurry, but easy to follow. I was thinking about dropping back further, when those taillights glowed brighter. Abruptly, the van stopped in the middle of the road.

I slammed on the brakes, but I was too close, going too fast. My tires rolled uselessly on the gravel. I saw the crash coming, but could do nothing to prevent it. The nose of my SUV rammed the back of the van.

It wasn't a violent crash, but the sound

of metal being mangled is always frightening. My driver's airbag didn't inflate. My seat belt kept me firmly in place. I leaned back in my seat and stared over my crumpled hood at the van.

Dazed, I saw the backup lights come on. I didn't have time to prepare.

Bam! The van hit my crippled SUV with a resounding crash. My neck popped. Pain shot up my spine and exploded in my head. Through the steam that roiled from the SUV's crushed radiator, I watched the van speed away.

Chapter Eighteen

I turned off the SUV's useless engine and looked out my window at the lonely night. A cell phone would have come in handy, but I didn't own one. At the flower shop the telephone was a lifeline for my business. When I was away from work, I didn't want to be tied to an instrument that could disrupt my free time. Considering my present situation, I decided I might have to rethink that personal aversion.

Without quick access to help, my feet were my only salvation unless I wanted to sit here and brood, which wasn't a bad idea. My head was splitting and my neck ached.

I flipped on the hazard lights and thought about my predicament. It was obvious I'd been set up by the driver of the van. I wanted to believe I'd done a fair job of tailing up to the point when that car had pulled out in front of me. I'd reacted by honking the horn — an action that had drawn the van driver's attention. My red SUV must have stood out like a beacon under the streetlight. Once I'd been spotted, the driver of the van had led me away from traffic, disabled my vehicle, and made a clean getaway.

Had he known my father was also tailing him? Where was my father?

That thought prompted action. I opened my door and was ready to step out when headlights appeared down the road. Hoping it was my father but afraid it could be trouble on this remote country road, I got back into the SUV and locked the doors.

I peered through the dusty windshield and caught my breath. It was the van. Scared that he'd come back to finish me off, I scrambled over the console into the backseat. If he rammed the SUV, I'd have the engine and dashboard as a barrier. I crouched on the floor behind the driver's seat tensed for the collision. I heard nothing except an idling motor. I peeked through the window.

The van had pulled alongside me. The driver's window was down, interior lights on. Staring directly at me was the old woman I'd seen in the alley. The rubber mask was as grotesque as I'd remembered, but it didn't have that second-skin look I'd noticed the first time I'd seen it. Beady eyes bore into mine.

The hairs on my neck quivered. Goosebumps pricked my skin as she raised her white-gloved hand and twiddled her fingers at me. The empty tips flapped. Her fingers didn't quite fill the fabric. My mind registered the fact that there were two people involved in the murders — one with a slighter build than the other.

I shifted my position so I could see Alicia. Her complexion was washed out in the pale light, but she didn't seem frightened. She gave me a swift look then turned her head.

I screamed, "Get out, Alicia. Run! I'll help you."

Alicia jerked around to stare at me. Her lips parted in amazement. I turned back to the driver. The rubber mask concealed her expression, but her spine had stiffened. She clenched the gloved hand. I thought she was going to get out of the van, but headlights appeared on the road behind her. She glanced up at her rearview mirror and hastily stepped on the accelerator. The van roared off, leaving me in a dusty fog.

A few seconds later, my father pulled up. Seeing him at the wheel was both a relief and an irritation. I was glad he was okay, but it irked me that my beloved vehicle had been rendered immobile while his was without a scratch.

I climbed from the backseat and plopped behind the steering wheel. I lowered my window, and Dad asked, "Are you okay?"

"I'm not hurt. Just shook up."

"Don't fret about your SUV. I've phoned for a tow truck and instructed them to haul your vehicle to the service garage we normally use."

I knew the answer, but I still had to ask. "Where'd you find a phone?"

Proudly, my father held up a cell phone. "I just got it this afternoon. Something told me I might need it. Hop in. No sense waiting around here." He gazed regretfully up the road. "The van's gone. If you'd called and told me what you had in mind, we could have double-teamed him. Tailing works better that way. One person is too vulnerable."

I picked up my purse, the framed photo, and the clipboard with my copies of the job application forms. Biting my lip to keep from spouting off, I got out and went around and climbed into my father's truck. Once we were under way, I said, "How long were you following me?"

"Since you left Alicia's house."

I frowned. "DeeDee didn't have Alicia's

address. How did you know where she lived?"

"I had the phone number. I looked it up in the cross-reference directory I picked up last week at the River City Chamber of Commerce. The woman there was most helpful. She told me how easy it is to find anyone in town. All I needed was a starting point. I had to have either a name, or a phone number, or an address. You want me to pick you up a copy?"

Miffed that he would assume I didn't know about such a directory, I said, "I already have one, thank you."

My father was too hyped to notice my bad humor. He swung into an explanation of his adventure. "I didn't know what was going on when you called DeeDee, but she was worried. I figured I might be able to help you. As I said, I was already parked on Florence Street when you arrived. When you didn't get out, I assumed you had a plan. I laid low and saw you follow the van with your lights off. I kept pace, but you really threw me for a loop when you got into that turn lane." He glanced at me. "Was that a tactical maneuver to confuse the driver of the van?"

"Yeah. That's it," I muttered, slouching down in my seat.

"Worked damned good," said Dad. "I didn't know what the hell was going on, but since I was already behind the van, I decided to stay with it. I tailed him for about a mile before he slowed down. Seeing as how we were on a secondary road with few turnoffs, I decided to pass him. I went another couple of miles and parked in a lane. I figured when he went by, I could pull back in behind him, but he didn't appear. I waited and finally decided I'd better find out what had happened."

He took a hand off the steering wheel and patted my knee. "That's my story, daughter. Your turn."

"My turn?"

"Yeah, tell me what happened to your SUV. From what I could see in my headlights, you must have had one helluva showdown with that van." His voice took on that I'm-not-going-to-lecture-you-but-you-should-listen-to-me tone. "Of course, you shouldn't tangle with a vehicle bigger than your own or you'll come out the loser." He glanced at me. "But I guess that's a lesson you've learned — the hard way."

I didn't reply. I squeezed my eyes shut and leaned my head against the window. My brain felt as if it were wrapped in cotton batting. There must be some action I should take. I could call Sid, but what would I tell him? I could ask him to put out an APB — all points bulletin — for the van, but I'd need a damned fine reason. Alicia had made it clear she was in the front seat by her own free will, so a kidnapping charge would be useless. I'd been hit by the van and it had taken off. Perhaps I should file a hit-and-run charge?

"Are you sure you aren't hurt?" asked my father. "Maybe we ought to have a doctor check you over."

"No, that's not necessary. I just have a headache."

"It's the stress. Once you're home in your own bed, you'll feel better."

I opened my eyes. "I need to go to the lodge. Natalie is there alone."

"Aren't deputies still patrolling the grounds?"

"I assume so. Donovan and Emily were visiting Natalie, but they've probably left by now."

"That was a Parker Greenhouse van. Do you know who was behind the wheel?"

"No, but I think it was a woman."

That admission was all my father needed. It opened the door for speculation, and he loved to theorize. His voice deepened. “I’ve been giving this case some serious thought, even though I’m not getting paid for my trouble.” He stopped, waiting for some encouragement from me.

I sighed.

Apparently, Dad was satisfied that I was interested. “Marnie seemed like an intelligent young woman,” he said. “When I spoke with her, I got the impression she was at Parker Greenhouse because she was looking for something. She mentioned she’d applied for the job at the request of another person. What got my attention was that it hadn’t been Marnie’s idea to work at Parker Greenhouse. Someone had put her up to it. If that was the case, then someone was manipulating Marnie. She didn’t seem upset, so I’m assuming this person was important to her, and whatever she learned working at Parker was beneficial for both.” He waited a second then asked, “Do you know who this person is?”

“Yeah,” I murmured, keeping my gaze on the flashing scenery outside my window. We were on the loop that circled River City. Thousands of lights cast their glow against the navy blue skyline. Neon signs from fast-food restaurants, from gas stations, and from convenience stores turned the locale into a kaleidoscope of color.

"Well? Are you sharing who it is?"

"In a minute." I picked up the clipboard. "Dad, does your truck have a map light?"

"Right here." He reached toward his sun visor and pressed a button. Bright light shone down on my lap. "What have you got there?" he asked, eyeing the papers.

"Give me a minute." I flipped Dixie and Shannon's sheets out of the way and studied Paige's application. I'd remembered right. Under the listing for "Former Employers," Paige had written that she'd worked for the Happy Hour Service Station and Food Mart, a convenience store located at the corner of Ohio and Blaine streets.

I turned off the light. "I need to get to the corner of Ohio and Blaine, Dad. Can you find it?"

"Let me think." My father leaned forward, peering out the windshield for a familiar landmark. "Yeah, but we'll have to backtrack."

"Let's do it."

My father made the necessary turns, which took us off the outer loop and back into River City. After several blocks, he asked, "What's on this corner?"

"A convenience store."

His tone was kind. "Still got a headache,

huh? I have some aspirins in the glove compartment, but I don't have any water." He pointed to a McDonald's that was just ahead. "I could turn in there and get you a drink to wash down a pill."

"No, thanks," I said. "I'll wait." My father's consideration of my needs never wavered. I couldn't count the number of times I'd cut him off while he was speaking or tuned him out. He wanted a detective agency, and I'd deliberately sabotaged the chance for him to have his first case.

"Here we are, daughter. Do you want me to go in for you? If your headache persists, I think we ought to go to the ER."

"I'm fine, Dad. I'll be right back." I climbed out of his truck and went in the front door. I grabbed a couple cans of diet soda from a cooler and went up to the checkout counter. The cashier was a robust woman with dyed black hair and ruby red lips. Her eyelashes were weighed down with thick, gunky mascara. It took a conscious effort on her part to pry her eyelids apart. While she struggled to see me, I glanced at the name — Juanita — stitched on her uniform pocket.

Juanita rang up my purchases and told me the amount. As I handed her my money, I asked, "Do you know Virgil? I understand he comes in here often." To myself I wondered if I'd remembered the name correctly. I'd only heard Mrs. Cooper mention it a couple of times.

Juanita's face contorted as she wrestled her eyelashes apart. "He used to come in, but his new address is the county jail. He got himself arrested."

"What's the charge?"

Juanita shrugged. "All I've heard is gossip, but it has something to do with drugs."

"He sold drugs?"

"Probably, but this has to do with making girls more receptive to his advances." She cocked an eyebrow at me. "If you get my drift."

I shuffled uneasily. Was she talking about a date-rape drug? I started to ask her, but figured all I'd get was more second-, third-, or fourth-hand information. I changed direction. "Do you remember Paige Cooper?"

Juanita nodded. "Yeah. She worked here for a while. Mousy but sweet."

"Did she date Virgil?"

Juanita's eyes opened wide, giving the impression that two hairy black spiders had crawled onto her face. "I hope to hell not. I warned him to stay away from her."

I didn't say anything more except thanks, and picked up my cans of soda and walked out of the store. As I approached the truck, I saw Dad talking into his cell phone. I took the time to lean against the truck and gather my thoughts.

Had Virgil raped Paige? I had a sick feeling that was true.

Why hadn't she reported it? That question had an answer when I remembered how the photographs portrayed her shy, bashful demeanor.

Paige had told her mother there was a problem, but she would handle it. If she'd been talking about the rape, how had Paige coped? Had she gone for counseling? Or had she simply run away?

I frowned and stared off into space. It was a fact that she'd left home. But had she run away from feelings of degradation due to the rape? Or had the rape created another problem altogether?

A knot formed in my throat, making it difficult to breathe. My heart wanted to shy away from the scenario my brain was piecing together.

Dixie and Jacob had been lovers.

Shannon had been wild and carefree.

Paige had been raped.

My shoulders sagged. I couldn't do this

without help. I turned to the one person I trusted. "Carl," I whispered. "Where are you?"

Since my husband's death, the sound of his voice has been in my head, especially when I'm unsettled about a case. "You always talk to me when I'm upset. I need you." Silence. I concentrated. "Please, Carl, talk to me." Nothing.

There's a place in my heart where I keep all my yesterdays — my memories of past pain and unforgotten deeds. I'd moved on. I'd made my decision years ago, but this case had stirred up former regrets to the point that I wasn't functioning in a competent manner.

I thought of all the people I'd questioned. All the miles I'd traveled. All the information I'd collected but wasn't able to pull together.

Carl was gone from me, but my father was here. What if I gave him everything I'd learned? Could he work out a solution that would leave my "yesterdays" undisturbed? It was damned tempting, but first I wanted to hear if he had any other theories.

I glanced in the truck and saw him watching me. I gave him a tiny smile and climbed in. "I was giving you some privacy," I said.

"That was DeeDee. She's the only one who has this number. She says Natalie called and is worried about you. You might want to call her." He held out the phone.

I waved it aside. "In a minute." I popped the tab on one of the cans and handed it to him. I opened the other can and took a drink. The cold, fizzy liquid felt good as it slid down my dry throat. I took another sip and put the can in the plastic cup holder on the console.

Rubbing the moisture from my hands, I lied, "I'm feeling better now." I waited while my father took a drink of his soda. After he'd put the can next to mine, I said in a fairly normal voice, "I interrupted you earlier when you were talking about the case. Why don't you continue while we drive to the lodge?"

At my direct request, my father's enthusiasm bubbled forth. "You'll have to bear with me cause I'm stretching my limited talents. But I think the note that was found near Marnie's body could be the key to this whole thing."

The note. Another point I'd neglected to consider. I massaged my temple. "You'll have to refresh my memory."

"I was eavesdropping in the foyer, but if I caught the sheriff's words correctly, they went something like this: *'Life is precious. There are choices. Meet me at the cornucopia sculpture tomorrow during the fireworks.'* "

He cleared his throat. "I think it's symbolic that the meeting was arranged near the cornucopia." His face was a blur in the dashboard lights, but I heard the embarrassment in his voice. "That's as far as I've gotten. I've hit a brick wall with my conjecture. I need more facts, and I just don't have them."

Grimly, I said, "I'm going to change that, Dad. I'm ready to tell you everything I know about this case."

Startled, my father shot me a swift glance. "I'll be glad to listen, daughter. This is what I had in mind when I came back to River City. I want us to work together."

I blinked rapidly. Once he had all the information, he was on his own. I had to back away from this case if I wanted to preserve my peace of mind.

Chapter Nineteen

Before I related the facts I'd collected, I used Dad's cell phone to call Natalie. After a couple of rings, she answered cautiously, "Hello?"

"Hi, it's Bretta. You sound odd. Is everything all right?"

She sighed. "So far."

I frowned. "What's that supposed to mean?"

"After Donovan left, the deputy came to the door and said he was being pulled off patrol here because of another emergency. I was uneasy being alone, so I invited Jake to come up here. We have all the lights on, and he helped me barricade the doors." She lowered her voice. "To pass the time, I suggested he watch a video. I hope I'm not corrupting him."

I chuckled. "I guess that would depend on your choice."

"It's an old Nicholas Cage movie. I find it depressing, but Jacob seems to be enjoying it, though I don't see how an Amish man can relate to all those car chases. Where are you?"

"I'm in River City, but I'm on my way back to the lodge. I should be there in about thirty minutes or so. It sounds as if you have everything under control. I'll be with Dad in his truck. We'll honk three times when we pull up to the lodge."

"I'll be watching for you. See you in a little while."

I said, "Bye," and pressed the button to disconnect. After my father had tucked the phone into his pocket, I settled back on the seat. "Natalie and Jacob are alone at the house. The deputy was pulled off his post because of another emergency. Natalie says they've turned on all the lights and barricaded the doors."

"That seems excessive. Does Natalie have a reason to think they're in danger?"

"The morning after Marnie was murdered, Natalie surprised an intruder in the house. It's understandable that she's taken precautions, but the killer might consider her a threat on another level. Natalie was with me when I made a couple of discoveries. She wasn't prudent when it came to keeping the details to herself." I waved a hand. "In other words, she blabbed to the suspects. They've been put on alert that I'm interested in three women who used to work at Parker Greenhouse."

"Three women? What's their connection to Marnie's murder?"

"Before I get to that, I need to tell you how I came across their names in the first place. Natalie found some old greenhouse personnel files in Dan's desk. She thought it was strange that Dan had these files at the house. At my request, she called Dan and he told her that Marnie had asked to see the records for employees who'd worked at the greenhouse in the last three years."

"Why did Marnie want to see them?"

"Earlier you said you thought Marnie had come to the greenhouse because she was looking for something. You were right. She was looking for information on her friend Paige, who disappeared three months ago."

Amazed Dad asked, "Disappeared from the greenhouse?"

I tried to give Dad an assessment of the facts without my personal opinions tossed in to color his judgment. He didn't stop me to ask questions, but listened intently to every word I said. I finished speaking just as we got to the Parkers' private drive. Dad made the turn. We coasted up the bluff a few yards before he pulled over and parked.

"I can't take all this in and drive, too," he said. "Let me get a couple of points straight. Three young women worked at Parker Greenhouse for two weeks, told a story to their family and friends that they'd been transferred up north, and then went away only to come back with money."

"Paige didn't come back."

"I got that, but money was mentioned before she left home, so we have to assume that a payment was involved just like it was with Dixie and Shannon."

"That's right. What other point did you want clarified?"

"Before we get to that, I want to know if you've determined what's going on with these women?"

I quickly shook my head. "I'd rather hear your theories."

"Why is that?"

I licked my lips, took a quick drink of my soda, and set the can back in the cup holder. "I've been too busy collecting information to try to make any sense from it."

My father studied me in the soft glow of the dashboard lights. "I don't think that's true. What's bothering you?"

Instead of answering, I said, "Have I told you about Dan's orchid house?"

Dad sounded annoyed. "Is that relevant?"

I fought the nausea that rolled in my stomach. When it came to interpreting the facts, was Dan's orchid program pertinent? I glanced at my father. "You'll have to determine that for yourself."

He sighed. "Let's hear it."

I swallowed. "Dan is trying to hybridize a new species of orchid. Natalie gave me a tour and a brief lesson in botany. I learned that plants have ovaries and male-sex cells. When pollination is successful the seedpods plump up. Natalie calls the area where these orchid plants are kept the maternity ward. Once the seeds have matured, they're collected and germinated in glass flasks. These flasks are placed in a room called the nursery. They stay there until the plants are big enough to transplant."

"I see," said Dad. "That's very interesting. I think I understand why you've told me about Dan's orchids. But just so I don't misconstrue your reason, why don't you continue on, tying it into this case?"

My heart was hammering again. "I'd rather you did it."

"Where is this reluctance coming from? It's as if you have a personal stake in the outcome."

A cold sweat broke out on my forehead. I wiped it away and massaged the throbbing pain. "I don't know what you mean. I've been too busy gathering information —"

"You've already used that excuse."

My chin shot up. "Let's drive on, Dad."

He reached for the gearshift lever but stopped. "I think you've already come to the right conclusion, but I don't know why you've closed your mind to it." He sighed. "You wanted my theory, so here it is. There are only two possibilities facing a woman with an unwanted pregnancy — abortion or delivery."

Silently, I added one more — miscarriage, but that didn't have a place in this scenario. I closed my eyes to keep the tears from spilling over. My voice was shaky. "Please go on."

"When Jacob told you that Dixie was giving away the last link she had to him, I can only surmise she was talking about a baby. As you said, we don't know if she was depressed when she learned about her father's death or if she arrived in River City already despondent. But I have an idea she was experiencing postpartum depression."

I had to make a contribution to this conversation if I wanted to keep my father talking about the case. "But why did these women go away? The stigma attached to an unwed mother hardly exists anymore. Pregnant young ladies march unashamed to the tune of "Pomp and Circumstance" as they accept their diplomas. Maternity wedding dresses are stylish and virginal white. Many unmarried women wear their pregnancies with pride. So why leave home to conceal their condition?"

"No reason that I can see unless a certain situation existed. One that would keep the woman from wanting her predicament revealed." Dad shrugged. "I'm a great one for what-if questions, but what if Shannon was pregnant? Her father supposedly told her if she didn't get a job and show some responsibility, she would be disinherited. What if Dixie was pregnant? She loved Jacob, but he made it clear he couldn't marry a woman who wasn't Amish. What if Paige was pregnant? Mrs. Cooper said Paige was a homebody, but she changed after attending a party. After you talked with Juanita at the convenience store where Paige worked, you and I both suspect Paige was drugged and raped by Virgil."

"Why do you think Shannon was killed?"

"I don't think her death was premeditated. After your visit, Shannon was probably worried that her past indiscretion was about to be revealed. She needed to vent her fear and anger. I would guess she called the one person who knew all the circumstances. That person arrived to console her, but Shannon couldn't be comforted. Things got out of hand. The murder weapon was handy. You said the wrench was hanging from a strange metal sculpture there in the entry hall."

"I hope you're right. It would ease my mind that I hadn't said something that led to her death."

"What else can I say to help ease your mind on other levels?"

I looked out my side window. My emotions were fragile and close to the surface because I'd kept a secret for years — from my family, my friends but, more important, from my beloved Carl. Since his death, when I'd felt used and abused and afraid, his voice had given me strength and guidance. I hadn't heard his voice in my head once on this case.

A lone tear trickled down my cheek. There could be only one reason. I wanted to think that his spirit had entered my heart when he passed away, keeping us unified forever. But if he was in my heart and knew my thoughts, then he also knew the sad truth I'd kept from him during our married life.

My father touched me lightly on the arm. "Are you thinking perhaps these babies were sold? I know that idea is reprehensible, but we have to consider these young women were desperate to get out from under the responsibility of motherhood. I'm not saying I understand what it would be like to take money for a child, but that's the obvious conclusion as to what happened. Witnesses connected to each woman admit that money was part of this plot."

I squared my shoulders and dashed a hand across my face. "I'm ready to go on to the lodge, Dad. It's been a long, long day."

My father shook his head. "You are one stubborn woman, but I'll respect your need for privacy. However, I do have one other point I need clarified."

Reluctantly, I asked, "What's that?"

He picked up the framed picture I'd taken from Dan's study. "I looked at this photograph while you were in that convenience store. It's a fantastic overview of this property. I assume you have it with you for a reason?"

Eagerly, I nodded. This was an area of the case that didn't have any dark memories associated to it. "Dixie's letter said she was in a cabin by the river. The Osage River flows across part of this property. I didn't have time to look at this picture before I left to go to Alicia's house. I snatched it off the wall on impulse."

Unexpectedly, Dad turned on the dome light. I blinked in the sudden brightness and averted my face so he couldn't see the tracks of my tears. But he wasn't looking at me. His gaze was fastened on the photograph.

I leaned closer and found our present location. "We're here," I said, pointing. "On our right are acres and acres of rough terrain, but on our left is the bluff." I tilted the frame so the light didn't glare off the glass. "See this ravine that's located up ahead of us? If we took that course we'd end up in the garden by the waterfall and ultimately by the cornucopia. It's a possible route the killer might have used."

Dad was thoughtful. "Sounds right, but, we have to establish if there's a viable route on the other side of these trees."

Silently, he examined the photo. "I'm getting my bearings now. The land is actually laid out in layers. First is the timber, which wasn't disturbed when the limestone was mined. When the trees peter out, the ground slopes toward the pit of water where excavation took place. Beyond that is a valley that might flood, further on is the river basin that most definitely would in the rainy season, and finally the river-banks and river."

He leaned closer. "Look here, daughter. I see something back under those trees. I can't make it out." He put his finger near the spot. "But it looks like a building of some sort."

I pondered the location. "I've been told there are a couple of old shacks still standing on the property. I can't believe they're habitable after all these years, but I suppose with covert remodeling, someone might call one a cabin —"

"— by the river," finished my father. "When you quoted the letter Dixie wrote to Jacob, you mentioned something about a spring. Can you repeat that part for me?"

I squeezed my eyes shut and concentrated. I prided myself on being able to memorize conversations I felt might be important. Softly, I said, " 'A spring keeps me in comforts that I need, but you do without.' "

I opened my eyes and stared at my father.

"I think Jacob must have misquoted that part of Dixie's letter. The only spring I can think of is a spring of water. The Amish do without many things we consider a necessity — cars, telephones, electricity. What would a spring of water have to do with any of them?"

"I've got an idea, but I want to check it out before I say anything." Dad turned off the key in the ignition. Without the deep rumble of the truck's engine, the night sounds crept into our space. Frogs croaked and crickets chirped a serenade. He opened the glove compartment and removed a flashlight. "Are you game for a walk in the woods?"

The thought of stretching my legs was agreeable. I nodded and climbed out.

My father locked the doors and came around the truck. Leaning on his new cane, he shone the flashlight at a break in the thicket. "Animals are creatures of habit," he said. "They frequent the same route to get to their feeding grounds. We might as well start here and take advantage of their trail."

I picked my way across the ditch. My knit slacks were ruined by the time I got to the other side. Thorns from wild rose bushes had snagged the fabric. Behind me,

Dad groaned as he hobbled to my side.

Concerned, I said, "That photograph is eight years old. The terrain will have changed considerably and not for the better when it comes to hiking. Are you sure you want to do this?"

"I'm sure," he said grimly.

He shone the flashlight ahead of us, and we entered the woods. Once we'd passed the outer rim of shrubbery, the brush was sparse, the ground spongy with leaf mulch and green moss. Gray lichen grew on the tree trunks.

"It's as dark as the inside of a cow," said my father.

I grinned. "The trees are close together so nothing much has grown under their dense foliage. It makes it easier for us to walk."

"But not easy enough." He stopped and swept the flashlight in a wide semicircle at what lay ahead of us.

We were at the edge of a steep grade that plunged downward. Below was the water pit we'd noted on the picture. Between the water and us were scrub oak, elm sprouts, and buck brush. Dangling from an occasional tree was wild grapevine as big around as a stout man's wrist.

"Nothing picturesque about this place," I said.

"We're not on a sightseeing trip."

Now that we were out from under the trees, the bugs had found us. The little critters nipped every inch of my bare skin. Before long there were nickel-sized welts on my arms and neck. Above us the moon was a useless lackluster crescent. The night air was oppressive. The trees had kept the day's heat from penetrating the forest. Here in the open, the warmth lingered. The squashy mulch of leaves had given way to rock outcroppings that were toe-catchers. We tottered down the rocky slope, picking our way over stones loosened by the changing seasons.

At the bottom of the slope we stopped to catch our breath. Dad had turned off the flashlight. Our eyes had grown accustomed to the darkness. I squinted and saw the ground dropped off again to a valley rimmed with trees. I pointed straight ahead. "I think the river bottom is on the other side of those trees."

"If I remember that photograph correctly, I'd say you're right. But we aren't interested in that area. We want the valley." He smacked his arm. "If these damned mosquitoes have their way, I won't have an ounce of blood left in me."

Brush rustled ominously off to our right.

Dad turned on the light and swung it in that direction. Three deer stood like statues. Their regal heads were held high, their necks arched. Eyes glowed in the light, giving us the impression that we were looking at alien creatures. We were the invaders, treading in their domain. We stood our ground and after a moment, the lead deer tossed his head and snorted before the three of them pranced off with their tails raised like white flags.

I patted my chest. "They were beautiful, but they startled me. Maybe if we walk closer to the water pit, we won't scare up any more wildlife."

"We can try it."

We didn't encounter any more animals, but the trail was treacherous. Shale slid under our feet. Pebbles skittered across the rocky ledge and seemed to take forever before they plopped into the water below. On our left grass grew waist high on the eroded slope. Around the lower end of the pit, mammoth gray boulders looked like a herd of elephants taking a snooze.

Once we got past the water pit, I heard the delicate splash of water trickling over rocks. Dad stopped and listened. "That sounds like something we need to investigate. It could be a spring. If I'm right, the cabin won't be far away. I'm dousing the light, so watch your step."

The splashing grew louder. I angled down the slope and banged into something about knee high. I tried to catch myself, but I sprawled flat.

My father scrambled to my side. "Are you hurt?" he asked.

All I could manage was a grunt of pain. I lay there trying to get my breath. Two things slowly registered — my shins hurt like hell and under my skinned hands I felt a smooth board. I sat up and tenderly touched the lump that had already formed on my leg.

In a hushed whisper, I said, "Dad, hand me your flashlight."

"Here it is, but should you turn it on?"

"I have to see what I tripped over. Look quick. I won't leave the light on very long." I cupped my hand over the lens and aimed it at the area in front of me. "Here goes," I said and flipped the switch.

The light showed a wooden box that was approximately a three-foot square with a handle in the middle. I turned off the light. "Well?" I said. "What is it? Do we dare open it?"

I heard the excitement in my father's voice. "I've got a good idea, but let me have the flashlight."

I handed it to my father and watched. He flicked the light on and shone it up the hill from where we were. In that brief illumination I saw a narrow stream running directly to the wooden box. Dad shone the light past the box. The water disappeared. He turned the light off.

"Where's the water?"

"Help me lift the lid, daughter, then I'll explain." I did as he asked. Again he flipped on the light. We stared down at a screen filled with leaves and silt. My father chuckled softly as he turned off the light. "Just as I thought. This is the filtering system for a hydroelectric generator. A pipe is buried underground and carries the water on down the hill. The cabin will be at the end of that pipe."

"Hydroelectric generator?"

"Water powers a generator that produces electricity. We shouldn't talk, and we can't use our light. We're too close."

I didn't know exactly how a hydroelectric generator worked, but I had a vague idea. We plodded on down the hill. I kept my gaze on the ground, though I couldn't see much. I was worried about falling and rolling unchecked over rocks and branches, when my father jiggled my shoulder.

I stopped and he whispered in my ear, "There's the cabin."

I squinted and searched where he'd indicated. Little by little I made out the lines of a ramshackle building weathered to a dusky gray that almost blended into the shadows.

My shoulders sagged with disappointment. "We've wasted our trip. This can't be it," I whispered. "It doesn't even have windows. No one would voluntarily live in such crude, depressing conditions."

"Don't be fooled by a first impression," said Dad. "Hear that?"

I tuned my ears past the crickets and frogs and heard a soft whir. Dad explained, "That's a hydrogenerator's waterwheel. If we could use the light, we'd see another wooden box where the wheel is housed. A wire leads into the cabin to a bank of six or eight car batteries where the energy is stored. From those batteries lights, a refrigerator, a television and such can be powered."

"Why aren't lights on? Isn't anyone here?"

My father took my arm, and we walked closer to the cabin. In a hushed tone, he said, "See that? The windows are shuttered."

We crept around to the front of the cabin. A Parker Greenhouse van had been backed into a grove of trees. I gulped when I saw it and squeezed my father's hand.

We'd found the hideaway. Now what were we going to do? I pulled my father away, putting space between the cabin and us. Once I thought it was safe, I whispered, "Let's use your cell phone and call Sid."

I couldn't see Dad's expression in the dark, but I heard the scowl in his voice. "Isn't there someone else?"

"Sid is in charge of this case, Dad. He deserves to be the first one to hear what we've —"

Suddenly the cabin door opened and bright light spilled out onto the porch. Dad and I shrank back into the shadows. Alicia came out and leaned on the porch railing.

"I love this place," she said. "Who would think to look at this rickety old building that it would have all the comforts of home." She made a deprecating gesture. "Maybe not my home, but the way other people live. I love the stereo system, and I've never had my own television. The video selection is up-to-date. There's so much food and games and things to do. The next few months will pass quickly."

I heard a low voice and strained my ears, but couldn't make out the identity of the person replying or what was said. Alicia unwittingly clued me in.

"— just a week earlier than we'd planned, but I'll make good use of the time. You've bought me the sewing machine. I never dreamed you'd buy so many different kinds of fabric. I love sewing and designing. When this is all over, I'll have money to go to college to become a fashion designer."

She stopped and listened. I did, too, but whoever was inside was staying out of my hearing as well as out of sight.

Behind me underbrush rustled. A tree branch cracked. Were there more deer? I'd heard stories about panthers and cougars roaming wooded areas in this part of Missouri. I looked over my shoulder, wondering if some animal was crouched in the dark, waiting to pounce. I strained my eyes and ears, but I couldn't see or hear anything.

Alicia said, "Being alone won't bother me. At home I don't have the space to spread out my patterns. Besides, someone is always nagging me so I can't concentrate."

"Who is she talking to?" whispered Dad.

Grimly, I said, "Think about it. Who has access to young women with problems? Who hears their woes and counsels them to make the right decision? Who was late coming to the greenhouse appreciation-day celebration? Who knows this property as well as Dan and Natalie?"

Before my father could speak, a voice behind me said, "You have it all figured out, don't you, Bretta?"

I whirled around to face a killer.

Chapter Twenty

Donovan switched on a powerful flashlight, spotlighting us like a poacher would his prey. I turned and saw the van was parked on a dirt track creased with deep ruts — probably an access road from when the quarry had been in operation.

Donovan said, "I told Emily a couple of busted flower shop windows wouldn't deter you, Bretta, but she wanted me to give it a try." Using the light he gestured toward the cabin. "Since you're so interested in what we've been doing, you might as well see it all. Get moving. I have you covered, so don't think you can run away."

My father said, "I haven't the energy to run. In fact, I think I'll stay here. Bretta, you go on with Donovan."

Donovan laughed. "Try again, Albert. That isn't an alternative." He shoved my father. While Dad recovered his footing, Donovan grabbed Dad's cane. "I'll take charge of this," he said. "And that cell phone you mentioned."

I thought Dad was going to refuse, but

he reluctantly handed over the phone.

Donovan said, "Albert, I want you in front of me. Bretta, you lead the way back to the cabin."

We threaded our way through the underbrush to the road and on to the cabin. As we approached, Donovan hollered, "Emily, we have guests. Turn on the porch light."

Immediately, the light flashed on. I glanced back at Donovan to see what kind of weapon he had trained on us. I saw nothing except Dad's cane and the flashlight. I stopped. "Where's your weapon?" I demanded.

Donovan shrugged. "I lied."

Outraged, I said, "You can't keep us here."

Donovan raised the cane and whacked my father across the shoulder. "Does that change your mind?"

My father nearly fell under the assault. Horrified, I tried to go to him but Donovan barred my way. Furious, I said, "I get the message, but leave him alone."

"That depends on you. Go on up the stairs and into the cabin."

We climbed the steps. I paused at the top and stared at Alicia until she finally met my gaze. She seemed embarrassed but not frightened by these events. "What you're doing is wrong," I said quietly. She looked away. Feeling Emily's hostile gaze on me, I turned to her. "Where's your mask?" I asked.

"It's in the van," she said in a clipped tone. "What difference does that make?"

"Just that it suits you. So much more in character."

Emily took a step toward me. Donovan shook his head at her and then nudged me with Dad's cane. "Keep walking, Bretta. Emily, you and Alicia stay out here on the porch."

Emily didn't say a word, but if looks could kill, I'd have dropped dead on the spot. Obediently, Alicia sat on the top step and folded her hands in her lap. Dad and I were herded into the cabin. Donovan shut the door and gave us a moment to look over our surroundings.

I had to admit it was cozy. We were in one large room. A light-stained wood paneled the walls. The luxurious carpet was a dusty rose. Paintings done in pastels brightened the room with color. There was a sofa and a recliner facing a television set. Bookshelves contained an assortment of videotapes. The sewing machine Alicia had mentioned earlier was still in a box by the bed. The satin coverlet was nearly hidden under the bolts of assorted fabric. The kitchen was equipped with an apartment-sized refrigerator and stove. The aroma of freshly brewed coffee lingered in the air.

Donovan gestured Dad and me to the sofa. He turned a wooden chair away from a tiny kitchen table and sat down. "I was unloading the van when I saw the light up by the water pit." Donovan nodded to me. "I kept track of your progress and heard you fall over the box that covers the filtering system." He waved a hand to the brightly lit room. "As you can see the hydrogenerator works very well. From the outside this old shack looks abandoned. But in here, I've double insulated the walls for comfort as well as a noise barrier."

He shook his head. "Where are my manners? I'm sure you're both exhausted from your jaunt through the woods. Can I offer you a cup of coffee or something cold to drink?"

"This is hardly a social call," I said.

My father rubbed his shoulder. "We don't knowingly break bread with a murderer."

Donovan nodded. "Events have gotten out of hand, but it's time the violence stopped. As I mentioned I have a proposition, but first I'd like to fill you in on a few details."

I said, "I can't imagine you'd have anything to say that I'd be interested in unless you're willing to turn yourself in."

Donovan's voice was crisp and businesslike. "No. I'm not going to jail. Until Marnie entered the picture, Emily and I provided a valuable service."

I smirked. "By selling babies? I assume the young pregnant women contacted Emily in her capacity as counselor. They poured out their hearts to someone they considered an authority figure. Emily probably asked the right questions so she could get a feel for their personality, their family life, and of course, their need for money." I cocked an eyebrow sarcastically. "Money was the objective, right?"

"Yes. We pay our ladies thirty thousand dollars free and clear to do with as they wish. There are conditions: they have to stay here alone. But they don't mind. They are committed to a goal. They understand that if a problem develops due to a faux pas on their part, the agreement is null and void, meaning the money is gone."

"But why bring them to the greenhouse to work for two weeks?"

"So they won't feel abandoned when we

leave them in this wilderness. They're comforted to know that good-hearted people are a half mile away."

"But they can't visit the greenhouse."

"Absolutely not. None of them care to. Emily and I have done this for five years. We research our clients well. We cater to each woman's goal or interest. Dixie wanted to be a singer. We furnished her with a Karaoke system and a high quality-recording device so she could perfect her voice. But radios, local television, and newspapers are not allowed."

"Five years, five babies. That's a lot of money."

Donovan shrugged. "Over a million dollars. Some prospective parents are willing and able to pay more than the going rate for a newborn. But we have expenses. We make sure our women are comfortable. We provide nutritious food and videos on natural childbirth. It all costs money, but we've never pinched pennies. Our women are a short-term investment."

In a droll tone, I asked, "Like brood mares?"

Donovan's eyes narrowed. "If that's what you want to call them. I prefer a more sympathetic approach. Emily and I think of these young women as victims of our nation's bureaucracy. If a young woman doesn't want her child, she either has an abortion or she gives up that child for adoption. If she chooses the latter, she doesn't receive adequate compensation for the mental anguish she has suffered. Emily and I make sure the amount of money she receives is sufficient to help her get on with her life. To become a vibrant, educated member of our society."

I whirled my finger. "Well, hurrah for you. But you failed to mention how you've prospered at the expense of these women. Or how Dixie spends her time rocking faceless dolls in a psychiatric ward. What happened to Paige? And don't tell me she's taken her schooling to a higher level. I think she's dead or she would have contacted her mother by now."

"She had a complicated pregnancy. The baby was born healthy, but Paige died. We gave her a dignified burial. Her body was wrapped and weighted and lowered into that water pit you passed on your way here."

Dignified burial? I thought. And you kept all the money, leaving Mrs. Cooper with nothing.

I took a couple of breaths to regain a modicum of control. "How much did Marnie know?"

"I wasn't sure. She kept asking questions about how long employees worked at the greenhouse, and why they left. I wouldn't have thought much about it except Mrs. Cooper, Paige's mother, had made several calls to the greenhouse, asking questions about her daughter. I know now we should have varied our story, but at the time when we told our ladies to say they'd been transferred up north, it seemed best to keep things simple.

"I set up that meeting in the garden with Marnie. Dan's plane was late, but not as late as Emily let on. I got back in plenty of time to park over here and hike across to the garden at the lodge. I learned that Marnie had talked Dan into letting her see old employee files, and that she'd told him about Paige's disappearance. Marnie was piecing it all together." Donovan stopped to give me a smile. "But not as quickly as you, Bretta."

A compliment from a murderer really made my day complete. "Why did you word your note — 'Life is precious. There are choices.'?"

"I wasn't sure if Marnie knew Paige was pregnant. If she did, that note would have a double meaning to her. If she didn't know, it wouldn't matter."

"What about Shannon Plummer?" I asked. "Why did you kill her?"

"A very loose end. She was scared and nervous, which is a bad combination if you expect that person to keep a confidence. Emily used every counseling tactic she knew, but Shannon was inconsolable."

"So Emily killed Shannon, and you killed Marnie." I gestured to my father. "We're loose ends, too. What's our fate?"

"That's up to you. After I explain my proposition, you can make your own decision."

"I don't know what you're talking about."

"Alicia is pregnant. Her baby is due in six months. Emily and I will waive our regular fee, though we'll see that Alicia is compensated. She has plans to become a fashion designer, and we want her to have the money to make that dream a reality."

My voice rose in outrage. "Do you think Dad and I can forget two murders because you're not taking money from the sale of Alicia's child?"

"Before you leap ahead, let me tell you what I propose. Alicia's baby needs a good home. Alicia needs a fresh start in her life. You have it in your power to grant both. All it will take on your part is to forget the information that brought you to this cabin."

"Forget it?"

"Have you shared this cabin's location with anyone?"

I didn't answer.

Donovan smiled. "I don't think you have." He leaned forward, talking earnestly. "There isn't any need for this to go any further. Emily and I will wrap up our affairs and leave River City. You have our word that we won't participate in another such — uh — operation. We've learned our lesson. There are too many unforeseen things that can go wrong."

I was astounded that Donovan would think that I'd take his word on anything. But I was aghast at the idea of meekly going on with my life while two killers went free. I wanted to rail at him, but I had to know what he had in mind. I said, "Why would I let you get away with murder?"

"You love Dan and Natalie. Natalie wants a child. Alicia's baby could be that child."

I was shocked into speechlessness, but my father said, "In other words, for our silence you'd see that Natalie and Dan Parker get a baby?"

"That's correct."

"There have been five other babies, so why haven't you approached the Parkers before you were backed into this corner?"

"Dan is too scrupulous. He would have wanted to know every detail of the adoption. A lawyer would have drawn up the papers with all kinds of questions asked. This situation can't tolerate that kind of scrutiny."

"What makes you think Dan still won't expect that?"

"Before he arrives from Oregon, Natalie will have signed the papers. They aren't binding, but she won't know that."

"I'm assuming you don't want Natalie to know you or your wife are involved in this. So who's your front person?"

"I don't see where that's important, but just so you'll know all the details, there's a woman who works with Emily who needs money. She called Natalie earlier this evening and talked over the adoption. I wrote the script for that conversation and I heard every word. Natalie has agreed. The paperwork will be delivered in the morning for her signature. As far as my niece is concerned, she's about to become a mother. Before Dan gets home, Natalie will have made a payment of fifteen thousand dollars. The baby will be delivered after the first of February, and the other half of the payment will be due."

I asked, "Where's Natalie getting the money?"

"That won't be a problem."

I said, "What if Dan refuses the child?"

Donovan laughed. "Come now. You know how much he loves Natalie, and you know how much she longs for a child. Do you seriously think Dan will deny her this opportunity when the agreement has already been made?"

"He would if he knew the circumstances."

"That's my point, Bretta. He won't know."

Another couple of points were bothering me. I said, "Let me get this straight. It was only you at the lodge this evening?"

Donovan nodded.

"Emily picked up Alicia, terrorized me, wrecked my SUV, and then came out here to settle Alicia into her temporary home."

"That's right."

"Why did you call the lodge?"

"To see if Natalie had told you anything about her previous phone conversation."

"But why did you come to the lodge? Was it for an alibi?"

"No. I had no idea what you were up to.

When I got to the lodge, I planned on saying that Emily had a headache and that's why she wasn't with me. I wanted to see Natalie for myself. If we could have an ordinary conversation without her telling me anything about the proposed adoption, then I felt sure I could trust her to keep it a secret."

I shook my head. "This is crazy. What happens if Dad and I don't agree to your preposterous scam?"

Donovan's voice didn't change. "You'll die."

I gulped. "Just like that."

"The decision is yours."

My father said, "I have to think things over, look at all the angles."

Appalled, I turned to him. "Dad, you aren't considering this?"

He lifted a shoulder and winced. "I'm not ready to sign my death warrant, daughter." He looked at Donovan. "You mentioned coffee earlier. Does that offer still stand?"

"Of course." Donovan rose and backed toward the cabinet, keeping an eye on us.

My father sat on the edge of the sofa. "I take it black." He glanced at me. "Don't you want a cup, Bretta?"

Short on patience, I snapped, "I'm not

in the mood for refreshments."

Ignoring me, Dad said, "Pour her a cup, Donovan. It'll settle her nerves."

I glared at my father, who met my stare calmly.

In a normal conversational tone, my father said, "Bretta never knew her grandmother, a wise woman, whose life was cut short by a bout of pneumonia. My mother's education didn't extend past the sixth grade, but when it came to understanding human nature, she should've had a degree. She had an adage for any and all situations. She could sum up life in an abbreviated fashion that was often astute and candid. She had a favorite saying that was tailor-made for this occasion."

Donovan smiled politely. "And that would be?"

"Sow a sinful seed, and you'll reap a wicked harvest."

Donovan thought a minute, then said, "On the surface it sounds apropos. The babies we brought into this world might have sprung from a sinful seed, but their births could hardly be called wicked."

Dad's stare was unrelenting. "The wickedness comes from your preying on the needs of people who can't have children of their own. You harvested those innocent babies like they were a field of corn and sold them for the almighty dollar. I knew the cornucopia in the garden was symbolic of this case. It represents a time of fruitfulness. The good book says, 'Be fruitful and multiply and replenish the earth.' "

Donovan frowned. "Let's leave religion out of this, shall we? I chose the cornucopia because it was close to the waterfall. The noise of the water flowing over the boulders would muffle my conversation with Marnie."

Dad's tone was disgruntled. "I was sure the cornucopia was symbolic." He turned a sharp gaze on Donovan. "Perhaps subconsciously you chose that piece of statuary —"

I closed my ears to this absurd topic of conversation. Everything around me had a surreal feel. How could I seriously consider letting Donovan and Emily skip out on a double-murder charge? It was ludicrous, and yet, I loved Natalie. I would do anything for her. But why did it have to come down to this? The fate of a child.

Stop it! I said to myself. There wasn't anything to consider. I would have to take my chances against Donovan and Emily. Surreptitiously, I looked around the room for something I could use as a weapon.

The kitchen table didn't even have a vase of flowers that I could crash over Donovan's head. No table lamps, just a ceiling light. No knives. No scissors. Nothing.

Donovan interrupted my thoughts. "Let's get on with this. Here's your coffee, Bretta." He handed me a cup, then turned to sit down. My father raised his steaming coffee like he was about to make a toast. Instead he tossed the contents at Donovan.

Donovan shrieked as the hot liquid burned his eyes and face.

Dad looked at me. When I didn't move fast enough, he grabbed my cup and slung it at Donovan, too. We were on our way to the door when it opened.

Emily took in the scene, put her hands up as if to physically stop us. I might not have known what my father had planned with the coffee, but I sure as hell knew what was expected of me at this moment.

I drew back my fist and slugged her. Blood gushed from her nose. My bruised knuckles burned like fire, but I didn't stop. I shouldered Emily out of the way and my father and I tore out of there, hobbling for our lives.

Chapter Twenty-one

My father had been sitting too long after vigorous exercise. His muscles were stiff, and mine weren't much better. We staggered down the steps, past Alicia who didn't utter a word, and away from the cabin, using the old access road for our escape. We made fair progress until Donovan switched on the van's headlights.

"I see you, Bretta," he shouted. "You aren't getting away. I treated you with respect. I gave you an alternative. Now to hell with you both." His voice dropped, but I heard him say, "Emily, get behind the wheel. Drive out there and cut them off."

Dad glanced back, but I kept my gaze on the road. We could hardly walk, let alone outrun a van. There was only one choice. We had to leave this trail and cross the open valley. We had skirted this basin on our way down, drawn to the sound of the spring. But that route was back by the cabin, and we were too far away to change course.

If we could make it safely across the open expanse of land, we'd have to climb the steep slope near the water pit. Going up wouldn't be as easy as coming down, but I didn't think the van had enough horsepower to navigate that rocky incline.

My heart pounded. Dad's breathing was erratic. I should have left him hidden among the trees and drawn Donovan's attention, but it was too late now. We were out in the open, crossing the valley that was as treacherous as an obstacle course. The ground was littered with debris that had floated on a turbulent river but had been stranded on dry ground once the water had receded. Cans, bottles, pieces of rusty tin were waiting to trip us up.

The van's lights quivered and quaked to a bebop rhythm as the vehicle bounced across the uneven dirt, closing the gap between us.

Abruptly, Dad stopped. "You go ahead, daughter. I'm slowing you down."

"I'm not leaving you," I said, pushing my shoulder under his arm. "Use me like a crutch. We don't have far to go."

He chuckled weakly. "We must be looking at different points on the horizon because the way I see it —"

"Don't talk." We moved a few more feet and almost fell over a piece of driftwood. The log was scarred and battered from having floated down the river. Caught on land it had been bleached by the sun, buffed by the wind, and was almost smothered by weeds. The van was bearing down on us. I had a plan but it involved getting my father to move faster.

Under my breath, I explained, "We have to maneuver Emily into a position so she'll drive over that log. If she hits it, it might slow her down, and we can get up that steep embankment."

Emily came at us fast and furious like a hawk that had spotted its next meal. "Please, Dad, keep moving, but stay in line with that log. We won't stand a chance if she doesn't take this path."

He didn't answer. My aching muscles screamed in protest, but I gripped him around the waist, and we moved forward. What if Emily saw the log? Could she swerve in time to dodge it? If she accomplished that, she'd have a direct path to run Dad and me down.

I looked behind me. Emily plowed into the log, wedging it under the van's framework. The engine roared as she gave it more gas. The tires spun, stirring up dust. The transmission squalled as she jerked the gearshift into reverse. But the van didn't move. The log was jammed under the chassis.

With the van off our tails, I slowed our pace. "That should keep her busy for a while."

"Where's Donovan?" asked Dad.

"I don't know. The last I saw of him, he was at the cabin, screaming at us."

Dad shook his head. "I saw him get into the back of the van."

I whipped around. Donovan charged us, whirling a rope over his head. The lariat formed a circle that grew bigger and bigger. "Run!" I screamed. "He's —" I took two steps and stopped. My father wasn't fast enough. The circle of rope snaked across the space and dropped neatly over Dad's head, sliding down over his shoulders.

With a flick of his wrist, Donovan pulled the lasso taut, pinning Dad's arms to his side. Donovan gave the rope a hard jerk, tugging Dad off balance. He lay on the ground, struggling to get free.

Donovan stretched the rope tighter and walked back to the van where he tied the rope to the bumper. Emily had stopped revving the engine. She handed Donovan my father's cane. I watched Donovan approach. He slapped the shaft of the cane against the palm of his hand. His gaze pierced mine.

Donovan spoke quietly, "I don't have an ounce of mercy left in me, Bretta. Get your father into the van."

I shook my head. "I won't do that."

Donovan stepped forward and popped Dad's thigh with the cane.

My father groaned. "I'm accustomed to pain," he said, clenching his teeth.

"Not the kind of pain I can inflict if your daughter doesn't cooperate." Donovan raised the cane. "Help him up, Bretta. Do it now."

I was afraid to bend over my father. With my head down, I'd be too vulnerable. I glared at Donovan. "Move back, and I'll do as you ask."

He took three steps away. Keeping my gaze on him, I put my hands under my father's arms. I strained and struggled and got Dad upright. He wobbled, but he was standing. We moved toward the van to ease the tension on the rope, but Dad shrank back when Donovan raised the cane threateningly.

I was ready to take my chances against Donovan, but I heard something in the distance. Caught by surprise, we listened to this strange noise that sounded like an enraged bumblebee caught in an empty fifty-gallon barrel. At first I thought someone had started a lawnmower, but on this unkempt tract of land that would have been absurd. The sound was closer.

I turned this way and that, trying to locate the source and glimpsed lights weaving in and out among the trees at the top of the incline. The headlights were close together. The motor's timbre was powerful. The engine accelerated, and the machine shot down the slope.

When I saw it was an ATV, my spirits leaped with hope. Those feelings turned to apprehension when I recognized Jacob at the controls, dressed in his Amish clothing, his straw hat pushed firmly down on his head. As I watched he gave the machine more gas. The sudden burst of power nearly unseated him. He hunkered over the handlebars and thundered toward us over the rocky ground.

I glanced at Donovan. His mouth hung open in surprise. His grasp on the cane had slackened. I took advantage of the situation. I made a quick grab for the cane and raised it above my head.

"Back off," I said, swinging the cane, driving Donovan away from us.

"Bitch!" he screamed. Running to the van, Donovan shouted at Emily to get the hell out of his way. He leaped into the front seat. The van's engine screeched in outrage as he tromped on the gas. He abused the transmission, putting the lever into drive and then into reverse.

The rope had Dad tethered to the van's bumper. If Donovan freed the van from the log, my father would be dragged —

I dropped the cane and worked some slack into the lasso that pinned his arms to his sides. My hands shook and my ears rang. The bedlam created by the two gas engines was deafening.

Jacob brought the ATV to a stop next to me. "Bretta," he yelled, "why is your father's truck parked out on the road? Mrs. Parker saw you pull off the highway. We've been waiting and waiting for you up at the house. She was worried so she's called the police."

I didn't answer, but kept working with the rope. I enlarged the circle and gently pulled it up and over Dad's head. Letting the rope drop, I turned to Jacob. "Help me get Dad up behind you."

Jacob shook his head. "Jess says it's too dangerous to ride double."

I yelled, "Then get off and let Dad on."

My father perked up. "I can go for help." He picked up his cane and handed it to me. "I won't need this, but you might."

Jacob climbed reluctantly off the four-wheeler. "Do you know how to drive an ATV?" he asked Dad.

"I'm a fast learner," said Dad, as he straddled the leather seat.

Jacob pointed to a thumb lever. "That's the gas. This machine has an automatic transmission, so you don't have to worry about shifting —"

I'd turned so I could see Donovan's progress. He was making headway, edging the van off the log. Agitated, I interrupted, "Forget the lesson. Dad, hit the gas and get out of here."

He pressed on the throttle, and the machine leaped forward. Dad clung to the handgrips and rode off. Now that he was out of the way, I said, "We don't want to be anywhere around if Donovan gets that van free."

Jacob finally figured out the scene. "He is Marnie's killer?"

"Yes. If we can get up that slope, the van might not be able to —" I stopped. Why talk when we could be moving. I took Jacob's arm, but he wouldn't hurry. He put one foot in front of the other, but it was as if his mind was far, far away.

"Jacob," I said, tugging on his arm. "You don't understand. We have to get out of this valley."

"I am understanding more and more, Bretta. Have you ever seen something that you thought had nothing to do with you, but after thinking about it, you realized it was a piece of your life?"

"I don't know what you're talking about."

He picked up the pace, both physically and vocally. "I have thought often about the link to me that Dixie said she was giving away. I didn't know what she meant, but I figured it was her English way of saying she was turning her back on our love."

Jacob shook his head. "But I have been stupid. I never thought that a mother would give away her own child, but I think that's what Dixie did. She gave away my child." His voice cracked with emotion. "The child she and I made from our love."

What could I say to get this man moving? Behind me the tempo of the van's motor changed. The whining transmission stopped. I knew the exact moment when Donovan freed the vehicle from the log.

"He'll be coming after us," I said. "We have to hurry."

"He is the one who took my child?"

"Yes, Jacob. He wants me dead. Since you're with me, you're in danger, too."

Jacob took a firmer grip on my arm and hustled me forward at a rate of speed that made my feet feel as if they were skimming the ground. Abruptly, Jacob changed direction. The slope was directly in front of us, but he was staying on flatland.

"No, Jacob," I said, pulling back. "We have to climb the hill." I cocked my head so I could listen. Sirens? I prayed my ears weren't playing tricks on me. But how close were the patrol cars?

Lights bore down on us. There was no place to hide. No place to get away from the van that spurted toward us.

Jacob stopped and searched the ground. He picked up a rock that was as big as his fist. Turning to me he said, "I will meet this modern-day Goliath." He walked away from me into the path of the oncoming van.

I stared in horror. Was this young man so miserable that he didn't care what happened to him? "No!" I screamed. "Jacob! No!"

A part of my brain noted that Jacob's Amish white shirt glowed in the van's headlights. He hitched up his suspenders, straightened his shoulders, and raised his arm.

In a calm voice, he said, "Lord, David I

am not. Thy will be done." He sent that rock soaring through the air. It hit the windshield squarely in front of the driver.

Emily's scream of terror ripped the night apart. Donovan applied the brakes. The van veered, hit a boulder, and flipped. I held my breath, expecting the van to tumble into the water pit. The abused machine lurched and skidded to a stop on its side.

Jacob stared at the destruction. "Deliver us from evil," he said quietly.

Chapter Twenty-two

"Happy Birthday, dear Bretta. Happy Birthday to you."

Fervently, Lois added, "And many, many more."

My guests solemnly nodded their agreement. We were seated around my dining room table. The room was decked in purple and lavender streamers. Flowers graced the table. The sideboard held the remnants of a hearty meal. A decorated cake waited for the candles to be lit. All the components were present for a happy occasion, but the party had fallen flat. Out of respect for Natalie and Dan, no one had mentioned last night's events.

While Lois and Lew entertained everyone with a humorous tale from the flower shop, I thought about Donovan and Emily's arrest. The greenhouse's ATV had gotten a workout. The sirens had stopped on the road to the lodge. I can only surmise what had happened. Since Sid had charged down the slope on the machine, I assumed he'd commandeered it from my father. I figured he'd pulled rank, flashing his badge for good measure. Sid had arrived at my side so perturbed he could barely speak.

Under heavy guard, Donovan and Emily had been taken to the hospital where their injuries were treated. Natalie, Jacob, Alicia, my father and I had been escorted to the sheriff's department. I don't know what the others said, but I'd held tightly to my composure while Sid questioned me. When he demanded to know why I hadn't told him that I suspected a black-market baby scam, I'd fallen back on the glib line I'd told my father — that I'd been too busy collecting information to put it together. Which had been true for a while. Sid hadn't believed me any more than my father, but at least he'd dropped the subject when the press came calling for his account on the arrests.

My mind switched back to the present when Lois said, "Enough of this. Bretta, don't you have something to say on this momentous occasion?"

As the guest of honor, I'd been seated at the head of the table. Slowly, I rose to my feet. Every muscle in me ached, but nothing could compare to the pain in my heart. I looked around the table. This party had been planned as a surprise for me, but at my request, DeeDee had curtailed the guest list to include only my closest friends — Lois and her husband. Lew and his mother. Avery Wheeler, my lawyer friend. My father. DeeDee. Natalie and Dan.

My birthday party might be small, but the love in the room brought a lump to my throat. I cleared it away. "Well," I said shakily, "I don't know what to say except that I'm truly blessed to have all of you in my life."

Abruptly, Natalie got up and left the room. Dan started after her, but I beat him to the door. "Let me speak to her," I said. "I want to make sure she doesn't blame me."

Dan's eyes were somber behind his black-rimmed glasses. Natalie and I'd always teased him that he looked and acted like an absentminded professor. Tonight he was just a sad man who was worried about his wife. He nodded and stepped away from the door.

I found Natalie on the front veranda, leaning against a fluted column, staring out into the darkness. I touched her arm. "Is this trouble going to ruin our friendship?"

She wasn't crying, but the tears were

close to the surface. "No. I don't blame you, but I feel as if I've been at fault."

I wasn't sure what I'd expected her to say but never this. "Why would you think that?" I asked.

"Perhaps I put the idea into their minds. I've spoken often enough about how difficult it is to adopt a child, about the wait and the expense. What Uncle Donovan and Emily did was wrong, but a part of me can see the goodness in finding loving homes for unwanted babies."

"But Donovan and Emily murdered two innocent women. Three, if you count Paige. They didn't provide her with medical aid when she needed it."

Natalie shook her head. "I can't think about that."

"You have to face the truth. Donovan and Emily were opportunists. They took advantage of a situation, but not because of their concern for the women and their unborn babies, but for the money they would make off the deals."

"All I can think about are the babies that were born practically under my nose, and I suspected nothing."

"Half a mile away was not under your nose."

Natalie waved a hand. "You're always so

literal. You don't understand."

"You've said that before, but I understand more than you give me credit. I also know right from wrong, and you do, too."

Natalie shrugged. "Dan has asked our lawyer if he will approach Alicia about adopting her child."

"That's wonderful."

"I'm afraid to hope." She straightened and took my arm. "This is your day. Let's go back inside. I want a piece of your birthday cake."

We entered the dining room to find the cake aglow with candles. Natalie squeezed my arm before taking a seat next to Dan. Trying to lighten the mood, she said, "Blow out those candles, Bretta, before they trigger a fire alarm."

Lois said, "But don't forget to make a wish." A devilish gleam danced in her eyes. "Make it a fan-damn-tastic one. You deserve the best."

"I don't know about that," I said softly.

My wishes were many. How could I pick only one? I wanted Natalie and Dan to have a child. I wanted Jacob to find peace with himself. He'd gone to see Dixie, but from what I understood, she hadn't recognized him. I wanted Bailey to come home as soon as possible. I wanted to be more tolerant of my father.

Finally, I settled on the one thing that was purely selfish. I took a deep breath and puffed out my cheeks. Leaning close to the cake, I released the air in a long, drawn out whoosh. The candles flickered and went out. Amid cheers and well wishes, the telephone rang.

DeeDee leaped from her chair. "I'll g-get it," she said.

I picked up a knife and sliced off the first piece of cake. "Who wants a corner with all this gooey icing?" I asked, then added, "Besides me, of course." Everyone held out his or her plate. I shook my head. "Come on, guys. There are only three corners."

We were laughing when DeeDee came back into the room. Her eyes twinkled with excitement. "B-Bailey's on the p-phone. H-he wants to w-wish you a h-happy birthday."

She didn't have to tell me twice. Smiling, I headed for the library where I would have some privacy. I picked up the receiver. "Hello," I said.

"How's my birthday girl?"

The sound of his voice washed over me, making my knees weak. "Oh, Bailey," I said, sinking down on the edge of the sofa. "I miss you."

"I miss you, too. I have a gift for you. I was going to give it to DeeDee, but I've changed my mind. If you can leave your party, go over to my house and look beside my desk."

I started to protest, but Bailey said, "I'd like for you to have it on your birthday. All you have to do is get my house key from DeeDee and walk over there."

"Okay. I'll go over while the others eat their cake." I paused, then asked, "When will you be home?"

"Soon. I'm cutting my visit short."

I breathed a sigh of relief. "That's the only gift I want or need."

His deep chuckle sent a delightful shiver through me. "I'll see you soon," he said and hung up.

I replaced the receiver. I wasn't ready to end the conversation, but apparently, Bailey had said all he'd wanted to say. I went back into the dining room. As soon as I walked through the doorway the conversation ceased.

"Bailey has a gift for me over at his house," I said. "For some reason he wants me to have it on my birthday. Please excuse me for a few minutes." I turned to DeeDee. "I need the —"

She whipped a key ring out of her

pocket. “Here it is,” she said.

I took the key and lowered my eyebrows. “What are you, a mind reader?”

DeeDee didn’t answer but escorted me across the foyer. “You’d b-better hurry so you c-can get b-back to your party.” She grabbed a flashlight that was conveniently lying on the table by the door. Offering it to me, she added, “Bye. S-see you l-later.”

“Yeah,” I said. “Later.”

I walked out the door and down the front steps. I turned on the flashlight and crossed my driveway to the path that led to Bailey’s house. Something was going on, but I wasn’t sure what. Maybe Bailey’s call was a ruse. DeeDee had been antsy all evening, not able to sit still for a moment. I hoped she didn’t have any more surprises planned.

I’d smiled and pretended to have a good time, but my heart wasn’t into celebrating and opening brightly wrapped packages. Sexy lingerie, seductive perfume, body powder, and flashy jewelry couldn’t compete with being held close by a pair of strong, loving arms.

I was thinking about Bailey, but murmured, “Carl, I am so sorry.”

Tears I’d held in check for hours ran down my cheeks. I stopped on the path and gazed up at the sky that was a blur of gray and black — colors that suited my melancholy mood.

It seemed only right that on this day, the date of my birth, I'd open my heart and my mind to the part of my life that I'd botched. Carl and I had only been married a couple of months when I suspected I was pregnant. A year, two years down the road, I would've been overjoyed, but at that point, I wasn't ready to be a mother. I was too busy, too young, and too inexperienced to care for a child.

I kept my suspicions to myself, never divulging anything to Carl. Alone with my anxiety, I'd ranted and raved and prayed that I'd misread my condition. A week after the doctor confirmed that I was six weeks along, I suffered a miscarriage. I was guilt ridden, dismayed that I'd somehow forced this baby from my body by willing it away.

Carl's erratic work schedule had made it easier to tuck my guilty secret away. When he was home, I was gone and vice versa. As the days passed into weeks, the weeks into months, and the months into years, all of life's unpredictable changes pressed down on top of my shame. Rarely did I think about the child that might have been. If I did, it was as if that experience had happened to another woman who didn't exist anymore.

The circumstances surrounding Marnie's death had gouged away the boundaries I'd placed around my remorse. In my heart, I felt that baby, who had been no bigger than a peanut, had known it wasn't wanted. And now, if I had it to do over again, I'd welcome Carl's child into my life. But Carl was gone. My time to be a mother was gone as well. I'd been chastised by never conceiving again. That was my punishment. That and facing Carl's disappointment each month.

For twenty years I'd kept my secret. Twenty years of loving a man with all my heart, but denying him the opportunity to grieve, to mourn the passing of his only chance for a child.

Fresh tears welled up when I thought about not hearing his voice in my head during this investigation. I'd pleaded with him to talk to me, but he'd remained silent. It was my own guilt that had stifled his beloved voice.

I turned off the flashlight and closed my eyes. From my heart, I said, "I have plenty of excuses, Carl, but it all boils down to one fact. I was wrong to keep what happened from you. I knew it at the time, but I couldn't bear to see your sorrow. I couldn't take the chance that you might blame me. Please forgive me, so I can forgive myself."

I concentrated, but I didn't hear his voice.

Dejected, I turned on the flashlight and walked on to Bailey's house. I stepped upon the porch and put the key in the lock. My birthday wish had been that I'd once again sense Carl in my soul. I knew it was ridiculous to feel at odds with the spirit of my dead husband, but I'd carried his memory in my heart for so long, I felt abandoned all over again. Anticipating what he would say in any given situation had brought me an inner peace. I wasn't asking for a bolt of lightning to come out of the sky. All I wanted was a broad indication that he knew my regret.

I pushed open the door. The smell of raspberries almost knocked me over. The scent stirred old memories. Carl used to bring me fresh raspberries when I was feeling down. I flipped on the light and nearly fainted.

Bailey lounged against the side of his desk. He was dressed in a pair of swimming trunks. A towel was tossed rakishly over his shoulder.

"Bailey?" I breathed. "I just talked to you."

He pushed away from the desk and held out his hands. "I told you I would see you soon. Is this soon enough?"

Laughing and crying, I started toward him, but stopped when I saw something blocked my way. I froze, staring at the child's wading pool in the middle of the floor. Dabbing at my eyes, I took another step closer. I bent down so I could have a better look. The bright blue pool didn't contain water, but the smell of raspberries was stronger. I touched a finger to the cool, stiff, glutinous mass.

My eyes widened. My jaws dropped. After a moment, I said, "Bailey, is that what I think it is?"

"Your Jell-O fantasy come true, sweetheart. We had to guess at the flavor. Natalie and DeeDee seemed to think watermelon or grape would be your choice, but for some reason, I knew raspberry was your favorite."

My voice trembled. "But why did you use a *child's* wading pool?"

Bailey's gaze was puzzled. "Is something wrong with that? It was the only thing I could think of that would fit in this room." Bailey came to stand next to me. Placing a finger against my lips, he whispered, "I did this because I love you, Bretta."

I closed my eyes. I loved him, too, but —

Was this my sign from Carl? I'd hoped for something meaningful and profound. I wasn't sure a child's swimming pool filled with raspberry Jell-O qualified. And yet what could be more significant than a man who professed his love, trying to please me?

Shyly, I asked, "So you're ready to make my fantasy come true?"

He kissed me lightly on the lips. "In every possible way," he said, pulling me into the circle of his arms.

I looked over his shoulder at the pool. We were standing quietly. There was no physical explanation, but the surface of the pool quivered ever so gently.

About the Author

Janis Harrison has combined her career as a florist with her love of writing in the Bretta Solomon series, which includes *Roots of Murder*, *Murder Sets Seed*, *Lilies That Fester*, and *A Deadly Bouquet*. She and her husband live near Windsor, Missouri, where they operate their own greenhouse business.

We hope you have enjoyed this Large Print book. Other Thorndike, Wheeler or Chivers Press Large Print books are available at your library or directly from the publishers.

For more information about current and upcoming titles, please call or write, without obligation, to:

Publisher
Thorndike Press
295 Kennedy Memorial Drive
Waterville, ME 04901
Tel. (800) 223-1244

Or visit our Web site at:
www.gale.com/thorndike
www.gale.com/wheeler

OR

Chivers Large Print
published by BBC Audiobooks Ltd
St James House, The Square
Lower Bristol Road
Bath BA2 3SB
England
Tel. +44(0) 800 136919
email: bbcaudiobooks@bbc.co.uk
www.bbcaudiobooks.co.uk

All our Large Print titles are designed for easy reading, and all our books are made to last.